MOMZILLAS

Jill Kargman

BROADWAY BOOKS

New York

PUBLISHED BY BROADWAY BOOKS

Copyright © 2007 by Jill Kargman

All Rights Reserved

A hardcover edition of this book was originally published in 2007 by Broadway Books.

Published in the United States by Broadway Books, an imprint of The Doubleday
Broadway Publishing Group, a division of Random House, Inc., New York.
www.broadwaybooks.com

BROADWAY BOOKS and its logo, a letter B bisected on the diagonal,
are trademarks of Random House, Inc.

While some elements of New York City parenting described on the
following pages may seem familiar, this book is entirely fiction! No mommies, kiddies,
schools, clubs, or real estate snafus are based on anyone or anything real.

Library of Congress Cataloging-in-Publication Data
Kargman, Jill, 1974–
Momzillas / Jill Kargman.
p. cm.
1. Motherhood—Fiction. 2. Rich people—Fiction.
3. Upper East Side (New York, N.Y.)—Fiction. I. Title.

PS3611.A783M66 2007
813'.6—dc22
2006024568

ISBN 978-0-7679-2479-5

PRINTED IN THE UNITED STATES OF AMERICA

1 3 5 7 9 10 8 6 4 2

First Paperback Edition

To Corinne Kopelman,
the anti-Momzilla and best
mother in the world

and

to Sadie and Ivy,
if you love me half as much
as I love your grammy,
then I'll know
I've done a great job

THE MOMZILLAS GLOSSARY
OF TERMS AND ABBREVIATIONS

AFFLUENZA: Malaise of the extremely wealthy; symptoms include panic over which color Bugaboo to buy and night sweats about which $20,000 pre-preschool to apply to. Common occurrences of dissatisfaction despite comfort of riches.

BALL-ON-STICK: Super-skinny pregnant woman who works out like crazy and counts calories, resulting in bony body with uterus as only evidence of pregnancy. Often wears stilettos.

BLUE RIBBON BIRTHER: Mom who brags about her natural childbirth and thinks she deserves a prize for forgoing drugs. See *EB*.

BW: Babysitter Worthy; i.e., *I haven't read the reviews for that movie, I'm not sure if it's BW* (since tickets + 'corn + bevs + sitter fee = $100).

COMPETITIVE BIRTHING: Racing to have more kids faster than everyone else.

EB: Epidural Basher; woman opposed to the use of anesthesia during childbirth. Generally brags about her own long natural labor.

FRESH BAKED BREAD: See *Glossary of Extinct Terms*.

GOALIE: Birth control; as in *We're ready for baby number two so we're going to pull the goalie*.

HYPOCHONDRIMOM: Mom who constantly thinks her kid is sick and/or that other kids are sick and will infect her kid.

J-RO's: Jack Rogers sandals, a cornerstone of the Momzillas' spring/summer uniform (metallic a plus), which also includes white cigarette-leg pants and beaded tunic.

LABORSPIEL: Endless, minute-by-minute playback of mom's labor; often peppered with unsolicited gory details, as if it were first birth in history.

LM: Liar Mom; i.e., *Madison slept through the night starting at two weeks old!*

MANNY: Male nanny. Usually attractive and younger than his charges' mom and dad.

MILF: Mother I'd Love to Fuck.

MNJ: Middle Name Junkie; mother who always calls her child by first and middle name; as in *Julia Charlotte loves Mandarin class*.

MOMOLOGUE: When a mother goes on and on about her kid as if s/he's the only child in the world.

MOMSICLE: Chilly, unaffectionate mom who never cuddles her kids; will probably call her son "Son" and will be called "Mother" in return.

MTD: Mom's Two Dinners; one at sixish with the kids, consisting of mac 'n' cheese or chicken fingers. Second dinner is with husband later on.

NAME POACHER: Thief of someone's already chosen baby name; as in *We're naming the baby Mabel but don't tell anyone 'cause we don't want some name poacher to steal it.*

NANNYJACKER: Mother who can't deal with screening/hiring a nanny so she hits the playground and tries to snatch someone else's.

NURSING NAZIS: Brigade of vociferous moms who compete over who breast-feeds longer; often judge/bitch out bottle-feeders.

P'N'P: Preggers and Proud; moms-to-be who bare belly in midriff-exposing shirts and/or often rub bump every two seconds. Often gush about how "alive" they feel.

PUSH PRESENT: Expensive gift from husband to wife for pushing the baby out, usually in the form of jewelry. C-section deliveries rate even though they don't technically involve pushing.

'REXIMOM: Mother who drops baby weight in two weeks or less.

SANTA MOM-ICA: Breed of L.A.'s west side mothers; see *Nursing Nazis*.

SANCTIMOMMY: Preachy mom who thinks she knows what's best for not just her child but also everyone else's as well.

SATURDADS: Fathers who can be seen desperately trying to entertain tots solo on weekends; often members of the DDC (Divorced Dads Club); usually seen with kids sans mom on days they have custody.

SIP 'N' SEE: A tea-time party to welcome home a new child from the hospital where guests *sip* tea and *see* the newborn. And bring gifts.

SPERMINATOR: Guy with four or more kids.

SUICIDE HOUR: Generally from five P.M. until husband comes home. "Happy Hour" for the rest of the world.

TECHNO TWINS: Trend of in vitro–fertilized Gemini; sometimes slighted by moms who claim to have "real" twins.

TOO POSH TO PUSH: Women who can't deal with labor and/or the possibility of a stretched-out vagina, who sign up for elective cesarean sections, often ten days early so as to avoid an extra week of pesky weight gain.

YUMMY MUMMY: Sexy, attractive mother; see *MILF*.

One

I am staring at the crystalline frozen tundra of ice-licked Alaska. Surrounded by an endless snowy desert, a little Eskimo girl pounds her way through the rushing, snowflake-laden wind as cheerful music plays.

"Put on your kami-kluk *to stay warm and dry . . ."*

No, I didn't board a flight to Juneau. I'm watching *Sesame Street* with my daughter, Violet. It's one of Grover's world-friendly segments where global cultures are profiled through the dewy, pure lens of a child's eyes. We visit a Chinese boy who is a top acrobat and can spin fourteen plates on his face and a little Indonesian girl who can balance six bowls on the top of her head. While dancing.

Today Grover has transported us to the forty-ninth state—and our local lass is suiting up to face the Arctic chill, with the help of her mother, who sews fur pelts together to fashion a *tikiyook*, or coat, to repel the subzero temps. The child rushes out into the crisp fresh air to meet other children, also clad in PETA's worst nightmare, and skips off into the fluffy white mounds, laughing sweetly.

It all looks so wholesome, so simple, so uncomplicated. No fancy schools to get into, no apartments to compare. It looked pleasant there, out in the bleak but weirdly alluring slate of glistening frost punctuated only by playful tykes toting their homemade lunches to school in swinging buckets.

But then the bilious pit in my stomach reasserted itself,

and I couldn't help but think this awful, impure thought: I bet one of the moms is looking over the other kids' *kami-kluk*s to see if the stitching is better. Or if the book sack one mom made is as creatively patterned as another. I am certain one family's igloo is grander, another's dogsled more impressive.

I was watching this on my television, in my apartment, not set in a downy white backdrop, but rather in the lion's den of competitive mommies: New York City's Upper East Side. In California, where my husband, Josh, and I lived before the re-location plunge a month ago, the one orange Bugaboo stroller on our block was so strange and uncommon a sight, people thought aliens had delivered it via flying saucer. In New York, the Rolls-Royce of strollers is as common as yellow cabs—and the streets are just as jammed with them, but instead of reek-ing of an overpowering air-freshener-and-curry combo, they smelled of Kiehl's-scrubbed babies.

It's gotten to the point where I don't even want to walk up Madison Avenue; while my kid looks like Baby Old Navy ex-ploded, I routinely bump into neighbors with children so per-fectly preened in smocked dresses, rickrack-collared linen blouses, shiny Mary Janes with lace socks, and enormous bows in their styled hair. My mother-in-law gives us baby clothes that are marked Dry Clean Only. Unless they're linen, in which case yours truly gets to crack out the ironing board. I just want to hide. Boy, am I living in a crazy place. Maybe I *should* call Air Alaska.

It all started when Josh got a call from Parker Elliott, his best friend from Harvard Business School. He knew Josh was sick of his job in San Francisco, dreading working the East Coast hours on the West Coast and getting up well before the ass-crack o'dawn. The bank that employed Parker was willing to make Josh an offer he couldn't turn down, so suddenly our laid-back California world was history. I was getting my PhD in art history at Berkeley right before Violet was born, but bagged after the Master's because a) of the impending stork arrival and b) I didn't know what the hell I wanted to do with a PhD. So when the call came for Josh, I was a perfectly transportable, abundantly educated, stay-at-home mom.

I grew up in rainy Seattle so the storm-whipped weather "back east" never cowed me like most California residents; in fact, even though I'm a born-and-bred West Coaster, I actually always felt more at home with the northeastern vibe—crisp autumns lazing indoors and avoiding the sun due to my ultra-pale, all-too-easily-burnable complexion. When I met Josh and we started dating, he told me straightaway that he wanted to move back to his native New York to raise a family one day. I was game; I just didn't know that day would come so soon. I'd liked our shimmering, carefree San Francisco bubble, far from his socialite mom, cozy in our solitude between our close group of friends, our favorite haunts, and mellow routines. I always loved Manhattan when I visited every fall, but it was all a glistening October collage of Broadway shows, plush hotel rooms, designer sushi, and kissing in burgundy-leafed Central Park.

The transformation from romantic tourist to entrenched inhabitant was bumpier than I had anticipated. The offer and subsequent arrangements happened so quickly; it seemed that within days I was loading up boxes, boarding a plane, and moving into corporate housing, all before I could even get used to the thought of it.

The night we arrived, Josh ordered a Chinese feast, and after we tucked Violet into her Pack 'n' Play, we chowed take-out cartonloads of chow fun and General Tso's chicken by the flickering light of nonaromatherapy candles.

"Hannah?" he said, smiling over his chopsticks.

"Yes, sweets?"

"Thank you."

He came over and hugged me and I blinked to release a lone tear, which he wiped away softly. Suddenly here we were: away from our friends, my family, my coast—and planted in a new world of the elite, his mom and fancy prep school pals included. My tear flow increased.

"As if I don't already have enough salt from this meal," I laughed as he kissed me, wiping my cheeks. "I'm already the fattest girl in this city and the MSG intake ain't helping."

"Shut up. You're beautiful."

I looked at him gratefully and sighed.

"We're going to be fine here," he consoled, stroking my hair. "Better than fine. You will love New York, Han, I swear."

Joshie has always wanted me to adore his hometown as much as he does, and he's done everything he can to infuse me with his passion for it—from Woody Allen screenings in our den to museum binges when we visited, to excited samplings of his favorite foods (the perfect bagel, the best hot dog), to showing me the most sublime walks, to pointing out the most diverse, most intellectual, most kaleidoscopic array of eclectic, sometimes freakish citizens. He was a real die-hard, love-the-gray, eat-up-the-noise, relish-the-smell-of-streetcart-food New Yorker. Ever since I'd known him, Josh had gone back home every few months for his fixes, like a junkie filling up on the buzz and heat and lifeblood of the twelve-mile island he thought of as the center of the universe. He was so ecstatic to finally be back, and I was thrilled for him. But gone were the days of him rolling home at four thirty P.M., taking evening walks as a fam, and eating early dinners in our favorite holes in the wall. He had warned me that in this new job he couldn't cut corners and would be pretty much swamped, handcuffed to the office at least for a while. And I'd be navigating the rough waters on my own. Waters teeming with sharks. Kelly-bag-toting, Chanel-suit-wearing, Bugaboo-pushing sharks.

"Bee is calling you on the cell tomorrow to meet up," Josh said, trying to lift my spirits. "Parker said she wants to take you to some children's clothes show or something. She'll introduce you to all her friends."

"Okay," I said, exhaling and nodding. I wanted to be supportive to Josh. He had been so down at his old job and I had hated seeing him miserable. This was a chance at a fresh start for him, and I needed to match his enthusiasm. But just hearing the name Bee made me nervous.

Two

Bee Elliott was pretty much the most drop-dead-gorgissima person I had ever seen up close—like that untouchable girl in high school two grades above you who all your friends stared at in the main hallway. With blond shoulder-length hair (that probably fell into place as she stretched and yawned at sunrise, barf) and a modelesque frame, she maintained her skeletore bod (or "lovely figure" as ol' school people would say, i.e., a stick with boobs) after giving birth to her son, Weston Burke Elliott. She was basically SuperMom, but not in that horrifying suburban soccer mom kind of way. She didn't wear pleat-front "Mom Jeans" like in the *Saturday Night Live* faux commercial featuring asexual, minivan-driving, baked-goods-wielding, newscaster-haircut women.

She was a stunning New York fashion plate. Her photograph appeared in magazines for her philanthropic efforts, which she managed to juggle between being class mom at her son's nursery school, running around the reservoir twice every morning, going to ladies' luncheons to benefit causes close to her heart, and showing up looking astonishingly beautiful when she accompanied her husband, Parker, to a dinner party or charity gala.

But don't get me wrong, she was no Stepford Wife. Some brain-free bimbo without wiles wouldn't make me nervous. Bee had gone to Princeton, which she let you know quickly enough to think "overcompensation," and had worked at

Lazard Frères up through the delivery of her son before taking the maternity leave that never ended. She nursed for a year, lost the baby weight in six weeks, and was in a bikini the weekend of my California wedding.

At the reception, while it was truly the greatest day of my thirty years next to the birth of little Violet, the one nanosecond of real stress (aside from my mother-in-law remarking that my dress was "so simple") was when I said hello to Bee. Everyone—I mean everyone, not to brag—gushed about how stunning the wedding was, how soulful, how perfect, but Bee said only a terse "congratulations." I know my reaction was my own issue and that I was probably reading too much into it or even searching for her approval in some odd way, but it was obvious that next to her blowout, high-society wedding, mine was a sandy, ramshackle beachfest with a barefoot bride and a clichéd sunset.

Bee's epic, peony-dripping, Colin Cowie–planned wedding to Parker Elliott was in New York, where they had both grown up. She'd gone to Chapin, he to Collegiate—both single-sex, old-line academies. They met in third grade at Knickerbocker ballroom dance class. Yes, *ballroom* dance, complete with white gloves. At age eight. I think at the time I was involved in the slightly less chic endeavor of frying bugs under a magnifying glass on our lawn. But Bee's life path seemed glamorous from her first steps, probably taken in satin ballet slippers. Her parents, who were old friends of Josh's mom, had an apartment in Paris, a ski house in Aspen, and an oceanfront estate in Southampton. So it should have been no surprise that her wedding was, next to Lady Di's, which I watched on TV as a kid, the most spectacular extravaganza I'd ever witnessed.

The four-hundred-guest University Club nuptials were captured on the glossy pages of *Town & Country*: her fourteen bridesmaids shimmering in crimson Vera Wang, four blond flower girls floating in white tulle skirts with white hydrangea wreaths on their towheads, and two ring bearers in tiny Ralph Lauren suits with little suspenders and bow ties. Joshie was up at the altar as best man, so I was alone in the pews for the ceremony, immediately feeling like a weird "plus one" on the guest list. It's strange when your guy is in a wedding and you're not; it's that "I'm with him" feeling, like you're not in the bride's inner circle and you don't fully belong. I sat next to Josh's mom, who raved about the "exquisite" and "sumptuous" Oscar de la Renta couture wedding gown, the towering bursts of peonies, and the fourteen-foot Sylvia Weinstock tiered cake. Forget the bride's inner circle—I kind of felt like I didn't even belong in the four hundred.

A year and a half later, when Josh and I got married, I met Bee for the second time, and she was just as radiant as she'd been on her wedding day, but this time with the added feather in her cap of being that hot *and* a mom, too. She was thinner than I was with my bridearexia and I hadn't even borne fruit. The thing was, Parker was the greatest guy ever, a true brother to Josh and always a kindhearted, lovely, fun person to be around. He came to San Francisco every couple months on business and our hilarious laugh-packed dinners together gave me those cackle cramps in my stomach. He was such a gem, always warm and sweet, and a loving dad who promptly whipped out folios of West's pictures while gushing about how much he missed him. So while I felt incredibly close to her husband, Bee was always a little bit of a mystery to me. It was also awky because I'm really a girls' girl and not one to bond with the boys; I have never been dicks over chicks. But I always felt it was so much more seamless with Parker. With Bee, convo seemed forced.

When my daughter was born, an extravagant sterling silver Tiffany baby cup arrived, hand-engraved VIOLET GRACE with a card that said "Welcome to the World—the Elliotts." I was suddenly so embarrassed by the dumb Baby Gap onesies I had sent Bee for Weston the year before. She must have thought that so . . . unspecial. It wasn't that I had, like, class-anxiety or anything, it wasn't about her having tons of money, it was more about *polish*. Bee was always so perfect, so put-together, I felt like a frigging slob-ass. I had met all of her Chapin friends, who just seemed so stylish and did everything right, by the book. Bee's hand-letterpressed stationery made my thermographed cheapola stuff look like I'd made it at Kinko's.

Take, for example, Bee's Christmas card. It was printed on stock so thick you could slash your wrist with it. Mine was flimsy and done with ink-pad stamps, total junior varsity Martha Stewart–style. The photograph of West was a full-on black-and-white professional portrait captured on the gleaming beaches of the Southampton Bathing Corp. Ours? A random snapshot I took of Violet playing with the seagulls by Fisherman's Wharf—hello cheesy tourist trap. I know I am overanalyzing and sounding all crazy, but it was little symbols like this, a tiny taste posted from her world into mine with a perfectly affixed seasonal stamp, that made me anxious to face my new life. Very anxious.

Three

Yet there was one other embodiment-of-chic humanoid that infused my move with spine-tingling stress. No sooner did I hook up our digital answering machine (which almost required an MIT diploma it took so effing long) than we got The Call. I'd gone to change Violet's diaper; it was a serious Code Brown situation, meaning I couldn't answer the ringing phone, and came back to the living room with my freshly Pampered tot to see a red "1" on the machine. I pressed play and instantly shivered as the poisonous timbre reverberated through the pad. It was Mrs. Lila Allen Dillingham, aka Josh's mom.

I know, I know: most peeps loathe their MiLs; it's the rule and not the exception. MiLs bug DiLs. They get up in their *bidniss*. They claim to know what's best for the kids. The list goes on. But this woman was not just a thorn in my side, she was a full *My name is Inigo Montoya*—hand-carved spear bisecting my bod. A true *Mayflower* type, she had married Josh's warm, sweet dad for love at twenty-one. But for a Greenwich-born *Social Register* member, love don't pay the country club bills. Josh's father, whose twinkling eyes and happy smile lit picture frames in our house, died when Josh was eight, leaving very little money—like my parents, he was a passionate teacher. Lila's parents, due to their lineage (but dwindling bank account, thanks to three generations of racquetball-playing Roman-numeraled peeps who felt "above" working), had vehemently opposed the marriage because he was Jewish. And though she must have loved him (by all reports, he was the funniest, most adoring man ever), her increasing anger about what her friends had and the pressures of keeping up with her childhood Greenwich friends mounted as her parents' dollars-in-eyes values seeped in. Josh said she got so crazy through the years, she used to obsessively drive him by Lauder Way after his father passed away, looking at the fancy houses in Greenwich before they moved back to the city, as she said to her young son—mere months after his father's death—"to find my next husband." She was this hardhearted patrician blonde, the only one who didn't sound psyched when we announced our marriage plans.

I cried to him after we told her because I could just tell by her Tom Cruisey clenched jaw that she was devastated that her only child, her prince, was wasting himself on a middle-class girl like me when I knew she had cadres of society swans fluttering around her that she'd prefer he wed. She had never been anything but ice cold to me (I called her "The Cube" to the Mooshu Mafia, my group of friends in SF who we had Chinese dinner with every Sunday) and always scanned me from head to toe, no doubt giving me the internal outfit-disapproval once-over. I'm sure even Christy Turlington wouldn't pass her MRI-like inspection, since no mortal maiden could ever be good enough for her "aaaaangel." And not to be cocky, but with every guy I've ever dated, the moms have loved me. I am always super polite, attentive, respectful, and leaping up as if my four-inch heeled boots were Air Jordans to clear the table or help in the kitchen. I am a girls' girl. I'm open, I watch Lifetime, I smile, I connect. And I fully understand that mother/son he's-my-baby thing. But this, unfortch, was way different, another beast altogether. Josh's mom had this strange worship of him that I found a little weirdo, like he was her chance to keep her lineage "on track" at a social level she had flouted by her first marriage; if Josh married someone to the manor born, she could right the wrongs of her past by sealing her grandchildren into the club of the elite. And she obviously didn't want him to make the same mistake she'd made.

And she didn't make the same mistake again herself: her second marriage, well, that was for cold hard ca$hola. Watson Dillingham was a British hundred millionaire slash former champion polo player who bought her a weekend estate on Conyers Farm in Greenwich and a penthouse on Fifth perched over the swaying trees of Central Park, which looked like their own personal backyard. He was nearing eighty—twenty years her senior—and while she lived it up with her credit cards galore, Watson, "Watts," had two daughters back in England who would surely get the bulk o' his dough when he went on to that great polo match in the sky. Maybe that was why she had been so desperate for Josh to marry someone wealthy. Maybe she just thought I was beneath him. Maybe she would plague me until I myself went nutso.

But thank God for my husband. Josh was the greatest. So many choruses of women have mother-in-law issues—obviously, even with my extremely tough-to-take MiL, I am not alone. And the only thing that can make it tolerable is how the husband deals with it. The worst is a Jocasta/Oedipus sitch I've heard lore about, where the guy lovingly defends his mom's behavior or even is "torn." Josh wasn't. He always told me he was well aware of his mom's craziness—he'd grown up with it: the constant quest to be on the right boards, the talking about other families' fortunes, the nonstop gossip about the so-and-sos' split or whose child got rejected from Groton or what family company stock was plummeting. "Just don't let her get to you, she's insane," he'd say, calming me down. "Hannah, you're the woman in my life." And it was true. At least while we were in our California perch, thousands of miles away from The Cube. Until I heard her throaty voice on the tin speaker and I froze all over again.

"Joshie! Welcome back, angel darling," she echoed through the machine's crap speaker. "I hope you're coming to Greenwich this weekend for my big birthday dinner. Watts and I are here having a great time. I'm going to pop into town tomorrow or the next day for some appointments. Call us in the morning, my angel."

No "Hi, Hannah" or even a mention of her only grandchild, Violet.

But I knew we had to face the music and go that weekend. It was her sixtieth birthday, after all. I could not have been dreading the sojourn more—every time we visited their country house during our dating days I felt so out of place in the Lilly Pulitzer explosion. If Greenwich was Hades, Josh's mom was the devil presiding over the lava-bubbling pit o' fire. And it would only get worse in a few weeks when her majesty was back in residence full-time just a few blocks from us. But I would have to take deep breaths and exhale my frustration and be strong. I thought I could do it. Sure! I could do it. Except that whenever we were with her, minutes passed like hours and I felt like I was in lockdown in Attica.

MEANWHILE, A FEW BLOCKS NORTH . . .

Instant Message from: BeeElliott

> BeeElliott: Bonjour—you there?
>
> Maggs10021: Oui, cherie. How art thou?
>
> BeeElliott: TERRIBLE.
>
> Maggs10021: Y?????
>
> BeeElliott: Went to my dermo today and got totally bitched out for my tan from Lyford.
>
> Maggs10021: Dr. Phillip? What'd he say?
>
> BeeElliott: That walking into his office with my skin is like someone walking into an AA mtg. w/ a bottle of Grey Goose.
>
> Maggs10021: Hilar.
>
> BeeElliott: So . . . Maggs, HUGE fave.
>
> Maggs10021: Sure, s'up?
>
> BeeElliott: This chick whose hub is friends w/ Park just moved here and I have to intro her around, ugh. Will u come?
>
> Maggs10021: K, so? What's her deal?
>
> BeeElliott: Blah. Lived in SF, grew up in Seattle, I think; nice-ish, but NOK. Dresses like Urban Outfitters threw up on her. Not a MILF like us ☺
>
> Maggs10021: HA. Gotcha. I'll totally come, no prob.
>
> BeeElliott: I know her hub and MiL since fetushood—u met her, Lila Allen Dillingham? She's chair of the WOG benefit committee.

Maggs10021: Wipe Out Glaucoma? Oh yes! Just saw her pic in T&C. Watson Dillingham's wife?

BeeElliott: Right—saw her at Swifty's and she practically begged me to intro her DiL to the gang; she's clearly stressed b/c the chick is v. left coast and NOK . . . dreading but please help!

Maggs10021: Of course ma cherie.

BeeElliott: Love u, thx! Let's get the boys together this week—I'll have my nanny call your nanny.

Four

There's something about Dora the Explorer, aside from the forced rhyme, that makes me want to chop her mop-topped oversized head off. Okay, that's too mean. She is a child after all, albeit a cartoon one. But after hearing her dumb jingles, say, eleventy times, I started to go nuts and suddenly wanted to clobber her à la Roadrunner and Wile E. Coyote with frying pans and destructive implements from the diverse Acme product line. I turned off the TV and tried to scavenge what I could from Violet's suitcases, retrieving a white eyelet dress that looked cute enough, even by New York standards.

I finished brushing Violet's hair, put on her best cardigan, pink, lined with a striped brown-and-white grosgrain ribbon, and began my walk to Central Park. The July sun was gleaming through the trees on the Fifth Avenue border of the park and I pushed Violet up the rows of hexagonal stones under a canopy of green. The trees, I mean. The other side of Fifth Avenue also was lined with green canopies: hunter green awnings, each with posh addresses written out in script—*Eight Twenty-Five Fifth Avenue.*

"Mommy, Mommy?" my precious daughter said, looking up at me.

"Yes, love muffin?"

"Birdie!"

"Very good! Yes, that kind of birdie is called a pigeon. Can you say *pigeon*?"

"Igin!"

"Good job, Vi! Pigeon," I said, patting her soft head. "We're going to see a lot of those here."

I thought about how even Josh's hero Woody Allen called them rats with wings.

As Violet's eyes slowly began to close for a nap, I looked at the pedestrian traffic of hordes of nannies coming toward me, pushing strollers, some out of *Mary Poppins*—huge Silver Cross prams with mosquito netting as if the coddled nugget inside were in the wilds of the Amazon. Some nannies were Filipino, wearing starched, pressed white uniforms, some Hispanic, some African American, all pretty much pushing these infant blondies with hair so platinum it was semi *Children of the Corn*. I looked at these white-haired kids and their diverse stroller-pushers and wondered what Martians would report to their mothership if they landed their space pods next to Central Park midweek. *"Captain, come in, Captain! We have found life! These creatures start out small and light and grow up big and dark!"*

I approached Seventy-second Street, my meeting point with Bee. She had texted me to meet her by the bench near that entrance to the park, and sure enough, there she was, perfectly turned out, in a full pleated skirt, kitten heels, a white blouse, and a Vuitton diaper bag, with her son, Weston, passed out in the stroller.

Within minutes of greeting Bee, I realized something right away: there was a war brewing. Whispers to the east of a dark, seething force, an echo from the west of an impending clash, a haunting rumble from the depth of the ground beneath our feet that tingles the spine of every soul who roams with inevitable doom.

I know this sounds straight out of *Lord of the Rings*, good versus evil. The problem with this bloodthirsty combat is that each side thinks theirs is good, the other, evil. And I'm not talking about Frodo and the gang versus the Orcs and those other beasty people that emerge from that weird flaming vagina thing. I am talking about the epic swordfight, the all-out, gut-churning violent, vitriol-laced battle between the most fiery of enemies: the working moms and the stay-at-home moms.

Back in California, while I was lucky enough to have just been wrapping up my thesis during Violet's first year, most of my friends worked and often made comments about the stay-at-homers who were so bored that they turned gossipy and malicious. I hadn't seen it with my own eyes, but I'd known a few moms at the playground to get a little too wrapped up in bullshit, but hey, it wasn't over-the-top or anything. But in

New York, everyone was wound tighter and I knew the two sparring factions were not just sides: they were poles.

Bee and her equally plucky and smiley friend, a very pregnant Maggie ("We were in the same eating club at Princeton!") Sinclair, said hello to me and then I stood by as they scanned the mommies on the playground and launched their assault, ushering me into their trench, arming me with staunch opinions and harsh *tsk-tsk*s about that other species of moms who journey daily to Hades. I mean, the office.

"Just look at her, poor Caroline Simmons," Bee said, shaking her head while looking toward the tire swings, where an attractive woman in a gray suit stood waving to her son, who was being pushed by his heavyset black nanny.

"Here for the fifteen-minute drive-by," Maggie said icily, rubbing her swollen belly. "I heard she works, like, literally twelve hours a day. Can you imagine?"

"It's just so sad, really," said Bee. "These women, they farm out the most important thing in life, the raising of their children! They're gone all day, they come home exhausted, and they miss the precious moments. Tragic, really." Bee looked around the playground and spied another woman who sparked a thought.

"Oh, Hannah—see that girl in the pink twinset? Okay, her name is Molly McBride and she used to be really really fat! But then she had her baby and got this weird thyroid thing so now she's all thin and is wearing skirts like that. I mean, hello, who do you think you are, the third Hilton sister? We're not twenty-four anymore."

"I think she does it to flirt with Scott from Mini Mozarts," said Maggie. "She has a massive crush on him."

"Everyone has a crush on Scott from Mini Mozarts," added

Bee with a hairflip. "Hannah, he's this hot guitarist who lives downtown but he does these baby music classes up here and has already slept with three moms!" she said excitedly. "He's banging his way up Park Avenue."

"That's three we know of. There could be loads more," added Maggie, eyes ablaze. "Oh! Which reminds me." She pulled out a contraption that said BeBe Sounds and proceeded to place giant headphones on her belly, pressing play on a CD player. "*Mozart for Babies*," she said, smiling. "It makes them smarter, studies have shown."

"Ugh, there goes Molly in her teeny skirt," said Bee, studying the leggy woman exiting the playground. "It's so weird how thin she's gotten. I just can't get the image of her old self out of my head. I mean she had chins, Hannah, *chins*."

"Well, that's the thing about getting skinny after being huge," said Maggie. "Everyone who knew you always remembers the old you. You can never shake the fat shadow."

I looked down and saw my thighs spreading over the painted green bench. Shit, what did they think of my tree trunks? Okay, I wasn't a lard ass or anything, I guess one would call me average. But "average" in my new habitat was certainly a size four to my curvier eight.

"And Molly's friends with this girl Lulita DeVeer, who has a kid out of wedlock with her, ahem, *partner*," sneered Bee. "Like I always say: Carriage before marriage is trashy trashy trashy."

Maggie chimed in, "I mean, this isn't California!" Then she caught herself, as if yours truly were hot off the plane from said state of sin. "No offense . . ." she added meekly.

"Look, Caroline Simmons has Tokyo on the phone, there she goes!" Bee observed as the harried woman took a call and waved a frantic good-bye and mimed a blown kiss to her child, who spun around in the tire swing. "She's leaving already. Back to the grind."

I decided not to mention that I was desperate to get back to work. I needed something in my life so as not to OD on unpacking boxes and wondering how to fill the day.

"So Hannah," said Maggie, looking me over. "Bee and I thought you might want to join our sessions with Dr. Poundschlosser. He's a genius in child psychology and we meet with him every week to discuss child development. He's the one who told me about Mozart on the headphones. He really gives some great insights and will definitely give Violet a jump ahead when it comes to nursery school interviews this fall."

"Oh . . . that's so nice. Um, yeah sure," I said looking across the park at a group of friendly-seeming nannies who were all laughing hysterically while bouncing their little charges on their knees.

"That over there?" said Bee, following my glance to their group of benches. "That's Little Trinidad. The nanny hangout. The mothers usually sit on this side."

"Oh," I said quietly, not quite knowing what to make of this. "They look like they're having fun."

"Oh, oh," said Maggie suddenly. "Six o'clock, look who's coming."

Bee turned around. "Yup, somebody cue the *Jaws* music."

I turned to see a petite woman decked out with seven different visible logos. It was like the alphabet had exploded onto her five-foot-two frame, which was covered with a sea of LV's, H's, double C's, and D&G's.

"Hiiiiiii, gals!" she said, her huge Gucci frames covering her tiny head. "So six weeks and counting to the speed dial! I am freaking out! Lester's guys at the office are trying to write a code this summer that will break through the phone lines! I am praying!" As she clasped her ring-covered hands in exaggerated prayer to the heavens above, the glint of her bling almost blinded me. "If we don't get into Carnegie, oh my gawd, I'll just die. *Die!*"

"They say if you don't get your kid into Carnegie Nursery School, well, there goes Princeton," smiled Bee tauntingly.

Huh? What speed dial?

"Keep your fingers crossed for me and little Stella Scarlett, 'k?" she said, leaving in a blaze of gold, gems, and zippers.

"Whoa," I said, amusedly watching her head to the swings in stilettos. "Who is that?"

"Gagsville," said Bee.

"The worst," added Maggie.

"Tessa Finch-Saunders. She is such a spoiled brat. I heard she just bought her husband a Jasper Johns oil for his thirty-fifth birthday," whispered Bee conspiratorially. "He's in private equity. Loaded. She runs around throwing her money everywhere, so tacky. Very nouveau."

I nodded. I was intrigued by her, but more than that, I wanted to know what she was talking about with this Carnegie place. "So, um, what's this nursery school?"

"Carnegie. The best. On Ninetieth Street. It's a feeder to all the best kindergartens," said Bee. "Everyone goes there, I mean, the class lists could be a page torn out of *Forbes!*"

"Uh-huh . . ." I felt my palms begin to sweat. "And what was that, like, speed-dial thing?"

"They have thousands of interested families. Literally thousands," explained Bee. "But there are only forty spaces. So they only print five hundred applications and they open the phone lines at eight A.M. the day after Labor Day for requests and you just have to just hope you get one. You have to get all your family to help you dial."

"Oh. Does West go there?"

"Yes," said Bee, proudly. "And Maggie's son, Ford. It's the best in the city. Someone donated a million smacks to get their kid in! It's harder to get into than Yale Law, but once you're in, you can write your ticket. But the first hurdle is getting though the phone line to get an application."

"Gosh, I didn't realize I needed to win a radio contest to be able to even apply," I said, shaken.

"Yeah, it's kind of nuts. I'm glad that's all behind me, since siblings are almost always let in," sighed Maggie. "I don't envy you beginning the process. It sucks."

Gulp.

"Tessa Finch-Saunders won't have a problem, though," said Bee, watching her far across the playground by the swings. "She sent her daughter to all the right classes. They always ask what Mommy and Me's the child took. Plus, I'm sure she'll send in her application along with a scroll of blueprints for a new wing."

"Like what classes?" I asked, fearing my hippie, barefoot Music Together in Berkeley wasn't the rigorous academic syllabus the advanced New York two-year-old required.

"Well, there's a few really important prerequisites for this age: music, art, gym, languages. Maybe you should sign Violet up for a summer course?"

"Okay, I mean . . . what did you guys do?"

"Well, I did Lucky Me, I'm Under Three. But . . . there's a three-year waiting list."

Great. "How is it a three-year list if you presumably go when you're under three? By the time you get in, you're over the hill!" I said, jokingly. Neither of them laughed.

"You call and put your name down the second you know you're pregnant," said Bee, dead serious.

"I called before I even told my husband I was pregnant," recalled Maggie. "I peed on that stick, thong around my ankles, and the second that the line turned blue, I was dialing them."

"So . . . that's out then." I smiled, imagining Violet going through metal detectors to get to her public kindergarten because I wasn't in on the fetal pre-pre-preregistration. "I guess my daughter will be home-schooled, serial-killer-style." Then I thought about Maggie wearing a thong. Were they taking over women's undies? I hated thongs. They felt like ass-floss.

"Well, there's a summer program at the Language Institute. You can sign up for that," suggested Maggie. "It's really key to learn a foreign language at this age because they develop an ear for the accent."

"Oh, and what about Milford Prescott Music School? They have a summer program, I think," mused Bee.

"We call it Juilliard 'cause they take everything so seriously. I mean, the kids are one and they're already learning the difference between violin and cello sounds. But it is the best pre-preschool." Maggie paused and looked at me. "Are you okay, Hannah?"

My pale complexion had once again betrayed my inner emotional quakes. As stress seized my body, my cheeks flushed without fail, rendering me a blank screen on which all my worries could flicker across for the world to see in Technicolor.

"I'm fine. I just . . . maybe I need to go, I'm still sort of, you know, jet-lagged and woozy."

"Oh, okay," said Bee. "Maybe you should rest. I know we're throwing a lot at you."

I quickly got up, head spinning, to venture home, but not to any comforting home I even knew. "Bye, guys. I'll see you tomorrow."

"Hey, wait," Bee said, getting up from the bench to walk alongside me. "I know this is all very overwhelming. And Parker and I are here for you. Really. And I'm sure your mother-in-law will help, too—she knows tons of people. She's lovely."

"I'm sorry," I said, hoping I wouldn't cry. I chose to ignore the kudos for The Cube. "I just feel a little lost with everything here. I want Violet to have the best of everything, and I feel like I got on this track a little late."

"It's okay," said Bee, consolingly. "Listen. I have a good tip for you. It's a broker. For your apartment?"

"Oh, really? That would be great . . ."

"His name is Troy Kincaid. His wife, Mrs. Kincaid, is actually the headmistress of Carnegie Nursery School. I am sure that if you buy a place through him, she will see to it that you will at least get an application."

I paused, wiping the sweat from my brow. "Can't you, like, get arrested for that?"

"No! It's just how things are done. Take his card." She unzipped a little metallic leather pouch from her bag and handed me a business card. "Call him. And we'll see you at the Pierre Hotel tomorrow for the Little Duke and Duchess trunk show!"

I nodded and waved, walking away as fast as my un-chic Chuck Taylors would carry me.

AND ON A NEARBY TITANIUM POWERBOOK...

Instant Message from: BeeElliott

        BeeElliott: Whatdja think?

        Maggs10021: She seems cool, actsh.

        BeeElliott: REALLY? You thunk? Yawnsville.

        Maggs10021: I feel bad for her—she def. needs
our help w/ schools & stuff.

        BeeElliott: I know, she's clueless! I heard
her mom-in-law is kind of horrified that she's so
out of it and like sloppy.

        Maggs10021: I like her style—more downtowny
but whatev, she dresses cool.

        BeeElliott: If you're hanging out at a punk
rock club. This is the UES, not CBGBs.

        Maggs10021: So are you going to write for her
for CNS?

        BeeElliott: Dunno. I can put in a good word I
guess but I don't want to blow chips on a non-
friend.

        Maggs10021: Wasn't her hub Park's best man?
He was a hottie.

        BeeElliott: He's not my fave. Express train
to Loserville.

        Maggs10021: Really? I remember him being
totally DDG!

        BeeElliott: Lameissimo.

        Maggs10021: Hmm.

Five

If there's one thing I hate, it's the pop-by. On TV when I saw bedroom communities filled with gracious neighbors bearing muffins in a gingham-napkin-covered basket, I would cringe, vowing never to leave city-dwelling. So natch I was less than thrilled when I was bent over a box with sweat dripping from my brow when the buzzer from downstairs rang. The doorman announced my unexpected visitor as "Mrs. Dillingham"—God forbid she just say my mother-in-law was here. Shit! Thank goodness I spotted and stashed Josh's morning good-bye note in a drawer—it had a list of would-be porn titles that we liked to come up with on our walks by video stores or cineplexes, it was sort of our thing, a running joke (e.g., *Forrest Hump, Booty and the Beast, Indiana Jones and the Temple of Poon*, etc.). With the list put away, in a human cyclone whirl, I put on some black buckled flats, tucked my gray vintage Blondie T-shirt into my black jeans, and shoved a brush through my hair so fast and furiously that I almost made myself bald. Just as I was applying a touch of Chapstick to my lips, the door-bell rang.

"Hiiii," I said. "Welcome to our new temporary abode! Sorry I'm so gross—"

She didn't challenge my self-assessment. "Hello." She walked right past me, surveying the plain, ordinary apartment. The skyscraping view was definitely mesmerizing, the rooms spacious and clean, but it was one of those apartments where all the good ingredients still made up a crappy stew vibe-wise. For example, there was one of those cut-out rectangle thingies in the living room wall and ceilings that seemed especially low given the piles of cardboard boxes. As I saw her take in what I'm sure she presumed to be a total mess, I realized I didn't feel well at all—my chunder was mid-esophagus and rising. Did I have some kind of social anxiety disorder like that drug commercial with all the warped, stretched-out faces? Why did I always get nervous around her?

"So. Hannah, daaarling, you must be itching to get out of here! It's positively claustrophobic! I detest these depressing postwar buildings, just horrible."

Oh, yeah. That was why—there was rarely a nice thing from her lips.

"Violet is napping and I was just unpacking the kitchen boxes—do you want to come see her? She's so cute, passed out in her little—"

"Have you seen Bee Elliott yet? She promised me she'd help you with the school process. Lord knows it can be daunting."

"Yes, yes. I met her yesterday with her friend and they were really nice—"

Lila sat down on our old Ikea couch but not before looking at it as if fearing it was stuffed with maggots. She tried to look comfortable but I knew she wasn't. Her massive Fifth Avenue penthouse was immaculately and stunningly decorated by El- lie Cullman, and I knew she was practically wincing at our def- initely unposh digs. The only thing worse than the home I was making for her son was clearly my outfit.

"You always have such . . . eclectic style," she said, staring at me nostrils aflare as if I were a stool sample.

I didn't know how to respond. I hate mean observations couched in faux compliments.

"And speaking of which," she said, delicately opening a pink shopping bag, "I have a few dresses for Violet. I know you tend to favor more . . . casual clothing for her. But this isn't the West Coast, you know. People *dress*. And with your interviews for schools coming up this year, I figured I'd help you get some more . . . conservative looks for her."

I thanked her meekly. While the beautiful Made In Portugal dresses were indeed exquisite and definitely so generous, I knew they were a 3D memo to spruce up my kid. I love how she said people "dress," as if in the jungle of California, our children run amok buck, peeing themselves. I knew what she meant in general; yes, children's clothes back west weren't as old-fashioned, and I did like the dresses. But you'd think I had Violet in leopard leggings and rhinestone tees that read "Daddy's Girl." I wasn't tacky, just . . . chill. She wore simple cords and cute tops from the Gap, so sue me.

"I simply want Violet to fit in here, you know, with the right families," Lila added.

I got up to get hangers for the dresses, which I carefully hung as I nodded.

"Violet's adorable, obviously, I mean she is truly Joshie's clone!" she laughed. "But sometimes when you've visited she's been a touch . . . bedraggled. And that ragamuffin thing can be sweet, but not in public, dear. We certainly don't want her going to preschool interviews looking like *une fille des rues*."

I took a deep breath and tried to slowly and calmly exhale the steam that was building inside. I thought I'd erupt like

Mount Vesuvius momentarily. *Fille des rues?!* My French was not *parfait* but I knew that meant "girl of the streets"—a street urchin. As if I made my ill-cared-for daughter look like tattered Cosette from *Les Miz*.

"So we're excited for your birthday this weekend," I lied, trying to muster kind words for the woman whose face I wanted to bludgeon with a borrowed polo mallet from her crusty husband's collection. "I'm excited to get out of the city."

"Yes, it should be lovely. It will be just us, thank goodness. Watts's daughters were due to come from London and thank the Lord they decided to just see him next month in Bath."

For some weird sick reason I was oddly psyched that there were people she seemed to dislike more than me.

"How are they doing?" I asked with fake interest; I'd met Watts's daughters once—they seemed very sweet but were clearly out of their father's life, as they had not only the Atlantic between them but also a chasm of intimacy thanks to a stepmom who would rather pretend they didn't exist at all.

"Nightmares. Just nightmares," she said, shaking her head. "They came to New York in May, and Fiona sat us down and said, in very dramatic style, that she was convinced that Victoria was anorexic."

"That's awful!" I said.

"Oh, please. It's all rubbish. Watts seemed quite worried and was practically about to call the plane when I said, 'You know what I think, Fiona? I think for the first time in Victoria's life, she's thinner than you. And you can't stand it!' They're quite competitive, you know."

"But . . . is she sick, or—"

"No, no, no, you know, girls gain and lose weight all the time. Victoria's twenty-four and pulling herself together, and Fiona is jealous, clearly."

I decided not to touch this with a thirty-three-and-a-half-foot pole.

"And how is your husband's health?" I asked, changing the subject. Watts had had a mini stroke a year before and I recalled Lila phoning us not from his hospital bed but from Swifty's, where she stuck to her dinner plans with friends. Nice.

"Fine, fine, you know. He's pushing eighty, so . . ."

"Mommy?" I head Violet's groggy cry from the other room. I leaped up and went to the makeshift nursery to scoop her into my arms. "Guess who's here?" (Lila insisted Violet call her Lila.) "Lila! Lila's here! Say hello to Lila, sweetheart!"

But Violet burst into tears.

"Oh dear," said Lila. "A lot of crying—"

Which was normal since she'd just woken from a nap and was, ya know, *two.*

"Sorry," I apologized. "She's still a little out of it."

Violet screamed and shook her little body in thrash mode.

"Shhhh, sweets, Lila is here! Look! Lila's here to see you!"

"AHHHHHHHHHH!!!!"

I began to sweat as if Violet's cries were somehow a reflection on me.

"I probably should go, then," Lila said, rising to grab her quilted handbag.

"Sorry—she just . . . she just woke and up and gets a little—"

"WAHHHHHHHHH!!!!"

"Well, all right then, I'll see you this weekend. Hopefully

she'll be in a better mood!" she said, opening the door. And with that she was gone, leaving us in her Ferragamo-wearing Roadrunner wake.

Six

"Happy Hour"—what a myth. Five to eight P.M., the time many yuppies are happily clinking glasses in bars dotting the map of Manhattan, is what I call "Suicide Hour," when I am so utterly exhausted I want to collapse, and it's still at least four hours until my husband comes home. I watch horrible soul-slurping shows like *Access Hollywood* and then being curious about Angelina Jolie's wild lovemaking in the Congo makes me want to kill myself even more.

Violet, my little scrumptious love, who can do no wrong in my eyes, crumbles into a fussy munchkin and I try to keep her busy with books, but after five or six I feel so tired I ultimately cop out guiltily and pop in a kiddie DVD, i.e., baby crack.

But that night, after an interminable day of unpacking boxes and nearly hanging myself with the very "ropes" Bee and Maggie had shown me as I Googled every nursery school in the neighb, I tucked Violet into her makeshift folding bed, sang her to sleep with soft rounds of "Twinkle, Twinkle," and was so excited I could hardly wait. My best girlfriend in the whole wide world, the spoonful of honey that made the medicine of my move go down, was coming over, and for the first time in about a month I got a sitter so I could go out to a civilized dinner and catch up with the only sister I'd ever known.

I met Leigh Briggs my first day of college. She was carrying a huge ficus tree, soil spilling out onto the flat stone path under a Gothic arch of our dorm. Leigh is my total übershrink/sage/partner in crime. She instantly struck me as a 1940s starlet. We bonded over boys, movies, and chowing, becoming pretty much add-water-and-stir insta-pals. She always offered wise (and sometimes old-fashioned) kernels of wisdom and was a true "lady," like a stylish dame from yesteryear, but with a gutter mouth. To outsiders, she was mannered and proper but sharply brilliant underneath all the immaculate beauty of classic clothes and old-world grace. We had been, despite the three-thousand-mile distance over the last five years, joined at the hip, and aside from Josh, she was definitely the person I downloaded the most stuff to. She always made me feel strong and ready to take on anything. And she didn't quite recognize me in my current state.

"What is the fucking matter with you?" she said forcefully, not half an hour into our visit. She was holding her wine in one hand and flipping through my *Us Weekly* with the other. "This is not you. Why are you such a stress case? Yes, you're living in this dump, but that's temporary! And so what if your mother-in-law is a beeyotch, take a number! You have husband and a baby, shut up."

"I know, I know. It's just that with a kid here, there is a whole new set of stresses—"

"*Puh-lease*. How about wondering if my shithead boss is ever going to tell anyone we're together after doing me for nine months? How about wondering if I'm going to die alone with my cat eating my face off 'cause there's no one to pour the Purina? I love you to death, but *get a fucking grip*."

Like I said, there's no one like Leigh. We greeted the sitter, Amber, a student from Barnard (I had discovered the college agency in the book *CityBaby*, which had become my overnight bible). We kissed Violet good-bye and walked down the street to Primola, a cozy restaurant nearby. As we strolled in the warm summer air, I felt bad for having bitched about my worries. After all, Leigh was right; yes, I had my own issues being new here in a sea of perfect, preened übermoms, but at least I wasn't *out there*; the recollection of that gut-churning time wasn't pretty.

After college I fell madly in love with Luke, a coworker at a dot-bomb, just before the millennial Internet implosion. Once the company melted down, I went back to grad school while he took a job in a tiny shitbox office at a little start-up called eBay. After three years together, living together, traveling all over, he wanted to get married. And something in me was . . . scared. It wasn't a fear of commitment, it was simply a pit of not being sure. Everyone thought we were the perfect couple, but deep down I was feeling like the *rest of my life* was a long time. So I confessed my doubts, and Luke and I split up. But not before he looked me in the eye and said, "Hannah, just so you know, you will never, ever get anyone as good as me to love you."

Ouch. He meant it to sting and it worked. But not nearly as much as it did when I heard, six months later, that he was engaged to a blond chick he'd met on a hike. A hike! Like me, he hated the outdoors. Their betrothal was a whirlwind that culminated in a majestic San Francisco wedding four months later, and there I was, single, lonely, and wondering what crack pipe I'd been smoking to let a great guy like him go. The next two years were a crushing, miserable montage of heinous dates and ill-fated relationships. The guy whose mom had him lick chocolate sauce off her finger at a fondue restaurant (ew, check, please!), the dude who tried to push my head down to blow him on the first date (you must be kidding), and even the guy who told me—deadpan—that he didn't have a sense of humor. Huh? Doesn't everyone, even un-funny people, think he or she has a sense of humor? Apparently not. Taxi!

And then there was Paul. The guy I thought I would marry. He was a blond stockbroker who played lacrosse in college (quote unquote lax) and we basically moved in together after a month of zero-to-sixty intense dating. He was almost the biggest crush I'd had in my life, second only to Tate Hayes, my college thesis adviser. Paul and I were like those creepy conjoined twins on that A&E documentary, attached at the heart. Despite his slight penchant for drinking, I woooorshipped him and was beyond smitten. Then one day, I came home to find him throwing a lacrosse ball at the wall and catching it and "cradling."

"Hi, cutie!" I said, going to kiss him. "Happy six-month anniversary!"

"Listen, Hannah . . . we have to talk." Nota bene: anything that begins with "listen" or "look" equals chiming death knell of your relationship.

Lump in throat. "About what . . . Is everything okay?"

Interminably long exhale. Second worst forecast of doom after "look" or "listen."

"No, actually. I came into work this morning and Nathan

said, 'How's your wife?' and it just . . ." (lax ball thrown at wall, cradle, cradle), "I don't know, it just really wigged me out. I'm just so not ready to get married and it just made me realize, ya know, like . . ." (ball thrown at wall, catch, cradle). "I just want to take it easy and I think we should . . ." (cradle, cradle in the fucking macramé basket on that long stick in that dumbest sport *ever*), "maybe see other people and maybe cool down a little."

Cool fucking down?

Yes. I was dumped whilst lax ball was hurled at tapestry-covered Sheetrock wall by a Patagonia-fleece-wearing white-baseball-hat preppy motherfucker. To say my shocked sobs flooded the Bay would not be far from the truth. Hysteria.

Over the next few days (during which I had to write a massive term paper, lucky me) I shut down and literally had a full-on Princess Buttercup *I shall never love again* melodramatic emotional seal-off. Could I ever really know anyone again? I was stunned. Shocked. *Gutted.* I knew it was "character building" to be dumped, and after a couple sob-filled weeks, I almost found solace in the fact that this was a rite of passage for me; suddenly I was in on the Top 40 lyrics about heartbreak. Now I knew what all those dumb happy people didn't—there's a whole subworld of the miserable out there—and it's so much hipper! I blared the Smiths. I pored over my childhood Edward Gorey collection. I brooded. The darkness was making me grow, and hey, everyone probably has one big heartbreak, right? Now mine was out of the way. I could play loud music and hate his guts and the world would be on my side 'cause, hey, everyone favors the dumpee. But that didn't make it much easier. Thank God, though I didn't know it at the time, Josh Allen had just moved around the corner and we would meet two months later.

Leigh and I walked into the restaurant and plopped into a corner banquette. I remembered the worries of my days alone and I felt horrible for even thinking of complaining to her about my dumb issues, especially because we were older now and that stress of being single compounds with age. I made a pact to myself to zip it about stupid motherhood stresses—I could vent to my best friend in California, Jenny, though the time diff was getting to be a challenge. And my parents, well, they were great and so understanding, but now that my dad had retired they were on this whole adventure travel kick, trotting the globe (currently on a four-month backpacking trip in New Zealand) and I felt like the rest of our posse was scattered, busy, and so when we talked I wasn't about to unload my problems. Leigh was the one I told everything to—aside from Josh (all three of us were only-children)—but Leigh was right, I was blessed to even have a kid, to have sweet Josh, and even though things people go through are all relative, I kind of had no right to complain. Here Leigh was, the coolest, most amazing, drop-dead-gorgeous woman, and it seemed that all the great guys were taken. I felt so lucky to have found Josh, but in my head, I always identified more with single gals than married ones—the whole couples-dinner thing and "There's this great couple you should meet" seemed forced to me. That's why I would never be a Bridget Jones "smug married": being lonely and miserable was not too distant a memory for me, and I'd never shove marriage in the face of someone single, since I myself could have easily missed Josh by minutes the night we met, and been freaking just like Leigh. She dated a ton but never met the right guy, and she was starting to get depressed. So she did the big no-no and started effing her boss.

"So," I started cautiously, as she knew damn well where I stood on her relationship, "how's Craig?"

Exhale. "Ugh. Totally in denial," she replied, shaking her head. "At first I thought the secret work fling was hot and it was totally sexy to have this clandestine affair, banging in the staircase, et cetera. Now I think it's just creepy," Leigh said, sipping her cocktail. "I feel like time's a-ticking, I mean what the fuck am I doing? I'm thirty-one. Cobwebs will start forming in my uterus in exactly five years."

"No they won't. It's 2005, and that woman had twins at fifty-three. I don't think you should worry about that. But I do think you've got to get out of this Craig thing, Leigh. This is bad. You deserve someone who will worship you and want to shout it from the rooftops, not this sneaky shit."

"I know, I know." She looked out the window at the twinkling lights.

"Hannah?"

"Yeah?"

You're in New York!

I laughed as she leaned in to give me a huge hug and we cackled like giddy winners on the *Price Is Right* showcase showdown.

"I mean, have we not been dreaming of this for years?" she said, glowing. "I am so happy you're here I can't even tell you. And little Violet. I have missed her so much, precious lamb."

"She missed you, too."

Leigh looked at me, fully scanning my insides, Robocop-style.

"Hannah, I know it's hard to move. And I'm sorry to wig

about your problems with everything. Of course you're entitled to have issues. I know it's all relative."

"No, you're right. I can't complain."

"So? Are you okay?"

I exhaled, not wanted to go into everything that was haunting me. But Leigh was already a New York expert and I still felt overwhelmed. "I just feel like there's such a scene here—"

"Here's what you have to learn, right now," said Leigh sternly. "There is no 'scene.' The scene is in your head. I mean, it is there, of course, but it is one of a trillion scenes. It's not like Seattle, where your mom knows everyone. You can do anything here—learn trapeze, take Finnish, start a sewing circle, anything! There are infinite ways to find new pockets of eccentrics and meet new people."

"I can't meet new people," I said lazily. "The friendship vault is closed."

"What?" she laughed, almost spitting out the olive she'd popped in her mouth. "What *friendship vault*?"

"There's no room. I'm closed for business, shut down," I said, shrugging. "I have no time! I'm exhausted and mushy-brained and also so not . . . myself. I'm such a zombie. How could I ever make new friends?"

"Well I know at least one person who will want to see you . . ." she taunted with a raised eyebrow.

"Who?"

"You know who," she said, giving me a sly look. "Professor Hayes."

Just hearing the name gave me chills.

"Leigh. I am a married woman. I'm in love with Josh, remember?"

"You're married, you're not dead! It's not like anything really ever happened with him! Plus he's married with two kids now, so it's like . . . safe to call him."

"No," I said, shaking my head. "*No way* would I call him."

"Why? I told you, when I bumped into him last year he asked all about you. And now you're both living in New York! You guys were, like, really tight."

"We were close. But . . . obviously I was obsessed with him and it's probably not a good idea. I mean, what would be the point, anyway?"

"You were inseparable back then," Leigh whined, trying to entice me. "There's good stuff there—a real friendship that excited you."

I took a deep breath and exhaled the thought, shaking my head. "I'm not seeking him out, it's too nerve-racking. It's so weird he's at Columbia now. He's the youngest tenured professor in the department . . ." I could hear my voice trail off as I caught Leigh staring at me with a mischievous face. She had heard me spill way too many guts out over him way back when. "He was like my idol for so long, I almost don't want to see him."

"You guys look like a couple of gossiping teens in the cafeteria," Josh interrupted, as he put his briefcase down by the door and came toward our booth.

"Josh!" Leigh ran to the door and hugged Joshie, who looked thoroughly wiped out but beyond adorable with his tie loosened and his suit slightly rumpled from a marathon workday. He came to kiss me. "Amber told me you two were here. Hi, love. You look hot. Is this a yummy mummy or what, LeighLeigh?"

"Delish!" she said, smiling, putting her free arm around me, pressing us into a triumvirate hug.

"Please. You could fry an egg on my face I am so greasy right now," I complained. "Want to order something? Ugh, sweets, I am the worst wife. I haven't made one dinner for you since we got here." Not that I'm any great shakes in the kitchen, though I do make a mean grilled cheese.

"Hey, we're in New York," he said, smiling, wrapping his arms around Leigh and me. "The only thing most wives have to make for dinner is reservations."

AND IN BEE-LAND . . .

Instant Message from: BeeElliott

> BeeElliott: So you're coming to the trunk show tom?
>
> Maggs10021: Totally! It's my fave one, gonna do some SERIOUS damage w/ my AmEx.
>
> BeeElliott: Me too. Let's go shopping after, I want to hit Christian Louboutin and Michael Kors for my outfit for the MoMA party.
>
> Maggs10021: I have pers trainer, can't . . . What abt day after tom?
>
> BeeElliott: Can't, have Pilates.
>
> Maggs10021: You're doing so much Pilates these days. Addicted?
>
> BeeElliott: Gotta get down to 108 bef we start trying for baby #2. Park's dyyyying to get me preg right now but must lose last 3 pounds.
>
> Maggs10021: You = stick, Bee! Crazy.

BeeElliott: Anyway, must go; Giorgio is
here to do my highlights—see u tom. Oh—and
don't forget, that Hannah Allen is coming too,
but let's ditch her bef we hit Madison.
    Maggs10021: Deal.

Seven

The next morning, newly empowered from my evening with Leigh, I put Violet in the stroller and headed to the nearby Pierre Hotel to meet Bee and Maggie. I had unearthed a few cool outfits from my dusty U-Haul boxes and felt way more stylish than I had the day before, when I had looked like such a recent San Franciscan import—i.e., sans edge.

I got to the grand hotel and walked in the gilded double doors. Maggie was inside fanning herself with her Fendi clutch.

"Uck, could it *be* any hotter out there?" she said with Chandler Bing sarcasm, delicately blotting her ever-so-slightly-misted brow. Her blond bob looked recently blown out and, like most moms I'd spied in the 'hood, she was using her huge Jackie O. sunglasses as a headband.

"I know, I hate summer," I said.

"What?" said Bee, who walked in, snapping her cell phone shut. "Did you just say you *hate summer*?"

I know it sounds so weird and almost call-the-cops criminal, but *yes*. I hate summer. I always feel slow and lethargic and dirty. Everyone else always slims down and perks up, but I just go into ice cream and nap mode, and the smell is so horrendous in the city that it should have those cartoon vertical squiggle lines over everything to connote stink, like that smelly kid on Charlie Brown. I'm more of the dark-hair, nontanned ilk, so grody pastels make me look recently exhumed from a grave. I love crispy cold invigorating air and turtlenecks and dark afternoons. The San Francisco weather suited me, even in the rain.

"It's just so humid and sticky and I just feel gross and uggles," I said, shrugging. They looked at me like I was certifiably insane. I sheepishly added, "I guess I'm a sort of fall-winter kinda gal."

"I can see that," said Bee, looking me over. "You have that Wednesday Addams thing going on."

When we got off the elevator, a sign stood in front of us, reading Little Duke and Duchess Trunk Show, suite 2415. The clothing company was founded by an actual duchess. Well, a New York girl who had married the French Duke of Burgundy. Lucky for him, as Bee explained, the duchess was a multibillionaire whose grandfather had invented velvet ropes. Talk about being born an insider. As we walked into the grand room, I beheld hordes of immaculate mothers selecting stunning clothes for their tots, who were all at home, presumably with uniformed nannies while their moms bought clothes for the following winter. I hadn't realized I would be the only one with a kid on hand.

"Mommy," said Violet.

"Yes, muffin?"

"Uppie, uppie!"

"Okay, sweets."

I unharnessed Violet from her stroller to let her run amok in the lavish space, which was a huge six-room salon with a sprawling buffet of tea sandwiches, cookies, Perrier poured in crystal tumblers, and coffee in huge silver pots.

"Okay, honey, you can play here, but stay right in this area, okay?"

" 'K. Mommy, Mommy?"

"Yes, Violet love?"

"Ruv youuuu."

I almost melted. I knelt down to give her a massive hug. When I looked up, Bee and Maggie were looking on. I assumed they were touched by the tender moment, but when I came over, Bee said, "Hannah, what are you going to do about help?"

"Oh, you mean babysitting?"

"Yes, are you looking into a nanny?"

A tall bejeweled South American–looking woman with an alligator Hermès bag was listening. "Oh, do you need a governess?" she interrupted with a shady pan-Euro accent.

"A *governess*?" I asked, almost laughing. "Like the Family Von Trapp?"

"I know one who's in search of placement. Live-in," she replied.

"Oh, no thanks, I'm not looking," I said. "But thank you anyway."

She drifted off and Bee turned back to me. "Ugh, Flora de Manteva, she's the worst. She added the 'de' to her name. Anyway, forget governesses. You need to get a nanny, how are you doing this all alone? I would *die*."

"Well, I would love to have some free time, for a few hours, maybe a couple times a week—"

"Well you'll never find *that*," said Maggie. "The good people all want guaranteed schedules. You must call Mrs. Brown's Agency. They have the best people. They all have impeccable references and work for the best families in New York. Mine used to work with the Bronfmans."

"Uh-huh," I said, feigning enthrallment.

"I have the most wonderful Indian gal. But I'd get a Malaysian. They're quite fastidious," said Bee. "I had just the best one as a baby nurse right after I had Weston."

"I thought Noona was Thai," said Maggie.

"Same noodle, different sauce," shrugged Bee. "But go with someone from Asia."

I was starting to feel very uncomfortable.

"And avoid the Islands," added Bee. "I had this one woman from Trinidad. So much 'tude. And lazy! She moved like a glacier, and was the size of one, too. I'd have to point out everything. Like, *hello?* This silver picture frame could not be more tarnished! And the South American nannies, they're all busy gossiping and speaking Spanish and meanwhile the kids are dangling from the highest rung on the jungle gym."

I sat silent, stunned.

"Everyone has issues. I mean, even with the Malaysians, be careful," Bee continued. "A lot are very sneaky. There's always a sick relative or some reason they need a day off or more money suddenly."

"Iceland is really big these days," piped in Maggie. "Tons of nannies on the scene from Reykjavik. I've heard good things."

"But be careful if you go that route," said Bee with a glint of warning in her eye. "You don't want a sitter hotter than you. Everyone knows about Janie Ribicoff's husband banging the Swedish nanny. My advice is *stay away* from Scandinavia. Clichés exist for a reason, Hannah. Do not get someone that might turn Josh's head."

What? Were they implying Josh's head would turn? Not that I was Miss America, but I was not worried in that department. To be totally honest, I probably wouldn't hire a supermodel doppelgänger anyway, but I barely knew Bee and Maggie, so the whole horrifyingly racist convo made me ill. How could they make proclamations about entire islands, let alone continents?

It was as if Bee truly saw herself as a superior being to her staff. I never grew up with "help." My parents were hands-on, and when they wanted to go out, we had a cool college girl come and hang with us—never a starched white uniform in sight. So the whole concept of my being someone's boss was too strange to me. I watched Violet giggling as she ran under the racks of clothes.

" 'Scuse me one sec," I said, pulling my ejector seat on the convo and bolting to go play with Violet.

I sat down cross-legged next to her on the floor, and when I looked up and saw a few blond-bob types looking down at me in more ways than one, I realized perhaps I shouldn't be plopped on the carpet of the suite. So I picked up Violet, put her on my hip, and began to peruse the clothes.

The handmade lace was more intricate and well tailored than anything in my closet. The little *dentelle* collars so delicate, the tiny cashmere sweaters softer than anything I'd touched aside from Violet's skin. The prices? Two hundred seventy-five smacks for the sweater, which I don't even spend on myself, unless it's a whole outfit. But a top? That she'll wear thrice? Sheesh. A little velvet holiday dress was $375, a wool pinafore, $250. A wool coat with a gray velvet collar and covered buttons was $450. I wondered if it would be tacky to bolt and not buy anything. I'd already snarfed five of those little tea sandwiches so I felt pressured to cough it up for something. Plus the loot was beyond adorable. Too bad Josh would cut my credit card into pieces if I even dared order anything that exorbitant.

"Hiiiii!" a somewhat familiar nasal voice said. "Tessa Finch-Saunders. Didn't we meet at the Seventy-second Street playground?"

"Oh, yes, hi—Hannah Allen."

"I just did some major damage!" she confessed with faux dread. "But this stuff is *to die for*, the cutest."

The logo-covered pixie gave me a wide smile as her sales consultant tallied her total on a Lucite clipboard. "Okay, that'll be three thousand six hundred seventy-two with tax," she said, smoothly swiping Tessa's AmEx black card. Tessa simply nodded casually and took out the pen to sign.

"I'm gonna go find Bee," I said. "Have a great day." I bolted, stunned by her purchase and psyched to report the "major damage," until I saw that Bee and Maggie were buying easily as much, if not more.

I peered into the boys' apparel section of the suite, replete with navy blue blazers, mini preppy striped ties, and crisp shirts like mini versions of those worn by their Wall Street daddies, who brought home the bacon so the wives could go on these crazy sprees. Bee and Maggie were chatting breezily while piling stacks and stacks of samples to order on their arms.

I walked in to say au revoir. "The stuff is gorgeous. Thanks for inviting me."

"Byeeee!" Violet said.

"Oh, good-bye, Violet. Are you leaving, Hannah?" asked Bee. "Did you even get anything?"

"Yes, I'm getting this little blouse," I said, holding up a cute Peter Pan chemise, which was the one thing I could actually stomach plonking down multiple dead presidents for. Maybe Violet was not a "little duchess" to their little dukes, but monarchies are getting crusty anyway.

"Okay, well, let's do lunch tomorrow. Why don't you drop Violet and my nanny will watch her with West? Sh'we say noon? I'll make a reservation at La Goulue."

"Um, okay, sounds good."

"See you tomorrow!" said Maggie, barely turning from her rack of miniature cable-knit sweaters.

AND AFTER THEIR SHOPFEST . . .

Instant Message from: BeeElliott

BeeElliott: Boys are sooo much better, girls are so difficult and bratty. Aren't you so glad we had boys?

Maggs10021: Oh, totally. Boys are delish,
they love their mommies.

BeeElliott: Thank God you're having another!
I'm so excited to meet little Talbott Xavier. I
hope when we get preg I have another boy.

Maggs10021: No, just as long as it's
healthy . . .

BeeElliott: No, I reeeally want another boy.
I love being the woman of the house, you know?
Just me and my boys. I just couldn't deal with
having a girl running around. They become the
apple of the husband's eye.

Maggs10021: I think girls are sweet
though . . . Violet Allen is a total cutie.

BeeElliott: You think so? I don't know.
Hannah kinda bugs.

Maggs10021: Why?

BeeElliott: Did you see she barely bought one
thing?

Maggs10021: Whatev. Psyched for lunch tom.

BeeElliott: Yeah, I promised Park I'd intro
her to the gang. I just don't want her to Krazy
Glue herself to us. She could turn out to be a
serious barnacle.

Eight

I showed up at Bee's apartment at noon to find a spread out of an editorial in a shelter mag—full lavish patterned drapes, overstuffed velvet couches, gorgeous gleaming white carpets—definitely a pad that little Violet would destroy in a nanosecond. She was used to humbler surroundings.

"Wow," I said, wide-eyed. "Your apartment is beautiful, Bee."

"Oh, thanks. We just had it redone last year by Huniford and Sills," she said.

"Oh, my decorator is Crate and Barrel!" I added with a smile. She didn't smile back.

"Hi, Hannah," said Maggie coming out of the kitchen, drinking a liter of Evian. "Shall we?"

"Hello, Weston!" I said patting his head. He stuck his tongue out at me and ran off.

I hugged Violet good-bye and felt a pang of guilt leaving her with strangers, but she seemed eager to bolt off into Weston's bedroom.

At lunch, Bee and Maggie introduced me to two other women whom I hadn't known were joining us: Hallie, a Julianne Moore–esque dark redhead, and Lara, a human skeleton with a diamond ring so big, Sasha Cohen could do a triple axel on it and still have room to skate into a double sow-cow.

Lara wore small, thin frameless glasses on her nose and put a hand through her shiny mane of platinum blond hair.

"Uh, I'm frizzing so badly. I just went to Fekkai and now you wouldn't even know it," she complained.

"No, you look amazing," said Bee, sipping her iced tea with fresh mint. "TDF." It took me ten seconds to realize that meant *to die for*.

"My hair is in two zip codes!" I added, pointing at the wavy frizzfest atop my noggin. No one countered.

"Hannah's mother-in-law is Lila Allen Dillingham," Bee said to her pals.

"Oh, she is so chic," raved Hallie. "I pray I look like her at that age, she's stunning."

I didn't feel like telling her if she wanted to shell it out for Dr. Dan, she could.

"Yeah, she's so out of the pages of *Vogue*," I said. "I feel like I'm totally bringing down the family's style quotient!" No one said anything to the contrary. The ladies perused the menu, all opting for salads, dressing on the side. No wonder they weighed the same as their kids.

After we ordered lunch, I sat quietly, barely contributing to the convo about schools, clubs, and people I had never heard of. After about fifteen minutes, I gleaned the lay of the social land as they gossiped about all things mommy—recent births, names that were tacky, who'd lost the weight, who "had a long way to go." While Bee was the definitely the ringleader, Lara, who had a son, Maxwell, was quite opinionated herself ("It's so strange to not at least try and skip the epidural"—she'd even had the words *natural childbirth* engraved on the lower left corner of her kid's Cartier birth announcement). I wondered what she'd thought of her friend Bee's elective C-section at eight and a half months. I remembered how a few years back

Bee, always the trend arbiter, was a huge proponent of the Too Posh to Push movement, telling me in a whisper that if I got sliced open that Josh would thank me for it. After that moment, I was somehow always haunted by her implication that now my post-birth vag was not unlike the Holland Tunnel.

Then there was Hallie, the crispy bobbed redhead, who almost immediately rubbed me the wrong way. Hallie had a two-year-old daughter, Julia Charlotte. Not Julia. *Julia Charlotte.* Like Sarah Jessica, one of those middle name junkies, and not just when they're in trouble, like, *"Violet Grace, you stop that right now!"* I'm talking *"Julia Charlotte could be in Baby Gap ads"* and *"Julia Charlotte is completely bilingual"* and *"Julia Charlotte is sooo brilliant it's frightening."* I also got the vibe that Julia Charlotte's mom, Hallie, was extreeeeemely competitive.

Within seconds of establishing that we both had daughters, she began her battery of statistics questions. What percentile was Violet's height? What percentile was Violet's weight? What percentile was Violet's *head circumference*? I rattled off the answers I knew as best I could (I really didn't keep track; my California doctor was not so obsessed with charts and graphs and rankings), and then came the doozy. Hallie asked me, dead seriously, what Violet's Apgar scores were. I had to stop and place what the hell those even were when I remembered reading about the quick post-birth tests in *The Girlfriend's Guide to Pregnancy,* my bible when I was knocked up.

"Gosh, I can't remember," I said, honestly. "I know they took Violet away to demucus her and put her under that French fry–warmer thing," I recalled. "Then they brought her back and said she was perfectly healthy."

"Did she get a perfect score, though? 'Cause Julia Charlotte got all tens. They only give out nines. Ever. But Julia Charlotte got tens. All tens. It's so funny, with almost everything she's off the charts!"

A feeble "Oh, cool" was all I could muster.

Then Lara started talking about how "gifted" her son, Maxwell, was. "Oh you guys, Maxwell is so genius it is *scary*. Literally, he says things sometimes and I am scared. His Mandarin teacher said he's a quicker study than the Asians! He is *scary* smart. Better than the Asian kids!"

Deep down I guess all mothers think their kid is the smartest and the greatest, but I still would never say stuff like that. I also would not send a toddler to Chinese class, unless maybe we were moving to Hong Kong. I of course thought about all the cute clever things Violet had said which seemed, naturally, even cuter and smarter than Lara's brags about Maxwell memorizing the ROYGBIV color spectrum at twelve months or doing times tables at twenty-six months. In Chinese. And what the hell was this "twenty-six months" thing. Couldn't she just say *two*? I mean, can I please do without the math? Even basic division is a hassle for me at this point. No months for me. Two. Two-and-a-half. Three.

"So, ladies, Thatcher and I saw the best film this weekend," started Hallie. "It's called *Memoirs of a Nobody*—have you heard of it?"

"Oh, yes! I'm dying to see that," said Bee, surprising me. "I read a piece about it in the *Wall Street Journal*. It sounds very powerful."

"Oh yeah!" exclaimed Maggie. "Is that the one from Sundance that was all made on an iMac for like forty dollars?"

"Yes, that's the one," Hallie said. "I cried for two days, it is so disturbing."

I hadn't heard of it. In fact, I felt so out of it, I wasn't even up on the latest splashy blockbuster, let alone an indie documentary. I guess these gals really kept up with their reading. I was so low-energy lately, the only thing I even cracked was fashion mags and cheesy celeb-packed weekly tabloids. I'm sure my lunch companions would be horrified that while I knew little about the current documentary scene, I did know plenty about Britney and K-Fed's marriage, who was suddenly obese, and what trendy baby names were sweeping H'wood.

"Oh, I heard the film is devastating, just gut-wrenching. But highly provocative," said Maggie.

"It's funny," I said, venturing to join the conversation. "So many people recommend these movies that they love, but get so upset after. I'm such an emotional freak, I never go because I don't want to get down," I said.

Silence.

"What do you mean?" asked Lara, as if I'd just said I eat maggots for snacks.

The sudden heat of their four gazes made me shift anxiously in my seat. "Well, it's just whenever people say something's disturbing, I kind of think, okay that's not for me." I shrugged, nervously. "I guess I'm just never in the mood to cry for two days is all."

"How sad!" said Hallie, astonished, looking at Bee as if wondering how on earth she could have dragged such a loser to their lunch. "I mean—Hannah, is it?"

I nodded.

"Don't you want to be stimulated and challenged and therefore be a better mother to your child by having a brain that's not mush?"

My heart was racing. Okay, my brain was mush, I'll admit it. But I wasn't retarded or anything.

"I guess since I had Violet I just don't like upsetting, tragic things or violence," I replied, defending myself. "Maybe because, I don't know, maybe having Violet made me feel more vulnerable or something."

"Fine," Lara said, lifting her Perrier. "Suit yourself. If you want to 'feel good' and sit around watching *Shrek* for the rest of your life, be my guest."

Ouch.

"I don't know, I guess I see your point," I said, feeling wounded by her belittling comment.

"Oh good, food's here," said Maggie, changing the topic. "I'm starving."

Nine

When I told Josh about my day, he seemed interested—particularly by some of the funny choice quotables—but thoroughly exhausted. His new job was sapping the life from him, but I knew he was so happy to finally be home that he didn't mind. The problem was . . . I minded. I missed him so much. So despite my visceral loathing of Greenwich and feeling stranded at Lila's house, I was just happy to all be a family again.

But Saturday morning when we woke up, while it was so nice to have Violet jump on our bed and watch Josh do "flying baby" with her (his feet on her tummy as she's lifted up in the air, giggling), I couldn't distract myself from the pit in my tummy. I felt like if I had a soundtrack at that very moment, it would be the noise you hear when Ms. Pac-Man dies: a slow withering followed by a putt-putt as the poor yellow circle-with-hairbow expires. We got into our rickety Volvo and hit the road for Connecticut, one of my least favorite states in the union. It's so fucking *Ice Storm*. On our way, we pulled over to Pick a Bagel and scored some carbolas for the drive—I always stocked up because the Dillinghams were so überwaspy the fridge was empty save for some Miracle Whip and white wine bottles, swear. I patted Josh's head; he looked so cute but I knew he was still so tired. We blared K-Rock and as we finally got on the FDR and shifted gears after interminable traffic on Ninety-sixth, I turned up the volume to eleven, *Spinal Tap*-style, and chair-danced to Nine Inch Nails. I got Joshie to smile as I got wilder, shaking my head and spaz air-drumming like Animal from *The Muppet Show*. I looked in the bag, deciding which bagel to devour first, and cracked open my apple juice. Ahhhh, elixir of the gods, this stuff. Like liquid honey.

I fed Josh bites of bagel as he drove, and we cruised pretty quickly, my staticky beloved hard rock station flickering on the Merritt Parkway. I knew we were officially in Creepsville, Suburbia, when strains of Thom Yorke's melted croon waned. That was always when the mental piranha set in, nibbling away at my freedom—I knew we were almost there when my music was gone. We wove through the swirling roads leading up to his family's house. I actually preferred going in the winter—at least then the empty black trees had a wistful graphic punch off the white sky, like a film still from a Tim Burton movie, crisp and bold and proud, not even wanting back their clichéd and gauche green leaves that covered us in wilted verdant canopies now.

We pulled in the grand driveway and parked as my heart raced. We unpacked the trunk and sprung Violet from her baby seat and knocked via the enormous lion's-head knocker on the giant double portal. A cute Latin-looking woman opened the door, in full black-and-white maid's outfit. Mrs. Dillingham fired the "help" (as she called them) so frequently that Josh and I could never remember their names—it was a revolving door of pressed, starched uniforms.

"Hello," Lila said, descending the large white marble staircase. "Josh, my aaaangel, come here." She approached him and hugged him, barely acknowledging me. "And Violet, love, you wore one of your new dresses! How divine you look!"

"Hi, Mrs. Dillingham!" Funnily enough I never knew what to call her—she never really told *me* to call her Lila, just Violet. So I usually just said hi or hello; it was like that Mulva episode of *Seinfeld*.

"You know, Hannah," she said, looking perturbed. "I should give you a bill for five dollars. We rented that film last night that you had recommended about that Cuban poet. I found it horrendous. Just awful! I can't think of a more depressing movie."

"Oh . . . sorry." I didn't know what else to say. "I mean, it was sad but brilliantly done, I thought." Gulp. I kept going,

"And not to be all film studenty, I mean I know it sounds pre-
tentious, but it was shot so beautifully. I felt like every frame
could be frozen and hung on my wall."

"Not a wall in my house," she sneered. "Come on, let's go
up and get you settled," she said, looking only at Josh, who
looked at me and winked, knowing I wanted to clobber her
bony bod.

After unpacking, Lila asked if we wanted to accompany her
to the "shopping center" to help with errands. Since I grew up
in a city, I had this obsession with malls, which Mrs. Dillingham exclusively called "shopping centers." I bet she'd spell it
centres. God forbid she utter the lowly M-word. But I was
thrilled to leave the grounds—even after only an hour that
panic had set in like I was Diane Keaton trapped in the Cor-
leone compound in *Godfather II*.

When we got to the ma—sorry, *shopping center*—I trolled the
stores, blissing out with all the fun people-watching and food
court frenzy. Do I go for the gigantor cinnamon pretzel or the
fries in a cone? I am also a fan of food on sticks, and there were
many options. The whole cavernous space was a pulsing
throng of tube socks and napkins and the kind of heavy grease
that smells intoxicating when you're starving and gag-o-rific
when you're full. You know when they distill vinegar to this
really intense mega-potent paste? Well, malls are like a bal-
samic reduction of America itself, an encapsulated 3D slice of
life, from old people who want to enjoy the air-conditioning,
walking around in those swish-swish suits, to "rowdy yutes"
making mischief and chasing skirts in their swish-swish
suits. Violet was overjoyed when I gave her a piping-hot Mrs.
Fields cookie, which she devoured in record pace, with evi-

dence of said snack in the form of chocolate all over her face. I was just about to go get a napkin to wipe it off, when Lila turned the corner to behold the mess.

"Oh my, Hannah, really, must she feast on sweets at this hour?"

"Well, she was hungry and there's so much stuff here I didn't want to deprive her," I said in my defense.

"Eating between meals is a bad habit to start now—"

"Mom, chill out," Josh said as he approached us toting his mom's new hair dryer and pharmacy bags. "It's fine!" He looked at me sympathetically with a smile. But his being on my side didn't make her comments less aggravating.

We piled back in the car since we had to shower and get dressed for Lila's birthday dinner. And I was actually psyched because in my duffel I had the blowtorch that would melt her frozen chest cavity, my secret daughter-in-law trump card that she'd never expect, a shiny elegant Tiffany sterling silver frame, hand engraved with her initials. And in it was the cutest picture of Josh holding Violet. No Hannah, just like she'd want. And the cherry on top was that Violet was in a Ralph Lauren pin-tuck blouse Lila had given her. It was, I must say, the perfect present. It was insanely expensive but I thought this was kind of an investment in, you know, not being treated like crap. Well worth the splurge. She would have to soften a little now!

I went into my room to get myself put together in pretty Greenwich mode, i.e., transform my being entirely. Full metamorphosis, bigger than Jeff Goldblum's in *The Fly*. It was funny being in the same room as Josh now—when we initially visited we had separate bedrooms and I was so scared of his mom that

I literally wouldn't let him sneak over since I didn't want her to have any Hannah's-a-Whore ammo against me. I packed perfectly preppy clothes, and even chucked in a new (gasp) headband. I felt like a traitor. Since most of my stuff is black, charcoal gray, or chocolate brown, my mom says I dress like a Sicilian widow. She's kinda right but because I have boobs and butt, darkness is slimming, and so me. I put on my new burgundy dress (steppin' out with that color!).

"You look pweety, Mommy! I like your pawty dwess!" exclaimed Violet, who I'd preened to perfection. The poor thing was so used to seeing me in my black jeans and little tees, my casual dress probably seemed like Cinderella's ball gown to her.

When we came downstairs, Lila had a very different reaction than her granddaughter. "Oh," she said, her made-up face like an 8¼-by-11-inch blank sheet of Kinko's paper. "Is that what you're wearing?"

Pause as I checked my reflection. Was there a gaping hole? A torn seam? Wrinkles? Period stains? Exposed ass-crackage?

"Um, yeah, I was going to . . . Why?"

"I don't know, I just . . . Forget it."

"No, what?"

"To be honest, I think perhaps you should try . . . one of my suits? This is a bit . . . Well, it's fine, it's fine. Really."

Crestfallen. "Oh, okay, well . . . What should I do? I only have this one other dress but—"

Josh came downstairs buttoning his cuff and asked what was going on.

"I was just going to run up and change—" I said. I gulped down hurt and annoyed feelings and went upstairs. When I returned in my backup outfit, Lila, who was in her usual full floral-pastel-pashmina mode, looked me over slowly. "Hmmm. Black as usual," she observed. I hope she dies a fiery death. I hope a crane falls off a construction site and kills her. I'm going to hell. Okay, Hannah, stop wishing death upon your MiL.

I looked down as she tousled Josh's hair and gently removed a thread from his lapel. She really hates other women, I thought. Just having another womb in the room after all these years freaks her out. She was one of those women who only can relate to men, seeing all other women as some kind of competition. I have always known women like this, and they have always scared me. Who the fuck is this beeyotch to judge my outfits anyway? She may have worn only designer duds, but I thought they were asexual and hideous. The color palette made me want to chunder. I may have dressed like a widow, but black was better than tertiary-color-wheel hues. Teal. Salmon. Coral. Magenta. Diarrhea.

Mr. Dillingham honked outside and we all piled into the car. Despite my husband's protestations, I offered to sit in the gimp seat in the station wagon's ass while Josh sat next to Violet's car seat in the back. But armed with my stellar gift, the frown would subside and I'd be let in; I'd be the Little Mermaid singing *Paaaart of your woooorld* . . . the second she opened the small trademark blue box. As we started driving, Lila did her usual spiel of which restaurants she had booked that evening. What never ceased to absolutely astound me was that she would regularly book three places and then select one at the last minute, depending on everyone's mood. How psycho and selfish is that? Sometimes she wouldn't even call the other two places to cancel! I'm talking new echelons of solipsism. No one matters but her and, of course, her *aaaangel*.

"Do we want the Bank in New Canaan, or Mediterraneo in Greenwich? I also booked Sakura—"

"Oh, I love that Sakura place," said Josh.

"Well, whatever you like, darling."

"What do you want, Han?" asked my hubby.

"Oh, um . . . whatever your mom wants, I mean it is her birthday."

"No, no, *you* choose, Hannah," she replied from the front of the car. "You're by far the most passionate about food."

I hope the cable in her next elevator ride snaps and she plummets to her death. Did I just say that aloud? No, okay, I'm fine.

"Well, I don't know, they're all great," I offered. Silence. "Maybe, um, yeah, Sakura is fun, I love that cook-on-the-table stuff."

"It's called *hibachi*," Lila said, as if she'd been born and reared in Kyoto. "Fine, if that's what you want."

"Well, I don't care at all, I just thought Josh—"

"If it's what Hannah's up for, that's great. But it is full of salt, you know. I'm not that hungry anyway," said Lila, shrugging.

The passive aggressiveness of this lady was enough to make me want to clobber her. The few times I actually expressed an opinion or desire—case in point, Sakura—her sickening passive-aggressive routine was enough to make me clam up for the next three decades.

"No, no, Mom—Watts, let's head to Greenwich, I know

Mom loves Mediterraneo," said Josh, looking at me in the rear with a smile and eye roll.

"Okay, if that's what you want, dear." Lila always got what she wanted. She'd pretend she was accommodating others but would slowly manipulate it back to what she desired. Passive-aggressive.

We got to the place, which is so average and, plus, she barely ate anyway, anti-food, anti-life, *Night of the Living Dead* zombie that she is. I always equate passion at a table with passion in the sack. No doubt Lila was a total frigid fish. Natch Lila barely nibbled a spear of her white asparagus with vinaigrette on the side. Violet ate her appetizer and then, as toddlers do, got a little shifty in her seat and Lila looked at me as if to say *Take her for a little breather*. Josh offered to get up, but I thought I'd let him be with his mom and Watts for a minute, and plus, I was psyched for a moment away from the table. Violet and I strolled down the block on Greenwich Avenue and then returned to the packed restaurant. The décor was pale peach and pink and I felt like I was dining in a giant tampon box. I twirled my un–al dente cappellini with a fork into a spoon, Italiano-style, which got a curious look from The Cube, and after our pasta course, she started cracking open the presents. Finally: my moment of redemption.

She unwrapped gifts, I might add, with zero gusto (another link to action in the bedroom). With me, it was Freddy Krueger–style shredded wrapping paper, bursting ribbons, ginormous eyes, excited grins, and gushing thank-yous. Lila opened every package like it might have a syringe hiding in it, or a Jokey Smurf homemade bomb. Watts got her some Van

Cleef diamond earrings and a weekend at Cliveden. Josh had bought her a Hermès scarf from all of us, and then I was so excited for her to get to mine, which already garnered a widened eye and a raised plucked brow upon viewage of the signature blue bag. As she untied the classic Tiffany bow and opened the box, my heart was beating so fast, I was like a pre–Jenny Craig Kirstie Alley after a flight of stairs. She looked at the frame; Watts and Josh, who hadn't seen it before, both oohed and aahhed. Violet giggled.

"Dat's me and Daddy!" she smiled, pointing at the glass with her little finger.

Lila simply looked at photo and said, "Oh, look at this great shot—I gave Violet that outfit, you know!" She put the frame back in its felt bag. "Now, shall we be very naughty and order some dessert?"

No thank-you or anything! This time I was just plain enraged. Watts perused the dessert menu, ultimately settling on another Dewar's on the rocks, the family Evian.

The next morning I woke up feeling paralyzingly sad. I always had the plum-size lump in my throat when I visited the Dillinghams because their house was so oppressive and bizarre that I missed my family so much and was glum to the guts with homesickness. Maybe I really am a West Coast person and not cut out for this northeastern pomp.

Josh woke up and kissed me sweetly. I loved him so much it hurt, and my would-be restorative weekend together was gone in a flash with him returning to work that next crack of dawn. He climbed on me and kissed me, going to take off my T-shirt, but I was too in creeps mode.

"Sweets, no—"

"Han, it's a huge fucking house! They can't hear us. Watts has a hearing aid anyway."

"It's not that—I just can't get into it here. It's too weird. Your mom probably has the house wired to make sure I'm not doing bad things to her angel."

He laughed, defeated, and rolled off me. "Fine. Let's go make pancakes."

We lifted Violet from her crib and went downstairs to find Lila and Watts in their wood-paneled den watching *This Week*, as the slate of Sunday news programs was their weekly fix. We had our usual table-pounding, political-discussion-packed brunch (they were die-hard right-wing Republicans, natch), and then we got in the car to come back to New York. Thank God. Pulling out of that driveway always made my heart leap, and the wheels on the pebbly gravel sounded like Mozart in *Shawshank*, a little bit of freedom that paved the way to refilled tanks of hope.

Ten

The next morning I kissed Josh good-bye at six A.M. and then finally roused my bones to get breakfast ready after eight. On the kitchen table was a cute note from Josh with a postscript of some new porn titles: *Lord of the Cock Rings*, *You've Got Tail*, *Doing John Malkovich*, and my fave, *Crocodile Dun-Me*. Smiling, I sat Violet down for our divine feast of Cheerios. I looked at the once-sunny box and thought of how Lila and her junior counterpart Bee and her friends had a no-carbs policy, and said that cereal was forbidden in their homes. In fact, at the lunch the week before, Hallie and Lara were discussing their organic cooking class for mothers about how to prepare healthy meals for their children. I had visions of them whipping me for cracking open the jars of Gerber I had fed Violet during babyhood. Or how about the salty pretzels and Goldfish she inhaled? Eternal sentence to the Shitty Mommy Layer of Hell. To them, a forbidden chicken finger might as well have been a vial of crack.

Grover came on the screen and Violet started yelping "Gwova! Gwova!" as I fed her the contraband oat-based wheels of sin. Today Grover was flying to Peru to a small village of brick-makers. The hot equatorial sun would bake the children's concoctions of mud, which was slathered into perfect rectangle-shaped molds and baked dry in a rudimentary outdoor kiln. The purity of the bricks, and the houses they'd build in the village, gave me a calming feeling, which motivated me to get my bathrobed ass dressed to take Violet out. I had signed up, at the behest of Maggie and Bee, for a music class, but it wouldn't start for a few weeks. To fill the day, I thought I'd hit the Metropolitan Museum with Violet. Perhaps the Met would be a nice cool playground for us, instead of the stressful playground with neighborhoods of benches and alpha-mom gossip.

After being told today's program was brought to us by the letter D and the number 7, I put Violet in the stroller and walked up to the stunning museum at 1000 Fifth Avenue. I remember hearing the address and thinking it was kind of cool

and that probably no one knew it. As Violet stretched her arms
to the fountain in front of the museum, saying "Mommy, wata,
wata!" I wheeled her in the handicapped entrance and up to
the grand main hall. You really realize with an unwieldy
stroller and little ramp access how hard it must be to be in a
wheelchair. And no one helps us open doors, not even men. So
much for chivalry.

"Wowie!" exclaimed Violet, visually swallowing the divine
space.

"Violet, sweets, this is the Metropolitan Museum, one of
the most amazing places in the world. Do you want to go up and
see some paintings?"

"Yeah! Paintings!" Violet already loved scoping artwork
and I'd ask what she saw. In a sea of colors, she'd spy the sun or
a face, and her eye seemed to me advanced for a toddler's. We
went upstairs into a gallery of Old Masters. For the first time in
New York, I felt mildly at home. The paintings were like old
friends welcoming me to the new city and I shuddered with a
wave of pure joy. We walked through gallery after gallery,
drinking in the Van Eycks and Brueghels and Titians. I felt a
soothing peace wash over me. A calm that was reversed the
nanosecond I heard his voice.

"Miss Hannah Greene. Or now it's Mrs. . . ."

"Allen," I said, almost choking. "Professor Hayes."

"I think you can call me Tate—now that you're, what, ten
years out of Berkeley?"

"Yes." I smiled, looking down at Violet. *Don't blush, don't
blush, don't blush.*

"And who is this cherubic little love?"

"This is Violet!" I started feeling like I was beamed back in time to my nervous freshman self. "Violet, this is Tate Hayes. Dr. Hayes."

"Hi," she said, reaching up to him for a hug, her new thing. He happily obliged.

"I heard you're remarried," I said. "And you have two little nuggets?"

"Yes, two boys, four and six."

"Herro, Ayes," Violet said, smiling brightly, and definitely flirting. It was funny how Violet picked up on people I loved or loathed. Without fail, when we ran into someone I detested, she'd scowl and refuse to say hi. And now she was her mother's daughter, practically cooing as the former crush of my life leaned down to softly pat her cheek.

"Listen, Hannah," he said, as my entire body froze at the sound of my name in his mouth. "I have to run, but I'd really love to catch up. Could I get your number?"

I obliged, rattling off my cell number as he wrote in a small leather-covered pad with an elegant pen.

"Four one five, hmm?"

"Yes. I've been here almost a month and I guess I'm clinging on for dear life. Can't let go of the old area code."

"Understood," he smiled, retrieving an old-school brick of a cell phone from his pocket. "Four one five, always."

I smiled.

"I'll call you, then. Maybe we can see the new etchings show at the Morgan."

"That would be great."

At home, still unsettled, I called Josh. I was cooking Violet eggs because I was such a loser I hadn't thought about dinner until the chowing hour was suddenly upon us.

"Hi, sweets!" I said.

"Hi," he said in a hushed tone. "Han, I'm so sorry I've got some people in here, can I—"

"Okay, sure."

Click.

An hour and a half later, Violet was crying for Daddy and Joshie still hadn't phoned. I called him again, feeling stalker-azzi, but I needed to get an ETA for sanity.

"Hello?" His voice sounded stressed.

"Hi, sweetie, sorry to stalk, I just—"

"Honey, I'm really busy here, I just found out I have to present tomorrow and I have a few more hours."

"A few more *hours*?" I was bummed beyond words.

"Sorry, sweetie, I can't help it. This is for us."

"I know, I know."

He told me he loved me, which warmed me up, but as I replaced the phone on the wall, I felt the now-familiar chill of loneliness.

After I tucked Violet into bed with *Goodnight Moon*, which I knew by heart, with her spotting the little mouse on each page, I sang her to sleep with "Tender Shepherd" then snuck out. Naturally, seven seconds post-tiptoe in the hall, there were wails.

"Mommieeeeee!"

I went back in, lay down on the floor next to her crib, and sang some more. As I'd quiet down and begin to slowly get up again, I'd see her sit up suddenly, her small face looking through the slats of her white crib, desperate. She'd see I was still there and lay back down. Back in California Josh had always been the bedtime expert, lulling her with his gentle voice that was at once calming but also strong, making Violet—and me—feel utterly safe. He was a master tucker-inner, exiting our daughter's room each night and leaving in his wake Violet's gentle breaths of deep and blissful slumber.

I, on the other hand, had a one-hour process—she even struggled so hard against my putting her in the crib that her little foot kicked me and her toenail was so sharp that she suddenly morphed from cherubic little nugget to Vlad the Impaler. I was so wiped out, she usually commanded me to lie beside her on the floor, which I would do and pass out myself, finally wakened from my dozing by Violet's heavier breathing, those little invisible *zzzz*'s coming from her tiny lungs.

When I got in bed after giving Leigh the Tate Hayes rundown, the clock read eleven thirty. I tried to stay up to see Josh, but as my eyes closed, I couldn't help but think of my chance meeting with Professor Hayes. It excited me, and I still felt the buzz. While I would never *ever* cheat on Josh, or even look at anyone for that matter, this teacher, this sage—no, guru—was so frozen in pedestal-mode from college, Leigh and I declared him an NGO—Never Get Over. But maybe Leigh was right—now we were both married with kids, so it was safe and relaxed. He seemed so happy and friendly, maybe it would be a nice intellectually stimulating afternoon, without having to see a "disturbing" film or forcing myself to put down *Vogue* in order to read articles in the *Wall Street Journal* that made me want to sleep, just because I was trying hard to know everything that was going on in the world like Bee's friends. Maybe seeing him and harking back to my more badass self would take me out of my obsessing about my fish-out-of-water status as a New York mom. Maybe etchings at the Morgan would be just what the doctor ordered.

Eleven

Professor Tate Hayes was the kind of man who made all the female students swoon, Indiana Jones–style, with bashful downward glances on their way out of class. He was tall with light brown curls, little gold glasses, and a Jermyn Street dapper edge that was especially hot because the tweedy and academic front had hints of a fire coursing below the striped-oxford-shirt and bespoke-tailored surface. To say that he was shrined by my friends was an understatement—Leigh and I obsessed about him, and I literally almost stalked him freshman year when I saw him at a Nob Hill art opening where he was holding the hand of a young sculptress. But it wasn't his green eyes and calm swagger that made us wring out our panties post-class, it was the way he spoke. There was simply no one in the galaxy like him.

He taught my first-year art survey with Bianca Pratt, a sexy professor we knew he'd had an affair with. Rumor had it they had this over-the-top fiery tempestuous relationship that ended with her throwing an alabaster bust out the window at him, which shattered on Fillmore Street.

I knew he'd divorced his grad-school love years before and she was now remarried, living in London. He was not your average playboy, because nary a lax-stick-toting buff dude could boast a PhD from Yale and a three-book deal. From my first class with him, I knew I would major in art history. So many classes at Berkeley were big lectures taught by cranky, bitter TA grad students, and any individual voices were squashed and buried. In the art history department there were twenty-eight majors in my class. It was so small and intimate, under the watchful eye of legendary professors. But none was like Professor Hayes. At thirty-four he had been the youngest full professor in the department, and his cult status made him a mini celeb on campus, at least among the girls.

But it wasn't his academic and analytical strength that made me weak, it was that he himself was an artist. He painted, but in words. In each class he dipped the soft-bristled, pinpoint brush of his musical, lilting voice into the deep spectral palette of colors, his unique lexicon of patented Hayesisms.

For a rowdy genre painting filled with rabble-rousing bar people, he pointed out the "legless cripples cavorting on crutches" and the "bestial peasant besotted with alcohol groping in a carnavalesque Falstaffian pursuit of earthly pleasure." A study of a bird depicted from three different angles was "uncompromisingly precise, with a neutral gaze charged with life in every feathered fiber; the heart is thumping beneath the blue breast, as if the painting screams *Believe me*."

That night, as I waited for Josh to come home from work, my bed became a Michael J. Fox–driven time machine because my normally restless solo self was cinematically transported back through a decade to freshman year. I wandered through all my courses with Hayes, and all our moments together, getting to know him as I worked on my thesis. Seeing him was like taking a balmy walk through my past—I drifted back to my college days, a safe place to nestle into, a soft hazy realm of fleecy nostalgia.

"Next slide, please," Hayes said to the projectionist that first year, and when the slide switched, a radiant Ruisdael landscape appeared before our eyes. Each time he saw a new slide, it was as if he were a man drunk on love at the first sight of the girl who would be in his bed only hours later. He inhaled, drinking in the breadth of colors, the warmth of the exhaling weeping willows, the depth of the rolling heathered hills, and sighed, quasi-aroused.

"This airy, wet landscape has this sweeping, transcendental, vibrant green," he said, almost air-caressing the color with his pointer on the screen. "The swirling motions meld description and invention, as Ruisdael turns up the volume on nature's whispers and we luxuriate in the glistening glow of a million sun-kissed leaves."

His recipe of words had baked me to a crisp toast, burnt to the core with utter love and over-the-moon devotion. To me, he was *perfect*.

The next slides and their verbally painted descriptions trickled over the stones of my mind like a violent, passionate cataract, completely awakening me to a whole new exhilarated side of myself, the sucker for beauty and the art of his teaching.

"Next slide," he said, delicately moving a piece of hair from his eye. Another landscape, "a sturdy monolithic cliff and tempestuous sea." The next slide was a woodcut, infused by the "rude, coarse, dynamic vigor of an artist charged with a forceful eye and vengeful burin."

In later years, we studied court portraits: Anthony Van Dyck's Charles the First had a "cavalier king's swagger; his insouciant, careless, flamboyant pose is dressed in glowing translucent hues, fabrics fashioned from sensuous slashes of color."

Hieronymus Bosch's insane *Garden of Earthly Delights* was filled with "the entropy of uglified self-delusional merry-makers, a monstrous, muscular mountain, a freak gallery of menageries, heraldic gryphon devouring the sinners all in a Dionysian release of ecstasy."

But of course, it was really the flesh that got him going. If a painting can speak a thousand words, Hayes had two thousand to describe it. And on one chilly November afternoon during my sophomore year, a Peter Paul Rubens illuminated the classroom screen. And that was the moment I knew, as Leigh and I joked, that I would never get over him.

When the slide came up, he gasp-moaned as if he had just begun making love. His voice soothingly floated over the "intimate tones of warm gold and sun-dappled browns" in the background, then zoomed in to focus on the skin. "Rubens doesn't offer an account of flesh, but the flesh itself," he said, and I'm not kidding, he was almost panting. "This flesh, almost a cream-cheesy richness, a beckoning softness incarnate." Most guys whack it to *Playboy* and *Penthouse*, but I swear this dude fully spanked to *Venus and Adonis*, and would choose the Met over Times Square's PeepLand in a New York nano.

We spent time together chatting in hallways or in the occasional office-hours-posed question about paper topics, and his comments through the years threw Duraflame logs on my fire for him. On my paper about the latent eroticism of musical instruments in Dutch painting, "Music be the Food of Love," he wrote, "Hannah, splendid as usual," which of course made me kill myself with every paper to impress him and be even more *splendid* for him. The ultimate obsession artifact, though, was on my wall to this very day, and was by far my prized possession.

My senior year, we had grown closer and had even hung out off campus, going to museum openings and various lectures. Once we walked all the way across town in a drizzly mist. He laughed at my weirdness and quirks, and I often thought he considered me a total freak, my worship washing across my whole face like a red Rothko. But we never spoke of personal lives and talked mostly art stuff. Together, we came up with the outline for my sixty-page senior thesis, and he mentored me through every scary step. When I handed it in, I submitted the three required copies to the department office (I'd be graded by a panel—horrifying) and left one on his desk with a note that read:

> *Dearest Proffy Hayes,*
> *Here it is. The big shebang, my life, my baby: the almighty*
> *Senior Thesis. It's a chunk whittled out of my soul all for you—*
> *I cannot thank you enough for all your sage guidance and*
> *tireless help.*
> *xoHannah*

I handed it in and felt a pang of regret that maybe my dumb note was too gushy. I wanted to say so much more. Something along the lines of *I fucking love you and think of you when I have sex with my boyfriend*, who at the time was Clay Fisher, a jock-ish guy who played football and was gorgissimo but frankly not the sharpest tool in the shed. I had come off a loooong dry spell sans ween and was psyched to just have someone; I'd been so lonely in the library jamming 24/7 on my thesis—watching disheveled couples emerge from the stacks where some girls opened books less often than their legs. I was thirsting for some affection and I knew I'd never get it from the object of my ridick lust, so I settled for what was available. Leigh once scolded me for my ill-fated, hopeless crushes, say-ing, "Hannah, like the guys that like you." Well, Clay liked me. He was semi-cocky, but sweet, unpretentious, and, hey, easy on the eyes.

I was walking hand in hand with him on our way to a party a month before graduation when we walked by Professor Hayes on Shattuck Avenue.

"Hannah—I just came from your mailbox, I left your thesis—"

Heart attack.

"Oh my God—no way! I thought we weren't getting them back 'til next week."

"Well, yours is back from the group. I think you'll be quite pleased." He smiled at me but then looked at Clay and nodded to him, looked back at me, and walked away.

I felt so torn in that moment, between the ecstatic glee that I'd obviously done well, and the despair magnet that was pulling me to watch him walk away into a café and out of my life. I'd heard he was moving to New York to teach at Columbia when the dopes in power at Berkeley didn't give him a raise. Would I ever see him again? I never got to tell him he changed my life and I worshipped him! I told Clay I wanted to run back and get the paper from my mailbox.

"Hannah, you are such a dork. Who cares at this point? You already know you're summa cum laude."

"I'll meet you at the party. I have to run back."

He seemed annoyed but I turned and bolted back to my mailbox. I walked past the heaving, breeze-blown trees, past the stoners, past the hippie stores, onto the campus I loved, and beelined for my box. There, with my A-awarded paper, was my prized possession. And because of what I found, I didn't give a shit about the panel's unanimous A.

Affixed with an almost vintagey paper clip was my original note:

> Dearest Proffy Hayes,
> Here it is. The big shebang, my life, my baby: the almighty
> Senior Thesis. It's a chunk whittled out of my soul all for you—
> I cannot thank you enough for all your sage guidance and
> tireless help.
> xoHannah

But the word *whittled* was circled with the familiar cobalt ink of his fountain pen. The circle was attached to an arrow that led me down the right margin to the bottom of the page, where he had written:

Dearest Hannah,

Your word choice, "whittled," suggests your sparkled soul is made of wood. In some ways, this is true; you are strong, clearly grained, and filled with life in so many golden layers.

In other ways, though, it is an inappropriate metaphor.

Your soul, sweet girl, is anything but wooden. Unless it is the honeyed wood of a lacquered violin, resonant and singing.

T.H.

My entire body grew heated and I felt the rush through my middle of a beggar who had happened upon a treasure chest of ingots. The paper shook in my hand and I read it again and again until I thought I'd faint. I had also never been more turned on. I wanted to find him and rape him. I couldn't bear to fold it, so I grabbed some crappy local arts magazine and slid it in, carrying it with me as if it were an original Declaration of Independence. The whole night at a birthday dinner at a Mexican joint, while everyone pounded tequila shots, I soberly felt the leather of my handbag between my ankles and thought of the gem inside it.

The next afternoon, I went to the department and nervously knocked on Hayes's door. I opened it slightly and he gestured for me to come in, while he wrapped up a call. I took a seat in his worn cognac leather chair and studied the books on the shelves behind him, including Simon Schama's works and ordered spines of *October*, the contemporary art criticism journal. "Very good then," he said, smiling and rolling his eyes at me, like the person on the other end of his phone line was a really Chatty Cathy. I could even hear the nasal tones of her squawk through the receiver, like Charlie Brown's teacher. At last he hung up. And looked at me. We said nothing.

Finally, I spoke.

"Your note . . . made . . . my life. I don't know what to say."

"I meant it. And I told you you'd get an A. The grade could not have been more well deserved."

"Thanks, well, thanks to you. I was so nervous. I didn't even care what they thought, really. What you thought was all that mattered. I didn't want you to think I was an idiot."

"Hannah," he said rising and walking to get his blazer, which was hanging on the door next to me, "how could I ever think that?"

I stood up also because I thought he was trying to leave, and I shrugged bashfully. My heart started to beat harder. This was the closest I had ever been to him—a few feet away. I looked at him and knew I'd fucked up when I looked not at his face but through the lenses of his little gold specs, past the glass into his green eyes. I wish I had his unique vocabulary to describe the green of his eyes, but I don't. Okay, I can try: the radiant, chlorophyllic green of an Albrecht Altdorfer oak. That doesn't even come close.

But in his irises, I lost track of time—about three seconds— and before I knew it, he was looking into mine. We paused, looking at each other, and it took a thousand mental stallions to hold me back from him. But then, he moved a hair closer, leaning in to me and I felt the space between us penetrated by his fevered step.

In a cloudy sweep more violently passionate than an epic war tableaux, he put his hand on the back of my neck, moved closer, and kissed me. I threw my arms around him with the vigor of a woodcutter, and he kissed me almost to tears. After about a minute of the most hell-bent, out-of-control make-out I had ever had the blessed rapture of experiencing, we pulled apart and we looked into each other's eyes. His were the same, but mine . . . uh-oh. Mine were stinging with the joyful, shocked dew of bliss. It was then that he snapped out of our late-afternoon moment. My coy spell had been suddenly broken by the mood-arresting wand of my obvious emotion.

"My God, I am so sorry," he said, flustered, rubbing his forehead.

"No, don't be, I—"

"This is very bad. You are my student. This is . . ."

"It was me, too," I stammered. "I mean, it's fine."

"No, it's really not," he said, straightening his jacket by a swift brush of the lapels.

"But—" I tried with futile effort to get him back into our heavenly zone.

"It's unethical and wrong. Plus, aren't you seeing someone? That man I've seen you with?"

"Clay is—"

"*Clay*, right. He gratifies the eyes, that's for sure, but he seems thin nourishment for your mind."

Whoa. Was he, like, jealous of Clay? My wide-receiver McBoyfriend of five weeks?

"Listen, I have been . . ." I trailed, humiliated and childish. I gulped before completing my sentence: ". . . mad for you for so long."

"I'm flattered. I can't deny there has been a connection, but that has to be all. I'm sorry."

He picked up his briefcase, looked at me once more, and walked out.

I never saw him again.

Until he spied me with Violet that day, when we saw each other among the still lifes. Perched in a sea of oiled flowers, the fiery hues seemed more charged in his wake.

Twelve

The next morning Josh woke me up with a kiss and apologized for coming home at two A.M. His work was killing him, but at least the guys were great (he'd loathed his assholic, alky, un-smart boss in California) and hopefully he'd be able to make our dinner with Leigh on time. He was all dressed to go in his suit, but came under the comforter with me and we had an eggroll moment, which made me feel cozy and toasty.

We started kissing and the smooch got deeper until that moment when it suddenly turns—that subtle spark of knowing (not to be so teen) that you're going to go all the way. My attempted Marilyn-coy glance was our lingo that his suit would come off for a quickie. But then Violet's little chirp rang out from the nursery, which was practically on top of our bed-room, which made getting on top of each other rather difficult.

We co-sighed that all-too-familiar sigh of *bang ya later* and went to scoop up Violet for a group hug and vertical cuddle. Then we walked Daddy to the door for an elevator-side kiss and said good-bye for what I hoped would not be fourteen hours. When we came back to the kitchen, I saw the broker's business card Bee had given me affixed to the fridge with one of Violet's magnet letters. I picked up the phone and dialed the number as Violet attacked the megabox of colored markers to draw. I was a little nervous since I knew this man's wife was the director of Carnegie Nursery School, so I almost felt like I was auditioning for him in a weird way.

"Troy Kincaid."

"Hi, um, Troy, hi, this is Hannah Allen calling, Bee's friend—"

"Yes! Hello, Hannah. Bee gave me the heads-up," his deep, gravelly British-accented voice replied. "I already have made a file for you and I have a few listings I think you'll really like."

"Wow, that was fast!"

"We have one exclusive one block from Bee on Fifth and Seventy-third. Prewar. White-glove. Top-notch." His Queen's English posh London accent made it sound extra-fabulous.

"Cool," I said, surprised. "How much?"

"Five three, but they'll come down."

Pin drop.

"F-F-F-Five . . . million three hundred thousand?" I stuttered.

"But it's not firm."

"Um, wow, Troy, listen, you are so sweet to have begun the search for us, and I hope I didn't waste your time, but . . . that's not really our budget. Like, at all," I apologized. "Do you maybe have any listings that are less? Like . . . four million less?" I asked, semi-blushing.

"Four million or less? Sure!"

"No, no, no," I said. "Not four million or less. Four million *less* than five point three million, i.e., something in the one-to-one-and-a-half range."

"Oh."

Crickets.

"In Manhattan?" he probed.

"Yes. I saw in the *New York Times* a three-bedroom—"

"No. There's nothing in that range with three bedrooms."

"Really? 'Cause—"

"Nothing. But I'll keep an eye out and get back to you. Let me run some searches."

His initially charming smoky voice turned very chilly when he understood our apparently chump-change range, which hardly seemed pauperesque to me. But alas, in our new burg what we could afford would buy a view of a brick wall and the square footage of a monk's cell. I hoped his wife wouldn't put our budget in Violet's file when we applied to the elite bastion of academia. For tots. Argh! Josh was doing very well and to me our budget seemed fine—it would have bought us a perfectly nice place in any other city in the union, save for New York, island of gazillionaires. But even though Parker Elliott and all Josh's friends have great jobs like Josh, they also have wealthy wives who chip in a mill or two, not to mention their own trust funds. I brought about $7,891 to the table—what was in my Wainwright Bank savings account when we left California. I was hardly pitching in for some ten-room layout as I suspected Bee and her pals were. No wonder Lila hoped for a more financially strategic marriage for Josh—in New York, even rich people find it hard to stay afloat in their gilded waters unless they align with other rich people. I definitely was bringing her family's stock down.

To block out the dread filling my midsection, I turned on *Sesame Street*. Today Grover had just returned from the Continent and was sporting a black beret, *très chic*.

"Hello, boys and girls!" the beloved furry blue monster said. "I have just crossed the Atlantic Ocean—and the Triborough Bridge—from Paris, France!" He showed a little girl hitting the *marché avec Papa*, where they scored fresh vegetables before visiting the local *boulangerie*, adding each delicious, fresh ingredient to a giant basket, or *panier*. As we watched the idyllic scene of gathering farm-fresh eats for the coming week, I contemplated the perfect setting and wondered if Josh would ever be into moving there. How great would it be to stroll the *fleur*-filled Tuilèries? I'd walk with Violet by buildings so richly ornate that if you just cut and pasted any old one, it would be the architectural toast of any city in the States. The rigorous *écoles* were free of charge and Violet would be bilingual! And I could have a killer *pain-au-chocolat* every morning. Bliss!

But who was I kidding, we weren't gonna bail and plop in France. It was fun to fantasize but I knew I couldn't do the expat thing. Despite the strip-mall-covered, freakish-right-wing land of junk food, I was a true American gal. I'd realized this when I was pregnant with Violet and Josh and I spent two weeks driving cross-country. We saw it all—the rocky red crags in the desert, a town called Zzyzzyx, population 4 (swear), those crop circles, the usual presidents-carved-in-mountains; we even stumbled upon a motorcycle rally in South Dakota with 600,000 Hog-ridin' badasses, including one whose T-shirt back read "If you can read this, the bitch fell off!" And yet the time in that car, with my husband rubbing my belly and feeding me delicious albeit greasy eats every few hours, had sealed my patriotic fate as a red, white, and blue–blooded citizen. (Although I must confess that when we were abroad, I was embarrassed to be associated with the loudmouthed, Larry Leisure–suit fatty crew that was constantly demanding ketchup.)

Later, after Elmo bid us farewell from his crayon-covered universe, I got Violet dressed to meet Bee and West for a walk in the park. I hoped that Troy would not update Bee as to our financial constraints. When she referred me, he probably thought he was landing some big fish ready to bite on splashy digs. Too bad we were minnows.

I pushed Violet up to the entrance to the Seventy-second Street playground and saw Bee talking to a handsome angular man. They waved good-bye and I watched him walk off in the distance. When I approached, Bee seemed surprised.

"Hannah, hi, you're early!"

"Yeah, I'm one of those promptness freaks." I shrugged, thinking she made it sound like a bad thing, even though she had been early, too. "Josh always wants to kill me when I make us park it at the airport two hours in advance."

She smiled but seemed distracted.

"So how are you?" I asked.

"Mommy, paci?" asked Violet.

"Sweetie, you don't need it right now," I gently said of the dreaded binky she still was addicted to.

"*Paaaaaaci!*" she wailed. Natch, I relented, unzipping the little compartment and handing her the sucky, which she promptly popped in her mouth, looking not unlike baby Maggie on *The Simpsons*.

"You know, Hannah," Bee said, with a serious tone. "It's really time you take that away."

"I know, I know, it's so bad," I agreed, semi-miffed that she had called me out on this sensitive topic. "I hope her teeth aren't fully buck."

"It's not just that," Bee said looking down at Violet. "It causes huuuge speech delays. She'll be way behind the other children. Way behind."

"Really?" I asked, now a tad defensive. "Because she's two and she speaks way more than a lot of three-year-olds I've seen . . ."

"They'll lap her soon enough if you keep that thing in her mouth," she said. "Luckily West never needed it. But I'll give you the number of Maggie's pacifier consultant."

No. Way.

"There's a pacifier consultant?" This town had kiddie consultants for everything. Walking, talking, peeing, pooing, now pacifiers.

"Oh yes. Dr. Poundschlosser referred her. It's four thousand dollars, but it's an investment in their independence. You can't have her with this on interviews. Especially Carnegie. Kiss of death."

"I guess," I said nervously. Maybe she was right, I wouldn't want to jeopardize Violet's chances. "Whenever I try and take it away, though, Josh says, 'Don't worry, Hannah, she won't go to college with it!' "

"Well, she won't go to a good college at all if she doesn't start off on the right foot with preschools."

Great. Now she was saying Violet would be in some commune for idiots, getting all doped up and sucking pacifiers all day while Weston and the others proceeded to PhDs all because their moms pulled the plug on the plug. With help of a consultant for four grand.

"Oh my God, guess what?" Bee started, changing the topic. "Maggie's friend Katie Slaughter of the Slaughter Oil Company just had a baby, like three weeks ago," she said, her eyes twinkling with breaking news of the billionaire family. I always thought Slaughter was such a weird name, like *Hi! I'm Susie Death!*

Bee continued, ablaze with hot goss. "She had a girl. Called Amelia Celeste. Anyway, they hired this baby nurse from Mrs. Brown's agency, and they send this very nice but clinically obese woman from Germany who ate them out of house and home. Total pig. But they liked her, whatever. So every morning Sabina, the huge baby nurse, would bring the baby in at seven so she could go to sleep and the parents could take over. So yesterday, they wake up and realize it's eight twenty! So they go in her room—the baby's still asleep in the bassinet and Sabina is lying facedown dead on the floor. *Dead.* Dead dead dead." Bee could hardly control her laughter. "Heart attack! From being so fat!"

Mortified, I found myself smiling, too, but it was more nervous than amused. This poor woman keeled in the service of their coddled tot, her expiration apparently now sending rippling gales of laughter through the Upper East Side. Suddenly my phone rang. I pulled it out and looked at the incoming number: 415 area code.

My pulse quickened as I flipped it open. "Hello?" I said, my voice lilting up in a question, though I knew damn well who was calling.

"Hannah, Tate Hayes."

"Hi! How are you?"

"Fine, I'm heading to a class, but I wanted to see if you wanted to meet a week from Wednesday at the Morgan. To see the prints—maybe around four?"

"Sure, sounds great—can't wait."

As we agreed to meet, Weston and Violet were holding hands, and even though Bee was cooing to them, I saw her brow crinkle in curiosity.

"Who was that?" she asked as I closed my flip-phone.

"Just this old friend," I said casually. "We're going to the museum next week."

"I'm dying to catch up on all the exhibits," she said, seeming frazzled by all the stuff on her plate. "Oh! I totally forgot to give you this!" she said, alarmed, fumbling through her Hermès bag to retrieve a huge, square envelope. As Bee handed it to me, my eyes widened in surprise. On the thick paper, in the most over-the-top flamboyant but beautiful calligraphy, was "Violet Allen" swirled in with curly letters and delicate inky flares. "Lara from lunch the other day? It's her son Maxwell's birthday and she wanted me to invite you."

That was sweet. I was touched, considering that I thought Bee's friends found me a *Shrek*-loving Hicksville moron. "It's for the whole family, so Josh can come," Bee added.

I opened the lavish enclosure, which was fancier than most wedding invitations.

"Whoa!" I said, reading the details of the bash. "The St. Regis Hotel?"

"The ballroom," she added. "His first birthday was there, too, amazing," she gushed. "The theme was Old McDonald and they had a tractor drive in plus all these live animals with handlers and pony rides—"

"This is in the hotel?" I said, incredulous.

"Oh yeah, with a sit-down lunch for two hundred. And every child got a barn from F.A.O. with their name hand-painted on the red doors to take home."

Clearly Bee was impressed. I knew the dumbass pizza party I'd had for Violet in our old apartment with some toys chucked in the center of the carpet would simply not cut it in the Big Apple. "Wow. That's intense."

"I'll tell Lara that you and Josh will come. No need to RSVP."

I looked the response number, which was to a Mrs. Caldwell, clearly the daddy's executive assistant. "Great, thanks!" I said, my head bursting with cluttered visions of the scene I was to behold that weekend, of how excited I was to meet Leigh for dinner out tonight, and—the most unreal thing, beyond even hotel-ballroom-hosted toddler birthdays—was that the following week I would actually be meeting with Tate Hayes.

AND A FEW MINUTES LATER . . .

Instant Message from: BeeElliott

> BeeElliott: Just got back from park w/ Hannah.
> Maggs10021: How was?
> BeeElliott: Fine. She's coming to Maxwell's b-day party. She seems so intimidated by us.

Maggs10021: It is kind of overwhelming tho—
felt bad for her at lunch the other day.

BeeElliott: Why?

Maggs10021: Dunno, just she seems not psyched
to be here.

BeeElliott: Well, she married a NYer, I mean
hellooo, eventually Josh would move back.
Meanwhile get this: her kid is TWO and still uses
a pacifier. I need to get the # of your
consultant. I didn't tell her you hired him at 12
months—can you BELIEVE her kid's a junkie at
26 mos?

Maggs10021: I gotta find the # will e-mail it
to you later . . .

Thirteen

I was playing on the floor in our furnished rental with Violet,
wondering if we'd stay there forever, when my cute Barnard
sitter, Amber, came in to take over. I told her I wanted to put
Violet to bed, so Amber plopped and watched reality TV while
I read Violet *Rotten Ralph*, a formative series from my childhood about a crazy cat that does everything to fuck up his
owner's life (like take one bite out of every cookie at her party
or graffiti his face on her dresses) but she loves him anyway.

After her little eyes closed, I snuck out and threw on my cardigan, knowing how freezing the subways were. On the train platform, a saxophone player was doing a slow rendition of Duran Duran's "Rio," which was so odd, but I loved it. I tossed a dollar in his case, boarded the train, and was hurtled downtown in a matter of minutes.

I found Leigh at the bar drinking a colorful concoction.

"Whoa, what's up with the antifreeze cocktail?" I asked.

"It's absinthe. It's coming back after a one-hundred-year hiatus."

"Random. But you look very Manet. Drinking away any sorrows?"

"Kind of. Bad date last night."

"A date?! What about Craig?"

"After I saw you, I thought, *What the hell am I doing? Hannah's right, I deserve better.*"

"Good."

"No. Because then I met this quote unquote movie producer at the shoot for this new band we signed, and he asked me out. So I go to his place, which totally looks like the bad guy in *Miami Vice* would live there—electronics, white leather couches, horrifying. Then, after he basically shoves his tongue down my throat and licks my epiglottis, I push him off and storm out."

"Oh my God!"

"Wait. So I go home and Google his ass and it turns out, he's not even some big movie producer, he's a scummy trial lawyer who won the biggest Fen-Phen case ever, like two hundred million smacks. So he like funded a movie or two and plays this whole big-time producer role, but he's a total loser. There is no one out there, Hannah," she said, crushed. Her dismayed look was one step away from tears, a major rarity for Leigh. "I'm so depressed there is literally not a soul. I am going to die alone."

"No, you're not," I assured her. "Guys worship you! At my wedding every one of Josh's groomsmen was like 'Who is that?' But you were taken with schmuckfucker Assholicus Maximus."

"Ugh, my ex-primate. What was I shooting to waste three years with him? I hemorrhaged precious time."

"You are young, Leigh. You have plenty of time."

"I don't for kids. I would love to be with a little pal the way you are with Violet. I mean, when I walk by the playground on Bleecker and Hudson, my ovaries literally start to ache."

I thought about how amazing a mom Leigh would be. I have always believed that people run on different numbers of cylinders. Probably most people love their kids to their full capacity, but some run on fewer cylinders emotionally, like three or four. Leigh and I are ten-cylinder girls. After theorizing on the subject together many times, we concluded that the more you were loved, the more you can love. Leigh's ginormous heart and endless vat of love had her practically bursting at the seams—for a man to pour it on and a child to forever shower with devotion. The lack of a vessel to unload this well of feeling was paralyzing for her and it killed me, especially when I saw Bee and her friends, who, yes, loved their kids but also had full-time round-the-clock nannies so they could shop and lunch and compare their children and work out like maniacs.

"What's up with peasant skirts?" Leigh asked, staring down one offender and crossing her legs in her sexy black pencil skirt. "I mean, why do people want to look like peasants? I don't get it."

"It's funny," I said. "All these wealthy uptown mommies are wearing them and I thought the same thing."

"These trends are so crazy. I look huge in those things but still people run and buy them even if they don't look good, which they don't. Most people look heavy in them, I think," said Leigh.

"Not these moms," I sighed, as I popped more salted nuts in my mouth. "They're all size zero. They all have personal trainers, Pilates studios, and when they drop off their kids at Carnegie Nursery School, they run around the reservoir for three hours until pickup."

"Okay, maybe I don't envy your mom world," Leigh said. Then her face brightened. "Look! There's Joshie. Wait—who is that *gorgeous* guy with him?"

I turned to see Josh walk in with Parker. Leigh and I got up to hug them all hello. Leigh barely recognized Parker from when she met him at our wedding; it had been more than three years and he looked a lot older now.

"I hope you don't mind my crashing." Parker smiled, hugging me. "Bee said she had some girls' dinner and West's fast asleep. I thought she'd mentioned you were going to the hens' night out, but then when Josh said he was meeting you I was happy to tag along. You look great, sweetie."

"I'm so psyched to see you!" I said, which I always was when I saw cute Parker. Although I must admit for some reason I felt . . . weirdly left out of Bee's girls' dinner. Maybe she told him she was inviting me and then decided against it? We weren't even close friends, so I shouldn't feel excluded and quite frankly I'd choose a night with the current company rather than that group, but whatever.

Within minutes, any lingering thoughts of Bee disappeared as we were regaled by hy-fucking-sterical stories that had me almost peeing in my pants with laughter. First Parker told us about this crazy Swiss client, Count Alexei von Hapsenfürer, who was a seventy-year-old billionaire eccentric who lived in an Alps-perched château that was so remote you literally had to helicopter into it. The dude wore an eye patch from some shooting accident and lived alone in his hundred-room estate with his staff of seventeen and his pet monkey, Josiah, who wore cloth diapers secured with a diamond safety pin. He took shopping trips to Dubai on his G5 and had a tank of piranhas that he'd feed with his killings from hunting trips. Parker said he had a contraption that would lower in his newly slaughtered wild boar and seconds later it emerged with only the porcine skeleton left, gnawed clean by the small but ferocious fish.

Then Leigh told us all this insane music industry gossip—she worked at Sky Records, a label owned by two druggie brothers who minted money and harvested Grammys. Between her tales of one country star who built a Texas-shaped pool in his backyard and a Brooklynite emo crooner who got caught banging a Lolitaesque sixteen-year-old who'd said she was twenty, Parker, Josh, and I were howling, doubled over with laughter.

We all had the absolute best time ever, and when dinner was over I was sad to have it end. Later on that night, we climbed into bed, and I told Josh how much I missed working; Parker and Leigh had so many fun stories and experiences and I felt like I wasn't really out in the world anymore. I was a shut-in with Grover and the gang. But I loved Violet and didn't feel like I could leave her all day. And plus, who the hell would hire me? I had no clue what I wanted to do anyway, so it was all moot.

"You can do anything, Han. You'll get any job you want. There's no one like you," he said, kissing me. I didn't quite feel reassured since I had no clue what would make me happy but I knew I was definitely soothed by his arms around me, which was becoming a rarity due to his late hours. And that safety zone would soon become even more remote.

"Hannah, um," Josh stammered. "I feel really bad about this, but you know that crazy guy in Switzerland Parker was telling us about?"

"Yeah . . ."

"Well . . . I have to go to see him."

"Like, there, in the alpine castle place? When?"

"Well, it's not definite. That's why I didn't mention it. But maybe Saturday."

"*What?* Like this Saturday? The day after tomorrow?"

He nodded, reluctantly.

"For how long?"

"I just found out. He wants me to come for like ten days on some hunting trip. Parker usually goes but my boss said I should spend some time with him since I'm working on his account now."

"This sucks. I mean, he sounds like a character but he also sounds clinically insane. Now *you'll* come home with an eye patch."

"Sweetie, I'm doing this—"

"*For us*, I know." I felt bad for giving him shit when clearly his hands were tied—in wild boar rawhide—but sometimes I just wished he'd have a normal job where you leave at six instead of nine. On a good night.

"Hey, Han, you said you had some new porn titles for me—"

"Oh yeah." I smiled to myself, though I was still bummed. "Okay: *Flesh Gordon*, *Frisky Business*, and *Wetness for the Prosecution*."

He laughed out loud. "Very funny!" But he saw my grin slowly fade into a frustrated pre-departure missing of him. "Don't worry," he consoled. "I'll be home before you know it."

Fourteen

Lila cleared her throat delicately, placing a dainty hand to her thin neck. Her emerald ring was not unlike a billiard table. "Hannah," she started in such a tone that I knew instructions were coming. "You know, to fully immerse yourself in life here, you're going to have to join some of the right charity committees and junior boards."

"Mm-hmm," I replied, eyeing Violet to make sure she didn't smash one of the thousand antique *objets* that lined the Dillinghams' penthouse. A maid entered the room and poured us scalding tea (did I mention it was 92 degrees out?) from a sterling teapot as I sat on edge, frantic with the thought that my kid would shatter a Tiffany lamp or Ming dynasty vase. "Well, I have been wondering how to keep busy," I said.

"Perfect. I'm seeing Bee's mother for lunch next week before she leaves for Southampton. I'll mention it to her because Bee has truly thrown herself into her philanthropies. You need to step up and make an effort in that milieu. It will be very rewarding. And to be frank, it's not like you have much going on."

I didn't mention that I was thinking more along the lines of working on something I could parlay into a career down the road, since she once scoffed at working moms as Bee and Maggie so vociferously had in the playground.

"It's truly necessary," Lila advised. "If you want to meet the right group. Get into the right clubs. Be a part of everything. You can't skulk around alone with Violet all the time. It's not good for her and it's not good for you, dear. You must—how shall I say this?—*play the game*."

I smiled at the now all-too-familiar expression. "So I've heard," I responded, while darting Hermes-like to rescue a small silver-and-tortoise box out of Violet's paws. "I know we have to face the same thing with schools this fall . . ."

"Well, you be sure to follow Bee on that. She is wired and knows exactly what to do. She is such a *great* mother," Lila said, starry-eyed. "Do you know she nursed West for a *year*? In my day, no one nursed, it was considered so bohemian, so hippie! But it's back in vogue now, I suppose, and she was determined to be the best mother she could be, bless her heart. That girl is a gem. A true class act." Lila had a girl crush on Bee! She would have been positively orgasmic had Bee wed Josh and been the dream daughter-in-law she could squire up Madison.

I didn't bring up that Bee said she had a live-in baby nurse, for which the going rate was $250 per day, during that entire nursing goddess period, which helps.

"And you simply *must must must* go with her to one of those lectures—Doctor . . . Poundsomething—"

"Poundschlosser," I muttered. I was starting to think this guy was the Manhattan Mommy High Priest.

"Yes. Please at least investigate it, you have nothing to lose. And you might meet some nice women through that as well."

Weary with the mandates from my MiL, Violet and I bid adieu to her gilded galleries of public rooms, and though the summer air stank to high heaven, I gulped a lungful, grateful for the fresh breath of freedom.

Fifteen

As I stare, zombielike, at the TV screen, I am wondering if the yellow-turtleneck Wiggle secretly detests children. Or whether he has, like, full bondage outfits and whips and chains in his closet. Four smiley Aussies can't all be perfect and peachy—one of them has to have some serious skellies in there. Then I think, okay, gun to my head, with certain death if I don't pick one, which Wiggle would I bang if forced? The thought was too disgusting. I mean, clearly Jeff the purple guy was out and the yellow-turtleneck guy was gross, too. Anthony? Ew ew ew. I had a husband I was attracted to, but I bet there were some moms who probably had a Wiggle pop up in a sex dream or something after seeing them seven thousand times. Vomit. I'd probably loofah myself 'til I was lobster red. The cheery quartet then broke into a line dance complete with added friends Dorothy the Dinosaur and a pirate, Captain Feathersword, as Violet joined in with the arm movements. I wondered how many moms were at that exact moment also enduring the stupid fucking songs but couldn't change the channel 'cause their kids were in heaven.

When the colorful foursome of glee signed off, bidding a musical adieu, I piled Violet into the stroller to buy a birthday gift for Maxwell, Lara's son. At home a little Melissa & Doug wooden toy set is a surefire hit, but here I probably needed to amp it up a notch. So I went to Mary Arnold, which was our first stop when we visited with Violet when she was six months old; it was Josh's childhood toy store slash utopia, filled with balloons and stickers and DVDs and toys galore.

"Mommy, Elmo!" Violet screamed with glee on sighting the four-foot-tall red monster, and begged to be sprung from her stroller harness to wreak havoc. I let her out and walked down an aisle, searching for an appropriate treat for a three-year-old, when I saw Hallie, the redhead model mom, perusing the rack.

"Oh hi," I started as she stared at me blankly. "It's Hannah, Bee's friend? We met at lunch."

"Oh sure," she said, so not sure. She was holding an art set in her hand.

"Are you getting that for Maxwell? I was just picking something for him—"

"This?" she replied, incredulous. "Oh no, this is for us. I got Maxwell two cashmere sweaters from Ralph Lauren, one red, one navy. So cute."

Oh.

"I have no idea what to get him," I said. "Three seems like a senior citizen to me!" No smiles.

"Maybe get that rocking horse. He's into all things equestrian these days 'cause of the grandparents' ranch in Millbrook. They collect Thoroughbreds—Lara's mom flies to Argentina to bid at horse auctions like all the time." I turned to see a horse with a full mane of blond hair, a leather saddle, and a $350 price tag. Um, no.

"I'll figure something out," I sighed, excusing myself to find Violet.

After retrieving my daughter from her perch amid the dolls, I went up to the cashier to pay for a fire truck I'd found for Maxwell. It seemed cool enough, with real ladders and hardware. My rule was always that if I would be psyched to play with it, it must be okay for a kid.

Hallie, as it turned out, was still in the store, with piles upon piles of educational toys, kiddie flashcards, and pre-K workbooks. They rang her up and she didn't even look at the total as she blithely handed off her credit card.

"Oh, Hannah?" she said, spying me approach. "You must come to a lecture I'm organizing, it's part of a parenthood series organized by Dr. Poundschlosser—"

"Oh, yes, Bee's mentioned him." Plus, Lila would be euphoric if I "threw myself in."

"He's truly a genius. Anyway, he's doing an Upper East Side lecture at the Y next Tuesday evening. You really would enjoy it. I take such copious notes, my hand is cramping afterward! Can you make it?"

Was I free? Yes. Did I want to go take notes on how to parent? Not really. Did I want to be rude and put her off *and* piss off Lila for not making an effort? No. "Sure, I can come."

"Terrific. I'll get your number from Bee and leave you the details." Hallie walked out with three huge shopping bags. I saw her quickly relieved of her ribbon-tied load by her driver, who squired her away in her Cadillac Escalade.

"Next," said the woman at the register.

It was my turn to pay, and Violet was begging for a toy. "Sweetheart, I'm sorry, but we barely have enough space for the toys you have, let alone another, love muffin."

"Pleeease?" She made her adorable pouty face cum smile.

"Sorry."

"Okay, Mommy."

"I will get you a balloon, though, to tie on your stroller."

"Yaaaaaaaay!" Yelps of glee.

"You can only get one, though—which color would you like?"

"Umm . . . blue, please!"

With that, the sweet woman behind the counter went to blow up a blue balloon for Violet. When she came back, she tied it on the stroller and looked at me.

"You're a good mother," she said, looking in my eyes. "Most kids, they come in here and leave with whatever they want. These children are so spoiled I don't know what they have to look forward to, I really don't."

"Bigger toys, I guess. Real Porsches instead of mini ones . . ." I said, shrugging.

"You keep doing what you're doing. Your daughter is lovely."

I teared up, not knowing why I needed the stamp of approval at all, but as I emotionally mustered a cracking "Thank you," I realized that this woman must see it all. Like the cool janitor in *The Breakfast Club*, she was probably the eyes and ears of the Upper East Side parents' scene and somehow her approval meant way more to me than some Dr. Poundschlosser dude's.

The next night Violet and I hugged Josh so tight in our elevator vestibule it was as if he were off to Tikrit. I started crying as he mouthed out "I love you" through the closing elevator doors, but quickly swallowed away the cataracts on deck before Violet could see me in full Oksana Baiul–style waterfalls. I felt so pathetic and 1950s antifeminist, like I was going to crumble without Josh around for ten days. What was the matter with me? At Berkeley there was this super-strict Jewish lesbian group on campus called OrthoDykes and they all wore T-shirts that said, "A woman needs a man like a fish needs a bicycle." I felt like a breathless fish out of my California waters anyway, and that bicycle was looking pretty good as he rode out that door. I had to get a grip and stop hyperventilating as if I'd been dropped in the Sahara with seventeen dollars and a compass. I was in the center of the universe (as Josh always thought of Manhattan), and I'd have to learn how to navigate it with my inner compass or die a shut-in collapsing from Wiggles exposure.

Sixteen

I approached the Y, where the sold-out lecture given by Dr. Poundschlosser was being held. In front of the building town cars and chauffeur-driven Mercedeses, Lincoln Navigators, and Cadillac Escalades were triple parked. Blondes were helped out of their SUVs by their drivers and scurried in, lest the faint drizzle frizz their immaculately blown-out hair.

I entered the revolving door and saw a sign that read "Curing the Disease of Affluenza with Dr. Emile Poundschlosser," as the hordes flowed past me with the soundtrack of stiletto click-clicks, air-kisses, and Chanel bags being zipped. I scanned the room for Bee, who I spied sitting with Maggie, Hallie, and Lara in the second row. I walked up to them but there wasn't a free seat left for me, so I ducked into the row behind them and was alone until two friends in matching tweed jackets and intermingling eaux de parfum sat beside me.

"Ladies," began the esteemed doctor. "I'm very pleased you could all be here to join me." *Yeah, espesh 'cause the four-hundred-strong crowd each shelled out thirty bucks*, I thought. "May I first ask, before I begin, that you please take this moment to turn off your cellular phones and pagers so as not to disrupt the lecture."

With that, every single woman whipped out a sleek Motorola Razr or a tiny silver phone, and the auditorium erupted in a brief symphony of whirrs and buzzes and rings. Black-Berrys were switched off, bags reclasped, and silence fell again upon the eager crowd, most of whom clutched Tiffany or Montblanc sterling pens and pads of paper for recording the golden kernels of wisdom Dr. Poundschlosser would share.

"Welcome. We are here tonight to discuss a brewing, festering, contagious disease: Affluenza. In our zip code, it's a pandemic. Yes, wealth has its burdens . . ." *Oh please*, I thought. There are people living in caves and mud huts and shitting in holes and dying of starvation, and this dude's yammering on about the burden of privilege? Gagsville. "The weight of competition, the pressure of material goods, having the best things, winning placement at the top schools, living in the best apartments—it's not just keeping up with the Joneses where we live. It's keeping up with the Rockefellers."

Granted, I knew there were certain afflictions that truly were rich people's domain. You don't, for example, hear much about anorexia in third world countries. And rich peeps *did* seem to off themselves a lot; just since our move, I'd heard of multiple heirs throwing themselves off Park Avenue balconies, skiing into trees in Aspen, or crashing their Duccati motorcycles. But as Poundschlosser droned on and on about how our poor kids had this huge uphill challenge of growing up in this hotbed of money, I was ill. These kids were so fucking lucky! Their every whim was entertained, their every desire granted. Their parents pulled strings to give them access to anything their little hearts desired, whether it was piles of toys at the register or toddler clothes worthy of a Parisian atelier. The dude was making me sick. I couldn't believe I shelled out thirty smacks, let alone that Bee and her friends—and all the other disciples—paid thousands *weekly* to guzzle down this guy's absurd pontifications and pick his brain. He finally wrapped up after thirty-five minutes of complete and utter bullshit. I scanned the crowd to see if I could pick out another soul who seemed disgusted or even bored, but all seemed positively rapt and under his spell.

"And now I'd like to open the floor for questions. Yes? You in the camel shift dress!"

Everyone turned to see a petite, chic woman rise.

"Yes, thank you, first of all, Doctor, for that *fascinating* insight. I just wanted to ask, how do I avoid spoiling my son when his grandparents insist on certain luxuries? For example, my in-laws just bought a huge antique carousel for our back lawn in Bridgehampton. And we do have a lot of property, it's not about the space. I just think it's a bit much . . ."

"Excellent question," he responded. "Gifts can be outside your control, but you must take a stand and rein in certain purchases. Perhaps accept the carousel, but then make it clear that they should give only one gift per occasion—birthday, Christmas, et cetera."

I seriously almost hurled. A carou-fucking-sel? Jeez Louise. Poor Violet literally got a doll chucked at her for her second birthday. My mom always said the fewer toys, the better, because it forced kids' imaginations to grow as they have to come up with new ways to play with the toys they have as opposed to constantly getting new replacements hurled at them. Sheesh. Finally, after ten more questions, Dr. Poundschlosser finished, saying that applications for his group meetings for the following year were available in the lobby, along with envelopes containing his brochures, and, always with a plug, that his new book would be hitting bookshelves in a month's time.

Afterward, as the crowd stood up to leave, I was about to

make a comment about the lecture when I was silenced by Bee's gush that it was the most amazing thing she'd ever heard.

"And how brilliant is he?" added Lara. "I mean, how lucky are we to be in his regular group?"

"Yes, there's a huge one-hundred-person waiting list, supposedly," said Hallie.

"What did you think, Hannah?" Bee asked.

"Oh, um, it was . . . interesting" was my tepid response.

"You know, we could pull some strings and get you in our group," Maggie kindly offered. Thanks but no thanks.

"Oh, you know . . . I just kind of do my own thing. But thanks anyway."

Hallie and Lara looked at each other, aghast. "I don't think you understand," Lara said, horrified. "Half of this auditorium would kill to be in one of his groups. *Kill.*"

"I know, I'm sure, I'm just sort of getting my bearings and . . ." I watched as they stared me down in shock. "Maybe next year," I lied. As if. No one's sending us carousels anyway.

Seventeen

Just when I thought I'd had a jolting enough brush with the excess of Affluenza, I found myself in the thick of an outbreak, staring at a dizzying, movie-about-drugs-type warped view of fire-eaters, jugglers, men-on-stilts, Las Vegas showgirls with pasties on nips and feather boas, Rollerbladers, acrobats, and clowns with rainbow afros. I was not at Ringling Brothers. I was at a three-year-old's birthday party. As in the old Studio 54, there were velvet ropes and tight security. People with black turtlenecks and headsets whispered into the stealth mics, touching base with the catering staff, the florist, the musical director, the emcee, the event planner, and the calligrapher, who was on hand to make any last-minute adjustments. It was a seated dinner for two hundred. Forget weddings, bar mitzvahs, fiftieth anniversaries: this was the most blowout fest I had ever seen.

Naturally, Violet was on cloud nine thousand, feasting on the sights and sounds and gorging on sugar to the point where she was so hyper and up I thought she might blast off through the gilded ceiling. There was a jumpy castle, a haunted house, a mini petting zoo, an aquarium, a make-your-own-sundae bar, a caricaturist, and a button maker. There was a face painter, a giant piñata, a temporary tattoo applier. The name Maxwell appeared in lightbulbs that flashed different colors ringing the room. As I drank in the sea of decked-out kids and parents, eating caviar and blinis while clinking Bellinis, I noticed the tower of gifts from Cartier, Ralph Lauren, Tiffany, and F.A.O. Schwarz. I thought three words: *Holy fucking shit.*

Violet and I entered the second ballroom beholding the scene as a man dressed as a toy soldier checked us off The List. My daughter's eyes had never been wider. Within a nanosecond, she bolted off across the room, leaving me in the dust, alone with the designer-clad skinny moms and their banker hubbies, mostly in blue button-downs and khaki pants with navy blazers. Not one square inch of naked ceiling was visible—just a dense forest of balloons, each painted with giant *M*s. Every single surface had a bowl with a different single color of M&M's—a rainbow of candy that the kids were stuffing down their faces. Through a blur of hues I saw a hand waving across the room—it was Maggie, summoning me over.

"Hiii, how are you, Hannah?"

"Oh, fine. Josh is away for ten days, so it's a little hectic. I do not know how single moms do it."

"Nannies!" Bee replied. I didn't bother telling her most mothers do it all themselves, no staff on call so they can dart out for a mani. I thought I'd change the subject.

"Oh, I wanted to ask you guys, do you have a good pediatrician for Violet?"

"It's all about Dr. Careth," Maggie said. "He's so great. The top in the city."

"And easy on the eyes, too," added Bee. "Your kid's screaming from the TB shot, but you don't care 'cause the doctor's so gorgeous!"

Oh.

"He's great," said Maggie. "If you have trouble getting in, give him my name. He's technically not taking new patients but he'll make exceptions for friends of patients. He's really the best."

Naturally, I wanted the best for Violet. And I was psyched they were willing to help me, phew. Who knew you had to name-drop patients to get in?

"So Hannah," started Bee. "I'm worried about you. We all decamp for the Hamptons soon, and you'll be, like, all alone. Maybe you should come up and stay with us. Then Josh

can come on the weekends? We have a guest home you're welcome to."

I was touched by the generous offer but there was no way I
could leave Josh. I was already pathetically aching since he had
left and I quite frankly never understood the long-distance
marriage thing.

"We have a hens' party every Wednesday night with a hundred and twenty women, it's great!" Bee continued.

I am such a girls' girl, but somehow that did not sound so
great to me. There was no way I would spend more time away
from Josh than his work already dictated.

"Thank you. That sounds nice, um . . . maybe," I started.
Bee and Maggie looked at each other, clearly reading my hesi-
tation. "I don't know, I just don't like being apart. I'm kind of
dying this week."

"How long have you been married?" Maggie asked.

"Three years, right?" Bee answered for me. "See, you guys
are practically newlyweds! Park and I have been together
for eight years, married for almost five. You'll get over that,
you'll see."

I nodded quietly, knowing damn well that would never
happen. My parents had been married thirty-five years and
barely spent one night apart; the whole commuter marriage
thing with the wife and kids plopped three hours away was just
so not a West Coast thing, and it was all very alien to me.

Hallie approached us, holding a flute of champagne. "Hi,
girls," she said, lifting her glass. "Cheers, ladies! I'm celebrat-
ing: Julia Charlotte is fully potty trained. Fully trained!
Thatcher and I are delighted," she bragged. "How's Violet doing on that front, Hannah?"

"Um . . . we're not quite there yet." I'd brought it up with Violet but, with the move and everything, I didn't want to start pushing the potty just yet.

"Really?" Hallie asked, agog. "We started at seventeen months. You really should get on it. Nursery school application season is just about upon you!"

Violet came running up to us with Weston, Maxwell, and a few other kids, including Julia Charlotte, who then walked up to Violet and smacked her.

"Ow!" said Violet. I was horrified.

"You're okay, it's okay," I said to Violet and Hallie, trying to play it cool.

"Kids will be kids," she sighed, not apologizing for her supposed genius's brutal assault on my child.

Then a few minutes later, Julia Charlotte was pulling Violet's arm. When she suddenly let go, Violet crashed to the floor, accidentally knocking into Maxwell on her way down. It was so not a biggie but naturally the birthday boy burst into tears, screaming and crying. Lara swooped in to scoop him up, shooting me a glare.

"I'm s-so sorry," I stammered. "Violet fell and accidentally bumped—"

"Come here, my sweet pea," she cooed to Maxwell while rocking him, holding him to her Dior-covered breast. "That mean little girl hurt you. We won't let her hurt you again."

I was stunned. My daughter gets whacked in the head and it's "Kids will be kids"! But when she was knocked into this fluent-Chinese-speaking pansy-ass boy, she's a mean girl. Fuck that bullshit. I gathered Violet up in my arms to get the hell out of that gilded circus.

"Maybe we should go," I said, looking at Maggie and Bee.

"Bye," said Bee, leaning in for an air-kiss good-bye. "Don't worry about Lara. She's just a little protective."

As I walked out I caught sight of Hallie cuddling Julia Charlotte while Bee and Maggie refilled their chardonnay, and the party raged on.

AND BACK AT THE SEVENTEEN-INCH COMPUTER SCREEN . . .

Instant Message from: BeeElliott

```
    BeeElliott: Hannah = lame.
    Maggs10021: Why?
    BeeElliott: I dunno. She bugs. Did you see
how she was so not into Poundschlosser? I mean,
the man is a god in child development. What, does
she think she's such an expert mom and doesn't
need him?
    Maggs10021: I dunno, I can see how he might
be overwhelming . . .
    BeeElliott: Whatevs.
    Maggs10021: Are you still going to invite her
to join the NACHO committee? You should—she's
nice, Bee. And she needs to meet peeps, etc.
    BeeElliott: Okay, okay. I'll do it.
```

Eighteen

The next day was Sunday and with my hubby away I was alone with little to fill my day and keep Violet amused. Save for a quickie e-mail from Josh with three new porn titles he'd come up with (*Saturday Night Beaver*, *The Touchables*, and *For Your Thighs Only*), I was feeling very blah. Leigh was away with a band, I couldn't reach any pals in California, and so Vi and I just walked and walked around for hours and found ourselves at the park, where we plopped for practically the whole afternoon. I got more than a few weird looks from moms who would never let their kids near the sandbox, so Violet and I sat alone playing in the sand, which wasn't filled with syringes or anything . . . just sand. I pushed her on the swings and was amazed by how much she had grown, the little rubber swing with leg holes being my barometer, like an outgrown sweater, of how she'd sprouted. They'd had the same swings in San Francisco and I remembered snapping away at her first giggle-filled ride just after she'd learned to sit up. Finally I hauled her out and we made our way home, where she promptly passed out. I carried her onto the couch and put a big warm blanket over our legs. It wasn't so much that it was chilly but that I wanted a physically soothing thing to comfort me and sought the basics: blankie, Spaghetti-Os. As I slurped my bowl, I smiled thinking how all these women had personal chefs and I did too: Chef Boyardee. I sighed, wondering how reviled I'd be were Lara and Hallie to see me eating such Britney Spearsian foodstuffs.

Sundays, for some, are all about long strolls holding hands, fluffy French toast, and relaxed absorption in the obese newspaper, but for me they are gut-churningly dismal. They make me want to either string up a noose or go on an insane carb binge. I think they are haunted by that acidic pit caused by what I call the Ghost of Homework Past. There's residual nausea from years of dreading the school week and piles of assignments that dauntingly faced you after the cereal bowls were washed and the milk and OJ cartons were back in the fridge. But that afternoon, it was pasta instead of wrist-slashage, and as I inhaled my trashy eats, I looked out the large window onto the chaos outside, and started to close my eyes before I could cry out the tears that were sizzling on deck.

I remember when I was little, my parents would order in from Hunan Garden (eleventh commandment: Thou shalt order in Chinese on Sundays) and they'd be glued to Mike Wallace as that stressful *60 Minutes* clock would tick at commercial breaks and make me want to hurl my scallion pancakes. That effing giant watch. It marked my life ebbing away from week to week, each monster-second-hand flicker scavenging a beat of my heart.

Okay, so I was being a melodramatic teen. And now I was having a relapse, but without hormones and high school to blame it on. Except I felt like I was in high school, the new kid who joined midyear and who the teacher introduces to the whole class, telling them to "reach out" to the newcomer in the hallways. I had to chill. People moved all the time, they had husbands traveling and did all the housework themselves, boo-hoo. And despite my meal choice, I was in a decent apartment and not some hovel. I was blessed! I knew I had to stop wallowing. Plus, some women were in towns of population 547, not a thriving metropolis with a world of fun stuff waiting outside! But none of it called to me at that moment. I snuggled under my blanket next to slumbering Violet and grabbed for the other magic nerve-mollifying device: the remote control. But nothing was on. Preachers, news programs, yawnsville. Ahhh, Sunday, the vat of salt in my bloody self-inflicted wound. There I was, feasting on the Os and wondering where my life would take me, as I did hourly. I flipped through the channels silently praying to the cloudy heavens for a Molly Ringwald movie to soothe my weary, self-battered mind. In her loneliness, amid the slamming lockers of the rich and the heartless, I'd find my heroine whose pout-turned-smile would get me through the afternoon. But no Molly to be found, alas. And she, poor thing, had it rough with those jerky white-blazer schmucks and meanie trust funders, but they were sixteen, they had a whole life ahead of them! And I was almost double, *double* their tender age. I settled for the Food Network, my new zone-out addiction, and eventually fell asleep during a sauce-making demonstration.

Nineteen

The message from Lila said it was urgent. Heart pounding, I ran to the phone, freaking that something had happened to Josh. I left three voice mails, which were probably inaudible thanks to my incessant panting, and then tried the apartment again.

"Deelinkham residence?" the maid answered.

"Oh, hi—it's Hannah again. Is she back yet?"

"No, meesus. She not—oh, she is here now I tink. Hold on."

After I'd been holding for a minute, Lila picked up with a cheerful chirp. "Hello?"

"Lila, it's Hannah, is everything okay?"

"Hello, dear. Yes, fine. I just wanted to see if you were free for a meeting? For the NACHO benefit committee. There's a ladies' luncheon coming up and I thought it would be a very important board for you to join. Many names, you know. In fact, Bee is a junior chair. Did she mention it to you, by chance?"

She hadn't. I don't know why that bothered me, I wasn't so into "luncheons" and I didn't even know what the cause was.

"What's NACHO?" I asked.

"New Yorkers Against Childhood Obesity," she said. "Very, very important cause. Our nation is becoming bloated beyond measure. And these poor children, poor little things. Well, I guess I shouldn't say *little*. They are huge. Enormous—we saw photographs of a third grader who weighed more than me! The tragedy. And sometimes it's because they eat everything under the sun like their fat parents. But sometimes, bless their artery-clogged hearts, it's not even their faults! It's *glandular*."

I found it interesting that, while sad, *this* was the cause Lila, her friends, and Bee were so ravenous to embrace.

"Sure," I said weakly. "I'll come."

The NACHO committee "meeting" turned out to be basically a ladies' cocktail party. I had taken Violet to the park, made her dinner, and had Amber come for two hours, planning to return before my little one went to bed. I walked to pick up Lila, who had a chauffeured town car waiting for us, and we cruised up Madison to Carnegie Hill, pulling around to a stunning Fifth Avenue building overlooking the reservoir. I knew instantly the ladies we saw entering the gray-awninged building were going where we were going—it was like a club of fashion.

Inside, Eloise Skadden Tiverton greeted her guests and had two girls from the charity filling out name tags for us to clip onto our clothes. (God forbid they have those sticky tags, they'd damage the outfits!) We walked in to find ten tuxedo-wearing cater-waiters passing hors d'oeuvres, all of which seemed to be declined. Groups of ladies chatted as I followed Lila like her shadow, not knowing another soul there.

"We're off to the south of France for a month!" one woman

gushed. "We leave tomorrow night. I'm ecstatic! Get me out of this pit!"

"We leave the first of August for Little Compton when the city becomes empty. Lawrence has to work 'til then but I am just counting the days. Prescott comes home from his Putney trip then and Fifi returns from Welby Van Horn the following day and we're off! Can't wait. I really need this vacation!"

I wondered why everyone seemed to really need a vacation. Meanwhile, Lila, who was gabbing away with her fellow oppressed city-dwellers, never introduced me to her friends. At one point I told her I was going to get a water at the bar, thinking maybe the reminder of my existence would give her cause to acknowledge me to her friends, but instead she simply said, "Do be a dear and get me a Pellegrino while you're there. Lime wedge, little ice."

Nice. I went up to the bar and was patiently waiting when I saw Bee and Maggie walk in. Lila went straight up to Bee and kissed her on both cheeks and shook Maggie's hand. I looked into her Pellegrino, which the guy had handed me, and just started counting the bubbles to distract myself from my welling discomfort.

Maggie saw me in the corner and came right up, easing my awkwardness. "Hi, Hannah!" she said sweetly. "I didn't know you were coming to this. I'm so glad to see you here."

"Yeah, I didn't know either. My mother-in-law just told me."

"Oh, I thought Bee was asking you—she told me she had meant to."

"It's okay, I'm sure she's been really busy."

Maggie suggested we go sit down somewhere as she was

passing out from the pregnancy-and-heat combination. I asked when the meeting was starting.

"Oh, this is it!" she said. "I know, not much of a meeting, really. It's more of a kickoff."

"A kickoff . . . to what?" I asked, idiotically.

"To the event. You know, it's like a pre-event."

A photographer from *W* snapped pix of the swans smiling together in clusters, including a close-up of Bee and Lila with their arms around each other.

Finally, Bee stopped vamping for the camera and came over to sit with us.

"I am pooped!" she wailed, putting a manicured hand to her head. "West is so sick, poor kid." She looked at her diamond-bordered watch.

"You must have to go back," I said sympathetically. "I actually have to go, too."

"Oh, I'm not going home! I have a dinner for LAMP—Less Acne More Pride—and then some friends are in town and we're going to Bungalow 8."

So much for rushing home to the sick kid.

I got up to excuse myself so I could go home to my daughter and tried to find Lila, without success. Finally, I turned a corner and heard her voice. I stopped when I heard my name.

"Hannah is simply no Bee," she said in confessional tones to another blond skeletore. "I need to talk to Josh about having her try a little harder. I just don't want my granddaughter to end up in the wrong world: playgroups, schools, activities, everything."

"Oh, Lila, that could never happen," her friend promised.

"With a mother like that, you never know! Look at Bee Elliott and her friends. They are just so charming and their children all go to Carnegie. I pray that happens for little Violet. Then she'd be on the right track for life."

Tears burned in my eyes and I quickly darted to the elevator vestibule before a lone tear could escape. I burst through the gold-bar-covered glass doors onto Fifth and burst into tears. All my worst suspicions were true: Lila saw me as a liability and not an asset. I guess I always knew it, but hearing it loud and clear was a wake-up call. While I wanted to say *Screw you*, I knew I needed to do everything in my power to keep her happy so she didn't go running to Josh about how I was a shitty mom and not part of the scene. Lila was Josh's only family and I didn't want to make him choose; I'd have to be on her team.

Twenty

There's nothing I hate more than a Sanctimommy. The more I thought about that beeyotch Hallie saying I had to "get on it" with Violet's potty training, the more I wished I'd told her to fuck off. But that wasn't me. I always wanted to have the great zinger, the right-back-atcha line, but I was the Monday-morning quarterback who always thought of what to do in hindsight. That particular Monday morning, the heat was unbearable. I was walking down the street, each step an effort, with sweat covering my whole body. Per Bee and then Lila's urging, I had tried calling Dr. Careth, society pediatrician, and was put on hold. For twenty-three minutes. "Baby Beluga" was playing on a loop and I almost hurled the phone out the window. I thought it must have been a mistake and they'd forgotten about me, so I hung up and called again. The woman who answered spoke as fast as those fine-print voiceover people in car and drug commercials, "Sideeffectsincludenauseaand-analleakage," whatever.

"DrCarethsofficepleasehold."

So I held for another *thirty-one minutes*. I thought I would go insane. I wanted to find the "Baby Beluga" guy and slaughter him. Finally, the woman came back on. "HellohowcanI-helpyou?" A trillion shrill phones rang in the background as if Jerry Lewis were conducting a telethon on the premises.

"Hi, um—I—my family just moved here and I wanted to make an appointment for a checkup? For my two-year-old. Bee Elliott is a friend and she said—"

"Pleaseholdonemoment." More waiting. "Hello? Yes, we can take you December seventeenth at eleven forty-five."

Huh? "You mean, like, in *four months*?" I asked.

"Yes. He's fully booked until then."

Great. What if Violet, God forbid, had a problem? I wasn't going to wait on hold every time she needed to see this guy, even if he was "the best."

"Okay. Um, I think I need to find someone sooner than that. Thank you so much, anyway—" *Click*.

Violet came scampering in, singing the "Elmo's World" theme song. Today Elmo was thinking about: airplanes! The TV showed a montage of children traveling to all corners of the

earth. I thought about how nice it would be to just jet off somewhere—Rome, Chicago, New Delhi, even the Alps to accompany Josh on his business trip, not that we were invited or that
I wanted Violet near tanks of piranhas. When *Sesame Street* was
brought to us by the letter *K* and the number 11, we went outside and hit Oren's Coffee Roasters, my daily crack dealer, I
mean, coffee bar. The cool-looking (un-Starbucksian) barris-
tas all knew Violet's name and gave her a happy shoutout every
morning when we wheeled in. It reminded me of my cool indie coffee joint at home, where all the nose-pierced artists
would work to make ends meet. After Josh and I drove cross-
country, we realized that in every small town the edgy cool
people all work at one of two spots: the local record store or
the coffee bar. As I waited for my iced coffee with extra half-
and-half and vanilla syrup (I liked it to taste like melted
Häagen-Dazs), a sweet-looking older gentleman was smiling
at Violet. She giggled as he made funny faces then smiled at
me. "You're great with kids," I said, as Violet beamed with a coy
smile.

"I'm a pediatrician," he replied. Jackpot.

"Really? Because we just moved here and I need a doctor
for Violet! Is your office nearby?"

"Right up the street," he said, handing me his card. "Dr.
Smith."

"She still hasn't had her two-year checkup, so I'm calling
right now."

"I think we can get you in there, Violet," he said, pinching
her cheek.

Phew! That was easy. I called his office from my cell after
he'd left with his espresso (which I would need to mainline

were I to have that job) and his sweet office assistant answered right away. And though there were still phones ringing in the background, they could get us in that afternoon. Bingo!

As Violet and I walked around, we passed a bus shelter with an ad for the Morgan exhibit. I felt a jolt in my midsection that I was actually meeting Professor Hayes and walked around in a daze until lunch. Violet and I strolled to Three Guys diner on Madison and Seventy-sixth Street, near Dr. Smith's offices, and got a table for lunch. The place was packed with toddlers and yummy mummies, dressed perfectly, some with nannies on hand to assist in lunchtime feeding. It was a kiddie explosion complete with cacophony of whines, thrown fries, and spilled milk. Violet sat in her high chair and ate her grilled cheese, which I'd sliced into strips. Just as I was realizing that this was the epicenter of mommypalooza—that all roads led to Three Guys for lunch—Bee walked in with Weston.

"Hi, Hannah!" she said, looking us over. "Great to see you! How was the rest of your weekend? You know, after the whole party thing?"

"Fine, we just relaxed. We spent a lot of time walking around, playing in the Sheep's Meadow."

"Really? Ugh, I hate that place! It's all these stoners playing Hacky Sack. Weren't you scared those ultimate Frisbee junkies would hit you?"

"Not really."

"I just always feel like I need to boil myself after spending time there. I mean, at Chapin we'd sit there and smoke with the guys, but I honestly haven't been back since."

"Oh."

"So, Troy said he hasn't heard from you in a while."

"Who?"

"Troy Kincaid. The broker? He said you all were rethinking the budget?"

So much for broker privilege. "Well, yeah, we may just stay in a rental, actually."

"Hiii guys!" Maggie then walked in with Hallie and Lara and broods. Great.

"Sorry we're late, Bee!" said Maggie. "Hi Hannah, hi Violet!"

The posse plopped at the booth adjacent to our table. We could still talk, but clearly they were one unit and Violet and I were another, with the aisle between us signifying a lot more than a path for the Greek waiter.

Just then, a blond woman, her six towheaded children, and three nannies came in and headed to the back, where the bigger tables were.

"Hi Cindy!" said Bee as she passed.

"Oh, hi guys." She waved, looking frazzled but still immaculately put together.

Bee leaned across the aisle to me after she passed. "That's Cindy Hetherington, billionaire. Her in-laws invented the reaper. She's a competitive birther."

I almost spat out my Sprite. "What?"

"You know, bangs out a trillion kids. She has six kids under six years old. Makes her feel superior to everyone. It's like she has something to prove."

"Wow, I commend her."

"Don't. Her family was so screwed up," said Maggie conspiratorially. "Her dad was banging the secretary and her mom became a lesbo afterward. Nightmare!"

I felt awful as I looked at the perky Cindy getting her litter settled at the massive back table.

"Dr. Poundschlosser said on the QT that clearly she's trying to right the wrongs in her family history by having this massive blond brood," Lara added in a confidential whisper. "Speaking of which," she said, looking over Violet. "Hannah, where on earth did Violet get her goldilocks? 'Cause you could not have darker hair."

I heard this all the time, but this time it was almost as if Lara was like mad at me that Violet was blond. Maybe it was because Lara was blond and Maxwell had brown hair? "Um . . . yeah, I know. I have blond in my family, though, and Josh used to be blond as a kid—"

"But I thought brown always wins," Maggie said, confused. Wait, were they like accusing me of banging the postman? Plus, brown *wins*? Did she mean genetically dominates?

"Well, it doesn't always . . . win," I said. "I must have recessive blue eyes and blond hair somewhere, ya know, like that big B, little b Punnett-square stuff?" Blank faces. "Ninth-grade biology?" Didn't these people go to fucking Princeton?

"Sometimes I see that," said Bee. "It does happen sometimes. Like a freak thing."

"I don't get it," Lara said, almost pissed. "I couldn't be blonder and Maxwell still ended up with dark hair! It's so unfair." Um, was Hitler reincarnated? If she wanted an Aryan nation, she should move to God's country in the rural Pacific Northwest.

Unfair? Okay . . . weird. I mean, *who cares?* Plus, it was semi-weird and overtly narcissistic for a blonde to just come out and say it's better to be like her.

"Maybe this summer in the Hamptons the sun will bleach it," she said, patting Maxwell's fluffy head.

Poor kid. I knew damn well she was about to pour vats of Sun In, lemon juice, and probably pure peroxide on his locks and come home chalking it up to sunshine at the beach. Gag. After a lifetime of telling dumb-blonde jokes, it was almost funny sometimes that my daughter would be one of them—except brilliant, naturally!

"Meanwhile," said Hallie, "I need a new weekend nanny. Do any of you know of anyone? I was going to use Miffy Henderson's but—"

"No, no, no, no," instructed Bee. "Never share help."

"Why?" asked Hallie.

"Bad idea. Miffy could use her to get information on you. Or just poach her back later when she needs more help. Trust me, not a good idea."

Jeez, who knew there was nanny espionage?

"It's hard to find a live-in just for the weekends," sighed Hallie. "It's just that Thatcher likes to go out and party, so we want to sleep in. Oh well, if you hear of anyone let me know."

Just then Hallie's perfect, amazing, potty-peeing, brilliant-IQ'd Julia Charlotte threw a fistful of peas at me across the aisle, which was our cue to leave. I said bye to Bee and Co. and gathered Violet for our walk to Dr. Smith's office.

We walked in to find a friendly waiting room filled with fun toys, rolling cars, dinosaurs, and a full play kitchen. "Mommy, kishen, kishen!" Violet was in heaven and darted off to fake bake. After a few minutes, Dr. Smith came out to get us by singing Violet's name, opera-style. It was so cute and she scampered across the room and jumped into his arms, giving him a massive hug.

She loved him immediately, and almost more important, I loved him as well. He was old-school, not just in age and granddad looks but with his glasses and lab coat and worn hands that had held thousands of babies. I felt immediately reassured I wasn't doing a horrible job. All was fine with the checkup, and after I'd inquired only out of curiosity, Dr. Smith told us that Violet was ninetieth percentile in height and weight and he practically laughed up lunch when I asked about head circumference.

"You're not serious," he said.

"Someone asked me," I laughed. "I'm not kidding."

"Listen. Don't listen to these crazy moms around here," he ordered. "They're all creating things to compete about. They're Momzillas."

I smiled, imagining Bee in T. rex form, giant and reptilian, carrying a huge Hermès bag with one claw, while biting the heads off unfashionable moms.

"I know, I just . . . get stressed out sometimes. I feel like I am the worst mother on the planet 'cause Violet is still drinking from her bottle!"

"She won't go to college with it." Dr. Smith smiled.

"Oh my gosh, that's verbatim what my husband says about her pacifier!"

"Sounds like a smart man."

"What about her attachment to her SpongeBob doll?"

"She won't walk down the aisle with it, I assure you," he said.

I felt soothed by the balm of his common sense. Like I said, old-school.

"She also still spits up once in a while—"

"Too bad your husband's not a dry cleaner."

I laughed. What other questions did I have? "She also gets diarrhea like maybe once every few weeks for no reason. Is that normal? I mean, she'll just all the sudden have it, but only once."

"Keep her away from juices afterward, and if her spirits are high, keep her away from doctors." He patted Violet on the head and I felt totally taken care of, like I was back in California.

As we walked home, I tried to tell myself that it wasn't all peachy keen everywhere else in the country—Momzillas are clearly not a New York–only phenom. My friend Victoria lived in L.A. and had told me about the nightmarish Santa Momicas that infested the west side of the city, preaching about nursing as they handed their kids off to a flock of nannies. Plus, with the showbiz angle, all these parents would work the room at every little birthday party since each tot was the child of a studio exec, power agent, producer, or famous actor.

But still, New York was different. I realized that Bee's friends, despite clearly lacking the understanding of how DNA worked, were all obviously bright. They were just bored. Being a stay-at-home mom was a ton of work, probably more than most day jobs. But these women all had hot-and-cold-running help and I suspected they were dying slowly of boredom. I couldn't engage in their hangups and worries about the best school, the best clothes, the best doctor. I just couldn't. Because I knew myself, and that slope was too slippery; if I became immersed in that world, I would wither on the vine. The problem was, Violet did deserve the best. So even if I hated that scene I had to suck it up and play ball. Bee and her posse made it look like they were supermoms, but it was kind of smoke and mirrors. They even had substitutes should their weekend nanny fall through. God forbid they were alone with their child!

I thought about what Josh once wisely said when I was wiped out one night after a long day with Violet: "Pay now or pay later." And it was true; maybe Bee's fancy friends needed 24/7 live-in people, but the Nobel Prize winner Julia Charlotte might rebel. Or Maxwell might be a performance artist. You can't control what your kids will be or how they'll develop. I just needed something to take me out of that world so I wouldn't get bogged down in it. And that something was coming the following afternoon.

Twenty-one

After kissing Violet's forehead as she lay sleeping, I tiptoed out, waving to Amber, and made my way down to meet Tate Hayes. It was four P.M. exactly when I saw him standing by the double doors of the Morgan in a loden green jacket over a white oxford shirt and jeans.

"Hannah," he said, drawing out the two syllables as if my name were the first word of a poem.

"Hi, Profess— Tate." I looked down, blushing. I still thought of him as my professor. How strange that now we would maybe become friends. But never equals, as he was too vaunted a persona in my life to be a mere peer.

"Shall we?" he asked.

We strolled the marble halls of the enchanted former home of J. Pierpont Morgan on Thirty-sixth Street and Madison Avenue. Even after watching movies that stylishly captured turn-of-the-century architecture, I could not believe that people had actually lived in the city's center in such lavish, all-enveloping velvety surroundings. Beyond the extensive collection of prints which we were there to see, the museum had preserved Morgan's library of rare tomes and a study so ornate and astonishing, you can't imagine how anyone could ever get work done: I, for one, would have been too distracted by the rich brocade curtains, the intricately carved furniture, and the oils that hung on the hand-stenciled walls.

We walked through much of the space, accompanied by the sound of my black flats practically tiptoeing on the marble floor. When we reached a small oil-on-copper, we paused to look at it. I remembered Professor Hayes always loved oil-on-copper, and he got up very close, as if to penetrate the frame's glass with his piercing gaze.

"See this enameling here," he said, gesturing. "Look at this fruit in the lower right corner." He put his hand on my shoulder and pushed me closer to look at the work; the subject was Adam and Eve. "The paint just sits on the copper, none seeping in as it would into a panel's fiber or canvas's pores. It's as close as we can be to the paint, this creamy, sensuous paint, with a vibrancy you really don't see on other surfaces. He delivers us Eden itself in these strokes," he said, as I studied the work in my own incredible private lesson.

He described the leaves as sighing and weighty with verdant glistening streaks of paint, and earth's first man and woman were supple with silken tones, as their fleshy bodies drew our eyes to their milky skin and up to Eve's buttery cascading hair.

Next we spied a landscape by Hendrik Avercamp, a glacial expanse of frozen canal, with skating revelers flying through the chilled air on stilled water. "This gray, gauzy filter," he said, gesturing to the smoky surface of the work, "doesn't dazzle with roaring lions or arch-backed nudes; it's a really muted, delicate reality, with all the classes melded—look at the rich man's carriage, here." He pointed. "Everyone is united by that harsh chill of winter, with the whole hierarchy frozen in that pond."

Tate Hayes was a true historian, guiding me through the tangled politics of the time. "The Dutch have written their history into the art," he said, showing me painting after painting that echoed the flux of the seventeenth century. "Political and religious metamorphoses were brushed into permanence." Just as when I was a student, I exhaled slowly, my skin tingling with an excitement that wasn't a sexual turn-on but a brain make-out. Some music can evoke that feeling in me, but then I'm a passive listener. Now, I actively felt myself learning, lapping up his words like a hungry, hardened sponge thirsting for information—especially delivered in such a poetic way. After two years of goo-goo-ga-ga with my beloved daughter, I realized, in an emotional tidal wave of hearing his words, that I desperately thirsted for this outing. To remember who I was, and to reawaken that latent passion for art that had been dormant until now.

When we were done looking at the newly installed collection, we sat in the sunlit tearoom. I actually secretly don't like tea but drank it anyway, dissolving spoon after spoon of honey in the cup like a kid in a candy store, which I was. We talked about his wife and two boys (Leonardo and Marcello—his wife was Milanese and taught Italian at NYU) and how he sometimes missed San Francisco.

"There's more texture here, more grit, more energy," he said of our new home. "And of course, more art, and not just giant museums but hidden jewel boxes, private collections. We were at a cocktail party last week on Fifth Avenue and the etchings just in the hallway to the kitchen were simply staggering. There was literally a Dürer in the powder room! All these people were hobnobbing and sampling the caviar, and I absconded to the ceaseless hallways to study their works; I barely ate a bite, but I felt replete."

Art was enough to sustain Tate, but I needed more. Thinking of sustenance, I looked at my watch and realized I had to leave to make Violet's dinner—it was a Cinderella exit, full of flustered good-byes and gathering of things. But no glass slipper was left in my flurried wake—only the hope that maybe he would call and invite me to look at art with him again soon.

Twenty-two

Thanks to Maggie and Bee, the Milford Prescott Music School, also known as Juilliard for two-year-olds, found a place at the last minute for Violet and me in their Mommy and Me series. Lila was overjoyed when I happily reported our acceptance to her. For our class, there were two choices: Parent/Child or Caregiver/Child. Since I was already calling in a huge favor, I didn't actually express my true desire to be in the nanny class; the mom scene kind of gave me the creeps and I would have probably felt much more comfortable with the nannies. I opened my letter from the director of admissions and found the school handbook with dress code, school rules, and instructions that should I change my mind, I must notify the office as there was always an "extensive waiting list," which I guess I had cut, thanks to a hefty donation by Bee's family foundation. Luckily, we got in the Caregiver class, which I was thrilled about. Apparently most moms preferred to be with other moms—choosing to avoid "aliens," legal or nay.

But I just wanted to relax; nannies didn't ask about height and head circumference percentiles. I also signed up Violet for ballet class since Rudolf Nureyev was her babysitter when Amber couldn't make it—as I unpacked boxes during the first three weeks, I plopped her in front of old, squeaky VHS tapes of *Swan Lake* and *Sleeping Beauty*, which kept her rapt for two straight hours. I was told by the Manhattan Academy of Ballet Studies that her uniform would be a pink leotard, pink tights, and pink ballet slippers, and her hair must be pulled back into a bun. A bun? Violet had never even had a haircut—she sported a baby mullet, her blond wisps barely able to make a ponytail without the assistance of added clips, let alone a bun. But hey, I guess in the big leagues you gotta sport the real ballerina 'do.

I had three weeks until Labor Day, which marked the re-entry of New York's elite into town: the gates opened and every Benz and Beemer cruised back into town from the Hamptons, loaded up with sandy summer gear as children shopped for back-to-school threads.

Bee and her clan had been shuttling back and forth but now were plopping for the final few weeks "out east" at the beach. Really "the beach" was all stilettos and oversized sunglasses and shopping in Southampton, not exactly flip-flops and sandy toes. It was club-chaises instead of towels by the waves, with dips in gleaming pools instead of the murky ocean.

For Bee's posse's last gathering before scattering to the places where they summer (yes, they used *summer* as a verb), we all gathered at the annual ladies' luncheon to support NACHO; Lara went to Millbrook then Martha's Vineyard, Maggie to East Hampton, and Hallie to Ewan's Peak, her family's private island off the coast of Maine where, Bee said, they hosted white-tie parties. I was picturing powdered ladies with Edith Wharton–style outfits and men in tails holding lobster mallets. I'd take burgers and dogs and jeans and a T-shirt any day over that supposedly glam stuff. I mean, the day I host a white-tie bash in my home is the day Hallie says Julia Charlotte did something dumbass, i.e., never.

For their August jaunt, Lila and Watts would be in England, and while all the women were itching to escape I was looking forward to quiet calm before the autumn storm, without Lila's pop-bys and Bee's sometimes stifling presence. I didn't know why, and maybe I was being paranoid, but I was starting to get the feeling Bee didn't like me. I hadn't done a thing wrong, I couldn't have been nicer. I just had this strange sense she was only semi-nice to me as an order from her mother by way of Lila.

Before the NACHO benefit, I spent the morning with Violet walking to Times Square to buy Broadway show tickets from the tourist-glutted booth in the middle, stopping at Toys "R" Us for a ride on the indoor Ferris wheel. Violet's face was as bright as the blazing LCD displays lighting up the store; she was simply in awe of all the activity. It was a nice feeling to really see her relish her new city, and it even gave me an excited buzz. I don't know what prompted me to go on a ticket-buying odyssey, but Josh and I loved plays so much and I think they triggered romantic memories of our trips to New York. I wanted to relive it the old way and remind myself how excited I used to get about the idea of living here. We strolled back uptown along the park and I had two hours before the famous luncheon. I didn't want to show up and displease Lila again with the wrong outfit, so to make every effort to make her proud, I walked with Violet to Bergdorf's, which was having a huge summer sale. Three dresses into my mini fashion show for Violet, I tried a plain, chic black crepe dress with buttons down the side that was part Audrey Hepburn, part 1940s, and entirely adorable. I felt good. My hair was pulled into a tight bun and I wore my A-plus shoes Josh and I had bought in London at Emma Hope. I read Violet her stories before her afternoon snooze, when Amber arrived to read *Us Weekly* and hang 'til I was done with the benefit.

The red tent covered part of Lexington Avenue as a bevy of paparazzi snapped various bold-faced names in New York society who were coming out pre—summer exodus to fight childhood obesity.

I watched them each pause for the camera, doing the movie star hand-on-hip thing and then fake-converse with each other as the fotogs snapped "candids." It was weird—fashionwise I seemed very out of sync with the Upper East Side moms; I always thought New Yorkers wore black all the time, but no: salmon cashmere twin sets, turquoise dresses, and a butter yellow suit were all fluttering by in a pastel parade. I guess we'd hung out more downtown before moving; now, ensconced among the blond barrage of pastel-wearers, I felt like the Sicilian widow my mother had compared me to.

"You're always in black!" Bee observed as she approached me, wearing a tight lime green dress. "I mean, isn't it like eighty degrees? You must be *broiling*!" Great, was I like sweating buckets or something?

"Oh, yeah, I'm Wednesday Addams, remember?"

She didn't smile. "Maggs!" said Bee, happy to see her chum.

Maggie came up and kissed both of us on both cheeks. Whoa. I knew New York was closer to Europe than California but the two-kiss thing threw me off. Plus she had never kissed me before. Maybe it was the upscale enviro versus the playground. Plus, everyone was playing the fancy role of grande dame philanthropist.

I saw Lila walk in and see me, then look away. I decided to go up to her and say hello.

"Oh, Hannah, hi!" She pretended she was just seeing me.

"Nice to see you, dear." She then had a pert brunette approach her in a hat with a huge bird on it and they air-kissed hello while I made my way back to the "kids'" table, where I was sitting with Maggie and Bee.

"So, girls, are we soooo excited for vacation?" Maggie asked, beaming. "We're all packed, I can't wait!"

"Ugh, *thrilled!*" gushed Bee. "I've been dying to get out of this pit. Oh . . ." she said, catching herself. "Sorry, Hannah."

There was suddenly an embarrassed awkward silence. Their pity over my being trapped in Gotham had quieted their excitement and I felt like the scholarship kid everyone felt sorry for.

"Well, we basically only just got here, so I don't care!" I said breezily. Crickets.

"Hiii, yummy mummies!" Hallie said, putting a jeweled hand through her red hair. "Sorry I'm late! Julia Charlotte was just reading all by herself and I couldn't leave! I swear, that child's memory is just unparalleled! She's a certifiable genius." Naturally, Hallie burst right into her interminable momologue about Julia Charlotte. It was a funny coincidence to me that Julia Charlotte's initials were JC, because her mom clearly thought she was the second coming.

". . . And then, she said, 'Mommy, more foie gras, please!' I mean, can you *believe it*? Even her taste buds are mature. Julia Charlotte is *such* an adventurous eater." Hallie was prattling on about JC reciting prime numbers in Mandarin when Lara arrived with an enormous flower-covered hat.

"Hi gals, I had to pick up my hat, and they were jammed at Plaza Florists!" There was a full fresh-flower arrangement atop her platinum head. Between my dark brown hair and my black dress, I felt like I was adrift in a sea of corn silk and bright flowers.

I heard a woman come on the microphone as we all settled at our tables, each place beautifully set with fine crystal, china, sterling silver, and calligraphed place cards. I'd thought, gee, if they'd just not hired the posh calligrapher and handwritten the names, they could have given even more money to fighting childhood obesity. Surveying the stick-thin crowd, I had a feeling this was a cause close to their hearts—God forbid one of these "yummy mummies" had a great big fat kid at home.

"Ladies, thank you for coming today," an older woman in a white suit said, welcoming the group of a hundred. "I'd like to begin by thanking our wonderful, devoted cochairs who have done sooo much for this gravely important cause: Mrs. Burke Tiverton the third, Mrs. Hyram Balsap the seventh, Mrs. Westminster Covington Junior, and our junior chair, Mrs. Parker Elliott." Golf-claps to reward their "efforts," which I suspected were just "meetings" that included tea sandwiches and photographers while the charity staffers labored in the background. Another woman got up to the podium as guests began to push their frisée salads around their gilded china plates. "Trans fats. Oils. Chemicals," she said sternly. "Childhood obesity is a dark, terrible, tragic, horrifying curse that is eating away at our nation."

No pun intended, I thought.

"And it's an epidemic of drastic and dire proportions," she continued, shaken to the core by this rampant, plaguing blight of fatness. "We don't even know what's in our children's lunches! I mean, let's face it, ladies, none of us here even makes our kids' lunch in the first place, but still!" Giggles from the crowd. She continued, discussing the virulent rash of giant roly-poly blob-like kids and I just started to tune out, missing Josh desperately and wondering if Tate Hayes would phone again.

Twenty-three

Later that night after putting Violet to bed, I spoke with Josh for the first time in thirty-six hours, which was unprece-dented for us. I felt so off-kilter and was acutely feeling pangs of longing for him to be home; I'd even made a laundry list of porn titles since I missed him so much, including *Lawrence of Labia*, *Star Whores*, and *On Golden Blonde*. He said he wished he was back, too, and asked what I'd been up to, and I told him how the benefit droned on and on, and how one woman burst into tears while giving a testimonial about her fat son, August, and all I could do was think of poor Augustus Gloop drowning in a river of chocolate, covered like a piggy in mud.

"I think my bris sounds like more fun than that lunch," laughed Josh. "Why'd you even go in the first place?"

"I thought you wanted me to hang with Bee and her hive," I said. "Plus, your mom is on the board. I really didn't have a choice."

"Sure you do! Sweet, I don't care if you go or not. Only deal if it's fun," he said, laughing. "Han, you can hang with whoever you want. I just want you to be happy. Who cares if my mom wants to you to be friends with them, it's not her life!"

"They're fine, Bee's fine. They're not Leigh, that's for sure, but she's always traveling for work, and I have no mom friends, I am such a loner, and it's better than nothing. Plus, I need to learn all the insider things here, your mom's right, I guess. I realize it really is better for Violet if I play ball," I sighed. "But I did all the school research, luckily, and I know exactly where we're speed dialing, so you better not forget to pen that shit in. I own you the day after Labor Day when the phone lines open."

"Okay, sergeant!"

"Oh! Sweetie, also, I got us tickets for this new play next week, *Swimming at Night*. Supposedly it's this really hot love story."

"Cool, I can't wait."

I asked him how the maniacal billionaire and his monkey with diapers were doing. He said it didn't seem possible before the trip, but that the guy was even crazier than he'd heard. Still, they were enjoying the hunt. In fact, with each "kill," Count von Hapsenfürer would ship the body to Asprey for it to be dipped in silver. Room after gargantuan room was filled with sterling animals with every bristle of fur preserved in an eerie King Midas freeze, but with silver instead of gold. Horrifying. James Bond villain times ten.

"How's the food? Sheep's brain with a sterling spoon?"

Josh laughed. "You're not far off. We literally ate, like, roast mutton or something. Total medieval meal."

"Ew! I'd die." Despite my longing to be with him, I knew the food sitch would not be remotely to my liking.

Finally Josh had to go to sleep, as it was three A.M. in Europe. We hung up and I crawled into bed with my new *Spin* magazine. Two seconds later, the phone rang again.

"Hi, sweetie," I said.

"Oh, hello, Hannah," a non-Josh voice said. Oh shit. "This is Tate calling."

"Whoops! Sorry, I just hung up with my husband—"

"Traveling, is he?"

"Yes, 'til Monday."

"Funny, my wife is away with the children in Como for two weeks. I have too much course work to prepare for, so I sent them off while I'm withering away in this heat."

"Tell me about it," I sighed. "The Upper East Side is clearing out as if an H-bomb dropped. I think tumbleweeds are rolling up Park Avenue."

He laughed, knowing exactly what I meant. "You're too much, Hannah."

He asked me if I was free to go to the Guggenheim the following Tuesday afternoon and I told him I'd love to, adding that I'd bring my roller skates—referencing Diane Wiest in my all-time-favorite movie, *Hannah and Her Sisters*.

"So what is on the agenda for you tonight?"

"Oh, I dunno. Some Jon Stewart, some magazines . . ." I said, feeling so weird to be lying in bed talking to Tate Hayes.

"You'll never believe what my bedtime reading was last night," he said.

"Harlequin Romance?"

"Nooo . . ." he mocked. "Your thesis, actually."

I was stunned. What?! I was shocked, elated, and wondered if he was on heroin. But played it cool. "Why, you needed to fall asleep? Was my essay Ambien in paper form?"

"Hardly," he said, dead serious. "It's truly beautiful, Hannah. You have a real talent."

"A talent for singing tunes by the Doodlebops these days," I said, feeling my mommy status had trumped my intellectual one.

"No, it's never left you. All that work you've done, your gifts, it's all there waiting for you when you're ready."

"Thanks."

"I'll leave you to your magazines, then."

"Okay," I said softly.

"Good night, Hannah."

Twenty-four

Finally, after what seemed like an eternity, Josh came home from Switzerland. I'm so pathetic, I mean, there were women with husbands at war for crying out loud and I was so lost without him, I pounced on him like one of those suction-cup Garfields in car windows. And while I did feel such a tight bond to Violet from our time together, being a single mom was exhausting, and my head was awash in a spin cycle of scattered toys, thrown peas, and the high-pitched voiceover lady from the Disney Channel (who sounded suspiciously like that secretary from *Moonlighting*). In other words, I missed the love of my life terribly, but I also missed the extra pair of hands. We snuggled in to a family dinner as I reported on Violet's latest words and caught up on his trip. New porn title conceived of on the plane that we both couldn't believe we'd never thought of: *The Rodfather*.

The next day Violet and I kissed Josh good-bye as he left for work and I tried to figure out what to do. It was 93 degrees and I thought I could barely handle walking one block, let alone roasting on a paved playground. I had read about a cool hang-out space uptown called Kidsplosion where you could pay a cover and let your kid run amok and jump in pools of foam and blow bubbles and basically go insane in a padded room. I fig-ured, hey, if it's air conditioned, I don't fucking care if the kids are juggling razor blades. Just kidding.

I was expecting the joint to be butt empty because in August it seemed like a neutron bomb had been dropped on the Upper East Side—the usual traffic of double-stranders (pearls) and their sailor-suit-wearing kids was nil, and the only things walking up Park Avenue were water bugs, which I realized early on was a New York euphemism for a huge fucking cockroach.

When Violet and I pulled up to Kidsplosion, I was stunned to see that it was pretty packed. There were a ton of nannies, so I assumed that some of the moms who worked couldn't take that time off. There was also a mom clique on the side. No sooner did I check Violet in than she ran off and hugged a lit-tle girl who became her insta-pal. I watched from the side and plopped next to the clique of moms, each of whom was hold-ing a Starbucks cup. The topic of their conversation was sex.

"Jonny rubbed my back last night and so wanted to and I was like, ew, I can't deal," one of them lamented. "It's been two months now and I just have zero desire. Zero."

"Just have a glass of wine, lie on your back, and it'll be over in five minutes! Make yourself do it," another responded, adding, "I've got news for you: if you don't fuck your husband, someone else will."

I was amazed; their conversation sounded so sad. But I had encountered this breed before: the Husband Bashers. It was a favorite pastime for some women, who bonded over how much their husbands worked, played golf, tried to sleep with them, etc. Truth be told, if I'd had a proper place to vent about Josh's hours since our move, I might be tempted to open up about how lonely I was. But even with my best friends it would feel like a betrayal of Josh; he was the main person in my life, my partner, my best friend. Clearly, most marriages were not the same. The only thing worse was kid bashing, which came next.

"Ugh, the terrible twos are killing me. Sometimes I want to die, Amory is sooo behind!" one woman lamented. "I mean, she's still using her bottle."

I wanted to chime in and say, as Dr. Smith did, that she wouldn't go to college with it, when one of her friends said, "That's ridiculous! You must take it away at once. Cold turkey! We took Harrison's away at ten months! He didn't even know how to hold the sippy cup, so he lost one third of his body weight from starvation. But sometimes you just have to show them some tough love."

I was almost dialing child welfare on my cell when Violet came up holding the hand of Mia, a little girl with black curly hair and a smocked dress.

"Hi Mommy! New friend!" The girls held hands and suddenly one of the blond moms nearby came over.

"Mia, sweetheart, who is this?"

"This is Violet, I'm Hannah," I said, smiling.

"Mimi Quackenbush Skite," she said, extending a mani-cured hand covered in rings. "And this is my daughter, Mia Skite." She looked Violet over, then glanced back at me with squinted eyes. "Is she . . . *yours*?" she asked, looking Violet and me over five more times each. "I mean, she looks *nothing* like you! I've never seen a mother and daughter look less alike!"

"Yeah, she's mine. Genes can be funny."

"But she's sooo blond! And you're *so incredibly dark*!" She made it sound like I had just passed through Ellis Island with a beard. I felt branded as a black pubic fur ball with a halo-covered flaxen cherub as my mistakenly switched-at-birth spawn. I simply shrugged, not quite knowing what to say. It was always the blondes who commented—clearly she was pissed her recessives hadn't passed on to her dark-haired kid, while my swarthy, grody pube head was forgiven in the forma-tion of Violet's soft light waves.

"Where are you applying to nursery schools?" she asked out of left field while looking over my outfit: black jeans, a gray T-shirt, and black ballet flats.

She, like all her friends who looked on from their perch, was wearing what I was realizing was the Momzillas' summer uniform: metallic Jack Rogers sandals (J-Ro's), white pants, and a Tory by TRB beaded tunic and blond ponytail.

"Um . . . I guess the usual suspects, you know," I said, un-easy.

"How many schools?" she asked, suspect.

"Four, the ones that are near us. I'm too lazy to schlep across town," I said.

"Only *four*?!" She was aghast. "Are you serious? Wow, you must be pretty confident. Most people apply to at least eight or nine. I'm applying to eleven, but that's me. Mia is a nightmare and has a craaazy temper, so I'm guessing she'll fully blow it at least three or four schools."

Evil. I mean, the kid was two, after all.

"Hi guys!" I heard a familiar voice say. I turned to see Hallie in the same outfit, flipping her red hair. "Oh, Hannah! Hi— I'm just in the city for the afternoon, Thatcher had a work dinner with the wives so I just hopped the jitney. Come here, Julia Charlotte!" The famous, sunshine-coming-out-of-her-ass Julia Charlotte came over and saw Mia and Violet and promptly stuck her tongue out at them. So much for the brilliant, mannered, Mandarin-fluent mini Einstein.

"Oh, you know each other?" Mimi marveled. "Hallie, please tell your friend—Hannah?—that she has to apply to more than four schools."

Hallie barely paid any attention to me and instead was extremely focused on one of her nails which—*gasp!*—had a chip in the pale pink polish. "It doesn't really matter," she sighed. Surprised, I felt relieved. Until she added: "If Violet doesn't get in anywhere you can always reapply next year."

Bitch. What she gained by dropping that doozy I do not know, but I thought it might be time to exit Kidsplosion before there was a Hannahsplosion. I politely announced I had to go and barely exhaled 'til I got around the corner, where I found myself panting. And then the perfect way to drown my sorrows pulled around the corner: Mister Softee. Even that semi-creepy serial-killer clown music sounded like the Philharmonic at that point, and with one cup and two spoons, Violet and I had a tiny taste of summer on the scalding pavement.

AND SO BEE COULD CHECK IN FROM THE CRAMPTONS . . .

Instant Message from: BeeElliott

> BeeElliott: Hamptons are boooring. How're you?
>
> Maggs10021: Fine, having a nice time pre-stork, trying to rest as much as possible!
>
> BeeElliott: Any goss?
>
> Maggs10021: No, just blah—it's kind of all about ice cream and sunblock ☺
>
> BeeElliott: Hallie IM'd me that she ran into Hannah at Kidsplosion and she was such a freak—she's only applying to like two or three schools! Clueless. How does Josh deal?
>
> Maggs10021: Whatevs. Violet is so smart, she'll get in.
>
> BeeElliott: Not so sure—Mom says Lila Dillingham is FREAKING and thinx Hannah sucks. Poor kid.
>
> Maggs10021: Hopefully she'll get in somewhere . . . it all works out in the end.

Twenty-five

Grover is visiting a horse farm in Saskatchewan. The stallions have names like Thunder and TriggerHeel and Feathers. The little girl who is our guide rides the horses, washes them, and feeds them crisp apples. It is miles to another house, the fields are dewy and endless, with a sunset dappling the high breeze-blown grasses.

I am trapped in an urban jungle of cement and stacks of people in towers that scrape the sky and gut my confidence. Violet, who is such a contented child she would have a blast at Alcatraz, is absorbed in Grover's northern romp as I stare into space, summoned back to earth by the piercing birdlike ring of our corporate apartment's incredibly annoying phone.

"Hi, honey," Josh said with a dark tone. Uh-oh. Just as I had feared the moment the nasal-voiced ticket saleswoman had said the words "final sale," Josh told me apologetically that something had come up and our long-overdue date night was now canceled.

"What do you mean you have a work dinner? I've got Broadway show tickets!"

"Sweets, I can't help it. Parker and I need to go over everything and it could take a while."

"But you just got home from a business trip! You've been working for ten days straight!"

Great. My romantic date night foiled. I had been so looking forward to a sexy New York night on the town. And with everyone away in the Hamptons for the last two weeks of summer, it would be a quiet winding down of sorts. The calm before the shit storm.

"Go without me, honey, ask Leigh."

"She's in Brazil at surfing camp. No one's in town!" Ugh. I hung up so bummed. Amber was already booked and the tickets were paid for. Maybe I could sell one in front of the theater to a Kansas person? An hour of stressing later, the horrifying, ear-splitting phone chirped again.

"Hello?"

"Oh—it's me, Hannah, Tate Hayes. I'm certain you're busy, but you mentioned your husband works quite a bit these days, and I just was wondering on the off chance you're free tonight if you wanted to do something?"

"Actually, this works out perfectly."

Twenty-six

"The moon is so beautiful, it looks like a picture," said the actress on the shadowy stage.

"Why does it have to look like a picture?" said the man who came up behind her, caressing her body, her arms, her breasts.

He slowly undid the tie of her bikini, letting the top drop to the floor. The highly erotically charged scene had me shifting in my seat, subsumed in a tide of awky blushing.

When the curtain fell twenty minutes later after said couple perished tragically, the lights came on and I looked at Tate.

"Uplifting!" I said, sarcastically.

"I think we need to get a drink. Or how about a bite?"

"Oh, um . . . I would, except I have to probably get back and pay my sitter."

"All right, I'll drop you home on my way."

In the cab, he thanked me for the ticket and we confirmed plans to see another exhibit at the Guggenheim. It was nice to have someone to spend time with, immersed in an old interest. But somehow being near him made me a little nervous, given my former obsession. Somehow I thought maybe we should keep our hangouts art-based, like an echo of the classroom. But in the face of my anxiety, I reminded myself that he was married, too, so luckily I knew his intentions were chaste and I could exhale.

We pulled up to my apartment building and Tate paid the driver, getting out of the taxi with me.

"I feel like walking," he said. "It's a lovely night. And the chill will be upon us before we know it."

"I hope so," I said. "This heat is killing me."

"Soon enough, Hannah." He reached for my hand, brought it to his face, and kissed it.

Whoa.

I thought I would keel over, I was so surprised. I mean, granted, it's a totally platonic thing, but . . . I couldn't see Josh kissing anyone's hand. It was as if his lips on my hand sent a bolt through that big vein that people commit suicide on and charged my chest with a happy nervous shock.

"Good night," I said, turning to go in the building. I

couldn't have turned away faster because I had to hide the fact that my cheeks, like an oiled stroke of a Degas tutu, were pink.

THANK GOODNESS FOR TECHNOLOGY! THE BETTER TO SPREAD GOSSIP WITH . . .

Instant Message from: BeeElliott

BeeElliott: YOU ON? YOU ARE GONNA DIE!

Maggs10021: Hi, am here, w'sup?

BeeElliott: Am FREAKING! R u sitting down?

Maggs10021: Of course. What, do you think I type standing up? Out with it!

BeeElliott: Hannah Allen is FULLY cheating on Josh!

Maggs10021: No way. I don't believe it.

BeeElliott: It's TRUE! I saw w/ my own eyes! Park said Josh is working 24/7 also and we came into the city to see West's allergist & I SAW HER w/ some hot guy and he kissed her and totally they are an item.

Maggs10021: Am in shock.

BeeElliott: I'm not. Nothing shocks me anymore. What a whore.

Twenty-seven

Tate had been right—August whizzed by and September was upon us. Labor Day weekend was here and not a soul was in the neighb. Josh adorably made me breakfast in bed and we had a late cuddle with Violet Saturday morning, then he announced he had to go to work because there was no Labor Day in Europe and that he had to crunch some serious numbers for Count von Hapsenfürer. I was so pissed and lashed out at poor Josh, but there was really nothing he could do.

It was amazing how different the empty weekend was from insane Monday. Labor Day was streams upon streams of deluxe SUVs parading back in from Cape Cod and the Islands, the Hamptons, and Connecticut. The Park Avenue that had been dead silent just twenty-four hours ago was now jammed with cars unloading piles upon piles of monogrammed T. Anthony luggage and preppy totes from the Monogram Shop. Moms were in a panic unloading all the children and loot, and tanned dads helped cattle-prod the kids off the sidewalks into their grand buildings.

My heart was racing all day Labor Day because I knew what the next morning held: the infamous nursery school speed dial. I had made my list of schools—Carnegie Nursery School was obviously my first choice since everyone said it was the "best" (one guy literally gave a million-dollar donation from his company to get his kid in) but I was instructed I needed backups so I also was ready to get my fingers to dial the Fifth

Avenue School (which was in a church basement), the London School (a British school with adorable uniforms so I wouldn't have to stress about how to dress Violet every day), and the Temple School, where Josh had gone. Bee had pronounced the Temple School "very B" and said it was a miracle Josh had gotten into Collegiate from there. Lila had left three messages on her way back from England to remind me to dial the next morning. As if I could forget—it was all anyone wanted to talk about.

Josh thought the whole thing was insane and ridiculous.

"Sweetie, she's *two*. I mean, *who cares*?"

"I do! Plus it's your friends that say you need a backup."

"But I'm a legacy at the Temple School!"

"I can't believe you moved me to a place where fucking two-year-olds need backup schools to play with blocks and it's a huge leg up to have a *legacy*!"

I started to get tears in my eyes.

"Okay, Hannah, you're being nuts. Why are you crying?"

"Because you worked all day! Because I'm always alone! Because I hate these bitchy women who make me feel like loving Violet isn't enough! Because they all compete over everything and because I am sick of doing nothing but obsess about where my life should be."

Josh came over to hug me but I knew he thought I was going off the deep end. Then, as I was wiping my eyes, he dropped the doozy.

"Well, sweetie, I have to go to the office very early tomorrow, so we should go to bed."

Silence.

"*What?* I told you, tomorrow is the day we call the schools!"

"That's tomorrow? God, this process is so nuts. Back when I was applying, my mom just dropped by and they handed you the application."

"But that's not how they do it now!" I screamed. "*I told you* this!"

"Sweetie, I am so sorry, I don't know what to tell you. I have a new job and I can't cut corners. Obviously I want to help you, but my hands are tied. I have a huge conference call with von Hapsenfürer and our Japanese office, and there're like eight guys on the call."

"Great. So I get to do this *alone*. She'll just end up in that day care where they beat up that little girl last year."

"Don't be such a drama queen."

"I don't think you understand that *I am alone all the time*! With your mother! With Bee and her friends and I'm *miserable* like this! I don't care about money."

"C'mon, Han, I'm sorry, I'm—"

"*Doing it for us*, yeah yeah. Quite frankly I'd rather have you be a public school teacher and at least have you home at five o'clock! I'm alone *all the time*! I'm the one doing everything with Violet while you're MIA at work! You didn't even know that Snuffleupagus wasn't invisible anymore until last week! You're never fucking here!"

"And who do you think would pay for these schools we're applying to if I was sitting at home with you?"

"What, are you implying that because I don't make any money I have to do everything else?"

"No—I'm just saying—"

"Forget it. I'm exhausted." Nice. I turned off my light and

rolled over. This is so not where I pictured myself. Let's face it, Josh's work is his life and I had to just think of myself as a single mother and then, when he was actually with us, it would be a bonus. Josh tried to rub my back, but I didn't respond, I just closed my eyes and slowly fell asleep.

Twenty-eight

I woke up as Josh stepped out of the shower with my heart immediately pounding from the moment I was conscious. I couldn't believe I actually had to win a radio call-in contest to just get an application for Violet's schools. Josh kissed me good-bye at seven thirty, and apologized profusely for our spat the night before and for having to leave me for the phone-fest. I had thirty minutes of trying to suppress a heart attack while feeding Violet her Cheerios and banana. I am the worst mother—I remembered as I was pouring from the big yellow box that Bee said West has farm-fresh eggs and organic bacon every morning. As did Lara's kid. "Brain food," they called it. Ugh. But they had help to clean the frying pan, utensils, and bowl covered in eggy film afterward. If that was brain food, what was cereal every day, thigh food?

I called Leigh to pick a place for dinner that night—hopefully Josh could meet us but naturally he "couldn't make any promises." I was starting to feel more and more stood up by my own husband. The phone rang and I thought it would be Josh to wish me luck. It was Lila.

"Hannah, dear, are your dialing fingers ready?"

I said yes and was hoping that she would step in to help me call, but she quickly mentioned she had a charity board meeting at the Waldorf for PIMP—People In Manhattan against Pimples, a not-for-profit outfit dedicated to the eradication of acne. She hung up, wishing me luck.

Soon enough the dialing hour was upon us. I set up Violet in her room with tons of toys and books and I sat beside her pretending to play but really having a nervous breakdown, my fingers shaking as I dialed the first number. Busy signal. And again. And again. And again. And again. And again. What was this, the 1970s? I hadn't heard a busy signal in literally twenty-five years! I kept hitting redial. Again and again and again and again and again and again and again and again and again and again and again and again and again and again and again and again and again and again and again . . . My pulse quickened even more. Fucking pick up, *please*!

Then I decided that maybe instead of hitting redial, actually dialing the numbers each time might make a difference. Nope. Then I decided to switch numbers for a different school. *Nada*, same shizzle. Panic ensued. Then I wondered: Do I try once for each school in a round robin or just pound away at one school until I get through? I decided the former, just because it seemed like there was more randomness to it that way. I kept dialing. Busy busy busy busy busy, busy, busy, busy, *busy*. *Arghhhhhh!* I had heard the expression "tearing one's hair out" all my life but never knew the meaning until the seven-hundredth busy signal and I swear I started grabbing the roots of my hair, ready to rip it all out, Sinéad-style.

I was starting to picture the *New York Post* headline "Mother Drops Dead from Dial-an-App" with a photo of me zipped in a body bag because I passed out from stress. I was literally panting when I heard "Hello, Carnegie Nursery School?"

"Hello?! Yes, hi! hi! Yay!" Gee, great opener, Hannah. Real cool.

"Hello?"

"Hi! Yes, hello, um, this is Hannah Allen calling. Um, I wanted to get an application for my daughter Violet?" Heart racing racing racing.

"All righty, this is Mrs. Kincaid, director of admissions. I can help you with that. Let me just start a file for Miss Violet."

"Okay . . ." I waited as I heard shuffling papers and a trillion phone lines ringing in the background.

"Full name?"

"Violet Grace Allen."

"Age as of September of next year?"

Shit, my math was failing me, shit! "Um . . . um three years and three and a half months?"

"Husband's profession?"

Huh? To, like, make sure we can cough it up?

"Hedge fund. I mean . . . uh, banker?"

"University you attended?"

"Berkeley."

"Mmm-hmm. And university your husband attended?"

"Stanford."

"All right, Mrs. Allen, we shall send that off this week."

Yippee!

Okay. Next school. Now maybe I'd be on a roll! Maybe now I'll get 'em all!

Wrong. Ninety-seven minutes later I finally got through to the London School. A woman in a clipped British accent took the same information and said she would send the application "straightaway."

Next I tried the Temple School. After one time dialing the number, I heard . . . ringing! Yaaaaaaay! Hooray! Angels on high! At this point the sound of a phone's ring was like Mozart's trumpets or Beethoven's *Ode to Joy*.

"Good morning. You have reached the Temple School. All requests for applications have been filled and because of a high number of siblings this year we are unable to send out any more applications. We wish you the best of luck in your nursery school process."

Click. Dial tone, which was like the sound of glass breaking. Fuck fucking fuck! They were sold out? And that was supposed to be our school with a connection, our "in." Dammit. I took a deep breath, not having time to waste, and tried Fifth Avenue School, which takes everyone's names and then draws out four hundred from a hat to receive an application. Why they do this I do not know, considering the calling in itself is a lottery. But hey, why not torture people some more, for fun? Their recording said we'd be notified via mail if we "won" the chance to apply. Night. Mare.

I then quickly whipped out my school guide to add one more to the pot and dialed the Browne-Madison School, which I'd heard a couple good things about. After only about eleven tries, Missy Baumgarten, the school registrar, answered and created a file for Violet.

"We will contact you in writing with your interview time," she said. "Do not call the school. We'll contact you." Same deal as Fifth Avenue School as per their Web site—don't call us, we'll call you.

"Okay—" *Click*.

Exhausted, demoralized, and convinced my daughter would be mauled in day care, I took Violet out for some air. We walked up a now bustling Madison Avenue, packed with mommies lunching in the still al fresco sidewalk cafés, and others bolting into stores stocked with new fall merch like Jimmy Choo, Barneys, and Hermès.

I walked by Ralph Lauren's children's shop on Madison, which was so glutted with strollers that there was a line to get in. Six pretty Orthodox Jewish women with wigs were carrying seven bags each on their stroller hooks, from Bonpoint, Polo, and Spring Flower. I walked up past Calypso and Flora and Henri—both mobbed—and then farther up to "Grandmother's Row" on upper Madison—Marie Chantal, Petit Bateau, Magic Windows, and the other Bonpoint (which Bee said has less 'tude). All of them had beautiful dresses in the window for fall already, even though according to the lower left-hand corner of NY1 newschannel it was still 81 degrees out. And while I must admit I did thirst for many of the incredible gorge duds for Violet, I didn't feel like I needed to wait in line, so we went to the park and I let Violet run rampant while I watched from the bench, finally able to exhale.

Twenty-nine

No sooner did I fall fully into relaxtion mode than I heard my name.

"Earth to Hannah!" It was Bee. "I've been calling you!"

"Oh, hi! You're back!"

"Yes, yes I am. We had the best summer. Gosh, it just flew by. Flew!" She looked me over from head to toe in a way I didn't like. She arched her brow and gave me a weird look.

"Yeah . . ." I said, in a wiped-out robomom tone.

"How are you doing?" she asked, seemingly concerned. "Oh my goodness! Hannah, I totally spaced! How did the calling go this morning?"

"Um, fine I guess."

She went on and on about what a horrifying experience it is and that—again—she did not envy me. Then Lara, Maggie, and Hallie strolled up in their rainbow fleet of Bugaboos. Bee announced that I had been dialing (thanks!) and they let out a collective, perfumed groan in harmony.

"Get ready for hell," Hallie warned. "It's such a heinous process."

"I just bumped into that Eurotrash bitch Chloe de la Vega," Lara sneered. "All I said was 'how are you' and she said she's *great* because she's sending Monique to Fifth Avenue and they only had forty-two spots from two thousand apps and forty were siblings! Can you believe they only took two outside families last year?"

"I heard Carnegie took one new family. It was all loaded with siblings and huge donors to the community center that is the umbrella for the school. And the London School took zero!"

Great. Now my chances were even smaller.

"That Chloe woman is trash trash trash," pronounced Hallie. "Her implants are so obvious!"

"And her jewelry?" added Maggie. "Tackissimi. There are just diamonds all over her. Does she think this is Dubai?"

"You know," said Bee conspiratorially. "Maybe she wowed some old lady admissions hag with her accent and bling, but that kid will not get into one kindergarten. They want classy, understated parents, not Riviera whores."

Great, after one hurdle, clearly here's another. I knew Bee and her posse had a couple years until they started trying to get their kids into school again, but it already clearly haunted them.

"So, Hannah," Maggie asked. "What did you do this summer?"

Before I could answer, she exchanged glances with Bee, probably feeling sad for me that I was in Manhattan the whole time while they skipped in slow motion under a setting sun on a sparkling beach.

"Oh, we just hung out, you know."

"I heard Josh was away a *lot*," Bee added. "That sucks. I mean, you have no help!"

I loved how moms here seemed to count other people's nanny hours. "Well, Amber has more and more free time now that she's a senior at Barnard," I said.

Bee smiled at me. "Lucky you."

Thirty

The next week brought Violet's first day of Milford Prescott Music School, aka Mini Juilliard. Lila had called to wish us luck, thrilled I was getting Violet "on track" at the right pre-preschool. I was also getting points because "we" had gotten applications to some of the "right" schools, which I'd filled out in record time and mailed back promptly.

When we arrived at the beautiful town house the school was located in, I suddenly got intimidated, beholding the stunning building that would house two-year-olds banging drums. How JV my hippie barefoot Music Together class in California suddenly seemed. The walls were lined with benefactors plaques with names of big donors, including several that were synonymous with Fortune 500 companies. I scanned the names, standing in the school's echoey hall under the twenty-foot ceiling in the lobby. Then we were greeted by women in suits who handed out packets and little cards that were required should someone other than the parent pick up the child from class, to prevent kidnappings. The thought gave me chills but then I saw one child enter with a bodyguard and a nanny, while another, in a full mini crested blazer, had a mom and a nanny on hand. The mother promptly whipped out her trendy phone.

"Tyrone, please go get the car washed at that place on First Avenue. Then pull around to pick us up in forty-five and we'll drop Ming and Gates and then go down to my lunch at the Four Seasons and you have to go to the dog groomer to pick up

Ducasse and Jean-Georges. And then we have to be at Central Barkers by four sharp."

I smiled when I heard Central Barkers.

"We cannot be late!" the woman warned. "All the It society dogs will be there—Dodo Trump, Bonnie and Clyde Kravis, Truffle Soros, Chelsea Lauder Zinterhoffer, Van Fanjul—everyone who's anyone with fur will be on hand!"

My obvious eavesdropping and dropped jaw were noticed by a cool-looking girl next to me. *"It" dogs?*

"I know, crazy, right?" she whispered as the instructions to pick up custom dog outfits at Z spot were given to the driver. "You can't invent this shit."

"We just moved here, so stuff like that is a little . . . surprising to me, I guess."

"Don't worry, not everyone in this school's like that," she said. I looked at her little girl, who was playing sweetly with her knitted blanket.

"Your daughter is so cute," I said.

"Oh, this isn't my daughter. I'm Kelly, I'm actually Morgan's tutor," she said, patting the girl's hair. "I have a degree in early childhood from Columbia."

"Oh, wow. That's cool."

"Yeah, her parents travel a lot, like two months at a time in Europe. They, like, started airport malls or something."

I hugged Violet, incapable of even fathoming leaving her for two days let alone two months. I kind of made a face because I didn't want to bash in front of the cute child and Kelly picked up on it.

"I know . . . intense," she said, looking around the room of moms in the Momzilla uniform. "This neighborhood is very intense in general. I live in Williamsburg when I'm not living with Morgan. You should come check out the mom group I go to there on the weekends. It's much much mellower. I bring Morgan with me with their driver and it's just a nice break from the whole scene."

"What is it, like a playgroup?" I asked.

"Kind of. It's called Tots 'n' Tonic. It's in this really cool lounge that's a club at night but is very mellow during the day. Cool group of parents, a lot of artists and writers."

Ooooh, I liked the sound of that! "Sounds right up my alley, I'd love to come," I said.

"Great, I'll give you my number—"

Just then the double doors of Violet's amazing classroom (which was so beautiful and huge it could have been a ballroom) opened. Not one, not two, but four teachers walked out to welcome us and invite us in. We sang songs in a circle and I was amazed by the piano player, who was straight out of New York Philharmonic and so incredibly gifted I felt like I was getting a free concert. Well, not exactly free—we'd hemorrhaged piles of money, which worked out to like seventy-five smacks a class, so it was hardly gratis (Josh had done the math). But incredible nonetheless considering I was expecting acoustic guitar and swaying. This was far from noodling to "Kumbaya": I'm talking airtight harmonies, drums, triangles, recorders, xylophones, and glockenspiels.

I was so impressed with the class, and the only sucky part was a mom-clique of blondes who were yakking the whole time. I could see the teachers' growing annoyance but their hands seemed to be tied—these women were probably some of the big donors posted on the plaques in the lobby.

I heard one woman, who I think I'd spied in the playground waving to Bee and Maggie, say, "So how are you?" to another decked-out mom.

"Couldn't be worse," she said, exasperated. I felt bad, wondering what had happened. Maybe a death in the family? "The contractor in Bridgehampton ran off to Puerto Vallarta. So now we have to fly in these craftsmen from Portofino to finish tiling the kitchen—it's all handpainted and so we can't risk some schlocky job. Prescott has to fly out there tomorrow on the seaplane to check up on things. It's a total disaster zone. I mean, forget Thanksgiving there. We'll have to fly down to Palm Beach with my in-laws." Gee, boo-hoo. Gagosaurus.

Next, one teacher pulled out a box of little stuffed animals and we all sang "Old McDonald."

"And on that farm he had a . . ."

The children all sat silently.

"Lion!" Violet said, smiling. I beamed with pride.

"No, silly," said Bridgehampton Bitch. "There aren't lions on farms!"

To say I wanted to vault, lioness-like, onto her gazelle self to make me some carcass is not an exaggeration. I wanted to kill her for raining on Violet's parade. (And by the way, her dolt of a kid didn't say shit. Better an animal name than a string of drool!) Fuck her. As if a two-year-old would know every natural habitat of the zoological spectrum. But I didn't say anything. I was too stunned and too annoyed.

"That's okay! On our farm, we have a lion!" said the teacher, giving me a wink.

Thank you thank you thank you. But still, Violet looked a little less proud.

After class I strolled Violet home and she passed out pretty quickly. I think the group enviros are too exciting for her—since I have no real mom friends, she gets all revved up by the company and then crashes. So as we wandered by the Whitney, I decided to go in and stroll through the galleries with my sleeping muffin. On the third floor, I saw a tour pass by and trailed a few steps behind, eavesdropping. Again, drinking in the drops of facts and descriptions made me feel full and brain sated.

When we left I started thinking that there must be some women like me out there. But how could I meet them? Maybe this Brooklyn posse would be the answer.

Thirty-one

That night I called Josh around nine to see when he would be coming home. Naturally, he couldn't budge from his desk until at least an hour later. Great. Meanwhile I was so hungry I thought I'd pass out. It took every fiber of willpower to not snarf the mac 'n' cheese when I made Violet's dinner at six thirty. I didn't want to get sucked into MTD (Mom's two dinners), a four-meal-a-day pattern that results in not only mom jeans but also the feeling that you can't fully enjoy dinner with your husband because you secretly chowed an entire fistful of chicken fingers.

As I flipped through menus to order in, I tried Leigh on the off chance she was free.

"Shithead lawyer schmuck *just* canceled on me! And I got a fifty-five-dollar Jean Louis David gloss and blowout at lunch just for this date. Fuck this. I'm totally coming over."

I ordered piles of Chinese food, and both the eats and Leigh arrived at the same time, thirty minutes later.

"Ugh, I'm ready to join Match.com," she lamented. "Last week I showed up for a date, and the guy was Danny DeVito's doppelgänger. Twin. Not Schwarzenegger twin, I mean identical. Clone. Porker. I mean mega, Hannah. Barrel-shaped. His fingers were Polish sausages. Kielbasas. I kid you not."

"Leigh, do not worry. I know you're gonna meet someone!"

"Oh really. What, you have a direct line to God or something? You don't have a crystal ball! I could be a shriveled hag."

"Let me be your crystal ball," I said, staring her down. "I know to the core of my being that you will find someone amazing."

"I just want my older self to come back to younger me, *Back to the Future*–style, and say, *Honey, don't worry! You'll be married with three kids one day, so have fun!* Then I'd breathe easy and take advantage of the fun parts of being free and single. Wait, what are those again?"

She told me she was trapped swimming against the tide of nubile assistants dumped in New York by graduations each spring. They took the summer off but had now landed in the Big Apple, scooping up all the one-bedrooms and all the single men our age. She refused to go on husband safari, because full-out hunts jeopardize your natural character, but then on the flipside, if you don't make an effort to meet people you might never get a chance.

"This is the age-old catch-22 I can't understand," she said, delicately nibbling a dumpling with her expertly wielded chopsticks. "They say don't think about it, but then it becomes the elephant in the room. If you truly don't think about finding someone, how can you ever? I mean, you have to be on the prowl a little, but not too much. I give up. I'm gonna be alone rocking in my chair in front of *Golden Girls* reruns."

"Let's see what your fortune cookie predicts," I said, cracking open one of them. "Oh my God! Leigh: it says 'Love is in the air'!!" I screamed.

"Bullshit. Let me see that." Just as she snatched away the small piece of paper, I heard the door open. "You're right! It's about time."

"Well hello girls!" Josh said, Parker behind him. "Wow, you ordered, awesome. Is there enough for us?"

"Totally! I got a ton so there would be leftovers for you." I got up and hugged Josh. I felt like he'd been gone forever, and it made me feel so safe to hug him. I squeezed hard like he was a ghost, then hugged Parker.

"So, workaholics, how's everything?"

"Well . . ." Josh said, looking at Parker. "Sweetie, you're gonna be really pissed—"

Uh-oh. My heart sank.

"I have to go away again in a couple weeks, but just for a few days this time."

"No way!" I was so bummed. I didn't want to freak in front of Parker or Leigh, though, so I just shook my head, clearly upset. "The single-mom thing is so exhausting!" I said. "Plus I miss you. You're, like, MIA. I do not know how war brides do it. Well, at least you're in some weird castle with a monkey that craps it pants and not getting shot at," I said, trying to look on the bright side.

"I'm sorry, sweetie, it won't be like this forever," he said, patting my head as I pouted.

"So Leigh, how's life?" Parker asked. "Record biz treating you well?"

"So-so, you know. How about you? Having fun with this one?" she said, gesturing to Josh.

"We manage to get some stuff done," Parker smiled. "We've been working so late lately—"

"Yeah, you're killing me!" I vented, ribbing him. "I'm here alone pacing for you like some loser!" Josh rubbed my back and kissed my forehead apologetically.

"Bee's out like every night. I swear, sometimes I don't think she notices!" Parker exclaimed. "She has so many benefits sometimes I come home before her," he said, shrugging.

Josh asked Leigh about her recent dates and she went off on her tirade, which literally had Parker lying on the floor laughing. He was so hysterical by the time she got to the "kielbasa fingers" part that I seriously thought he'd barf up the spare ribs he'd just downed and would need the foil-lined red bag they'd come in to hurl in.

"Stop! Stop, Leigh, you are killing me," Parker said, breathless. "You are so fucking hilarious, I'm dying."

"Yes, Leigh and Hannah have their own language. It's definitely a unique way of speaking." Josh winked at me. I smiled, putting my arm around Leigh. It turned out to be a nice unexpected foursome dinner. The Pottery Barn dripless candles burned their way down to our wedding registry Tiffany candlesticks and finally at midnight we all decided to hit the hay. Parker said Bee would probably be home soon from her benefit for FloGaM, the Flower Gardens of Manhattan, which planted fresh bulbs around the city. Only for designer poodles to crap on.

In bed I cuddled Josh, slowly rubbing his tummy, which was clearly stuffed with pan-Asian pan-fried food. "Not tonight, hon," he said, moaning. "I ate too much." Within minutes, he rolled over and passed out. Nice. Isn't it women who are supposed to "have headaches" and "be tired"? I lay awake staring at the ceiling, thinking that I never knew you could be both married and lonely until that moment.

AND ALSO ANALYZING THE STATE OF THE ALLEN UNION . . .

InstantMessage from: BeeElliott

```
BeeElliott: Guess what Park said last night
when he saw Hannah and Josh?
    Maggs10021: What?
    BeeElliott: He mentioned they "looked really
cute" i.e., she was all over him, and v/
affectionate.
    Maggs10021: So?
    BeeElliott: So! That's Guilt 101! She's
clearly trying to make up for fully CHEATING by
smothering him with affection! She is going to be
so busted.
```

```
    Maggs10021: She so doesn't seem the type . . .
    BeeElliott: PLUS Park said she was
 "devastated" that Josh had to go to Europe when
clearly she's gonna be sneaking off with the guy.
    Maggs10021: Gosh, poor Josh, he seemed nice.
    BeeElliott: She is toast. Lila Allen
Dillingham will kick her butt in court. Her son
could do a lot better and she knows it.
```

Thirty-two

It was Friday afternoon, the end of the workweek, and though I wasn't in a suit and hose like the actual workforce, I still had the TGIF spring in my step because it meant Josh would finally be home. We'd be a family unit, whole and strong. The November breeze rattled the trees and I felt a sense of calm now with a fun chilly fall weekend ahead. Violet and I headed for the subway and bumped smack into Bee and Maggie on the street. For a city of ten million people it's amazing how often you bump into people you know—our neighborhood was more of a designer Petri dish.

"Hi, Hannah, where are you two off to?" Maggie asked.

"Oh, just this playgroup I heard was fun."

"Is that the PR playgroup?" asked Bee.

"Huh?"

"Oh, there's this playgroup with all the kids of top publicists, there's a PR woman for Celine, one from Vuitton, one from Valentino, Tod's—"

"Um, no, not that one," I responded, incredulous. "I don't think I could dress for a playdate!"

"Wait," said Bee, looking down the subway steps we were standing beside. "You're not going down *there*, are you?" she asked.

I followed her disgusted gaze to the station entrance. "Uh . . . yeah, well, we're going to Brooklyn."

"Ha! Very funny," she said, looking at Maggie and smiling. "You're serious . . ." Bee looked so appalled I thought she was about to speed-dial child welfare. These are women who have private cars and drivers to run to Gristedes—they never take any public transportation, not even the bus, let alone something *underground*. And I was going to an outer borough, to boot.

Maggie looked at Violet with sad eyes, as if I were dragging my precious cargo through a mine-filled desert, where we'd certainly be shot at.

"Bee, Maggie, is that you?" We turned to see Tessa Finch-Saunders, the logo addict.

"Guess what, gals? I'm pregnant again!" She beamed.

"Oh, that's great. Wow, number three?" Maggie said, with a detectable hint of jealousy.

"Yeah, in three years. Can you believe it? I must be craaaazy! My husband literally winks at me and I gotta bun in the oven!"

"Well, you know what they say," Maggie said. "Three is the new two!"

"True, true." Tessa nodded. "People always say, why do the so-and-sos just have two kids? They only used to say that about onlys! It's all about three. Well, it's always been my magic number. B-bye! Off to my Temple Emanuel Nursery School interview!" She did a double finger cross on both hands, which were covered in rings.

Tessa sped off in a sea of leopard and the sound of her five-inch Jimmy Choos echoing in her wake.

"Hate her," Bee said.

"She is so losing that baby weight in five minutes like last time—she's just one of those naturally thin people," said Maggie.

"Yeah right," laughed Bee. "She had a little help from Dr. Baker. And she didn't waste any time. The placenta came out and the lipo tube went in!"

"A lot of people are doing that these days. Crazy," said Maggie.

"She's like out to prove something," said Bee, leaning in conspiratorially. "I mean, her dad's an FBI agent."

"That's cool!" I said.

"Not really. He's not like out in the field doing Mafia raids or anything like that," Bee said. "I heard he busts film coun-terfeiters. You know those warnings on the beginnings of DVDs? He's the guy who enforces that, supposedly. Anyway, she married this hedge fund guy and has reinvented herself. You should have seen what she wore to the Manhattan Fights Cystic Acne ball last night. It was as if the two most disgusting dresses got married and she was wearing their baby."

"Oh, Bee, you're too much," said Maggie, nervously.

I bristled. Bee scared me. Maggie looked at me and there was a flicker in her eyes that somehow related that she, too, was fearful of Bee's verbal stings. What in the world did Bee say about me? Whose hell baby were my un-chic outfits? I looked at my watch and said we actually had to bolt. I could not wait to get to Brooklyn, where there would surely be nice cool artsy moms, away from the evil materialistic bitches in my neighb.

I walked in to find a mom sitting in a full-lotus position with her three-year-old sucking her boob. She was braless, with a few tattoos and a streak of blond hair in her waist-length brown locks.

"Hey, welcome!" she smiled. "This is Titus. I'm Darby." Funny that her nursing three-year-old had the word *tit* in his name.

"Hi, I'm Hannah, this is Violet."

"Hey, Hannah."

Titus unhooked his mouth from his mom's chest and walked over to Violet, took her hand, and led her to Darby. "Want a sip?" he offered. "It's my mommy's milk!"

"Um—that's okay—" I dove in, practically grabbing Violet from the giant heaving lactating boob.

"You sure? It's fine with me," Darby said.

"Oh, she just ate, but thanks so much," I said, vom mid-esophagus and rising.

"You breast-feeding?"

Great. I was up against a grade-A Nursing Nazi. "Um, no."

"Really? How old is she?"

"Two."

"When did you stop?"

I felt the back of my neck get hot as my cheeks flushed. "Um, two months. It wasn't really for me—"

"Well, sure, it's not for you, it's for your child," she said, the easy maternal vibe melting away. "The World Health Organization said people should do at least a year. There are antibodies that exist only in breast milk that ward off certain diseases."

I felt like telling her that this is true. Except what she didn't add was that those diseases only exist *in the Congo*, not the United States. Fuck her for trying to belittle me.

She flared her nostrils and raised a pierced brow, adding, "Also, supposedly it makes them smarter."

"Well, I was bottle-fed," I said, shrugging. "And I turned out okay." And I sure as hell was smarter than her with her effing ankh burned on her arm.

"Hi girls," I heard Kelly say. "So you two met."

"Yes," we both said in unison. Then we were silent.

"Hiiiiii guys!" said a cute young guy with a little tyke. He turned to me and said, "Hello, I'm Rufus. I'm not the manny, I'm an S-A-H-D."

"Oh, great," I said, wondering why everyone said that when it was just as many syllables as "stay-at-home dad."

Two more parents showed up, a musician girl with an on-purpose mullet (hipster 'do du jour, think *Lost in Translation* Scarlett JoHaircut), a guitar on her back, and her kid in a camouflage sling. Another woman had spiky bleached hair and a daughter in a No Sleep Till Brooklyn T-shirt. I noticed that on the Upper East Side, every little girl was in pink. I myself favored chocolate browns and beiges but still loved some girlie pink. But every girl I'd seen in Brooklyn hadn't a stich of rose-colored anything near her body. It was all about mustards and puce and black. I even saw a little girl wearing a sweater with Che Guevara's face silk-screened onto it. I didn't quite get it, but assumed it was an expression along the lines of not just cool rebel baby, but also "down with The Man." But still, I was intrigued and wanted to learn more about the scene across the river.

We all hung out and chatted, and yes, they were interesting and did different, cool things: the SAHD had his own video editing facility in his loft, where he edited commercials and indie films; the musician had a band, The Saints, who played gigs at Lux and other local venues; and the spiky-hair chick worked at an art gallery in Chelsea but was on maternity leave with her second, a baby boy named Dexter, who was at home. All of them seemed young—maybe late twenties or early thirties. They weren't much older than Bee, but she and her friends—they just dressed like they were forty. I read enough cheesy magazines to be able to spot all their fashion logos and knew they spent a fortune on their clothes—even what they wore to the playground. This group was more relaxed and young and cool seeming. But just when I was starting to feel slightly at home with the more artistic posse, they started talking abut this one nursery school in Brooklyn, St. Ann's, that was really hard to get into. The applications were at a record high this year. Same shit as the mothership!

That's when I realized: You can run but you can't hide, Hannah. Momzillas are everywhere. Some might compete about being thin, or having better-dressed kids, but others compete about being cooler or a better breast-feeder. People would always self-create echelons for themselves to ascend in order to feel better about themselves. It's a competitive world and New Yorkers strive for success. All their ambition doesn't just evaporate when kids come—like the Newtonian law where energy remains constant; that rabid drive doesn't dissolve into lullabies and ABCs, it gets channeled into the kid. All parental hopes and dreams go through a funnel straight to their children, and even if I moved to some rectangular state in the middle, I'd probably find the same thing to be true. *Little Iris learned how to milk a cow first! Roberta can whipstitch faster than any other girl in quilting class! My, my, can Missy bake blue ribbon rhubarb pies at her tender age!*

After about an hour, I told Kelly we had to get back and I said good-bye to the parents and kids of Tots 'n' Tonic. The great white hope of a cool posse that I'd feel at home with was dashed on the screeching tracks of the L train, and I wondered if I'd ever find what I was looking for, whatever that was.

Thirty-three

We came home and I collapsed in a chair. Violet plopped right on my lap, newly entrenched in a phase of affectionate hugs and kisses at all times. "Mommy, I love you," she said, as my heart melted. Maybe all I needed was her.

"Heroes! Heroes!" she begged; she seemed to instinctually

know when *Higglytown Heroes* was coming on TV. The show chronicles a town where everyone—from the pizza boy to the grocer to the Park Ranger are, yes, *heroes*. It's a nice idea, except I would like it if it were, say, firefighters and cops and teachers, not deli meat slicers. Also semi-annoying were the lyrics, like "Never fear-o, it looks like a time for a Higglytown Hero!" *Fear-o?* Nice try, guys. C'mon, people, can't we find a real word?

Violet watched with wide eyes. A monkey was eating a banana on the TV.

"Mommy!" she squealed, dying laughing. I mean guffaws. Howls. The kid was doubled over. It was the cutest thing—I loved when she lost herself in laughter that way, no sound on planet Earth was happier. "The monkey's eating a banana!" She cackled so hard she almost fainted. It was a moment of truly seeing how innocent children are. I mean, I don't know any monkeys personally, but all grown-ups just know monkeys like bananas. Somehow, Violet's not knowing reminded me that she is a vessel waiting to be filled with knowledge. Watching her, I loved motherhood so much, and knew any of the hassles I was now experiencing were trivial.

The phone rang, interrupting my reverie. "Hi Hannah, it's Bee," she said. "How was 718-land? What're you up to?"

"Oh, nothing, just watching TV."

Silence.

"Gosh, Violet watches a lot of TV. I feel like every time I talk to you she's in front of the boob tube."

My daughter was not a boob.

"Well, I don't have that much help, you know, so it's a nice thing for her to focus on," I said defensively. "We also read tons of books."

"Weston doesn't get to watch TV. I just worry it will make him, you know, slow. I figure they don't call it the idiot box for nothing!"

Death to Bee. Why did she care what Violet watched? I watched more episodes of crappy *Brady Bunch* and *Silver Spoons* and *Smurfs* and *Bugs Bunny* than any human ever and I'm fine! But I didn't say any of that. "Whatever," was my meek response.

"Anyway," she said. "I was wondering if you wanted to join Maggie and me and the kids in the park Monday."

"Oh, umm, sure . . ." I said, dazed. "Oh! Wait, Monday's not good—we actually have our Carnegie interview."

"Interesting . . . Well, best of luck to you."

"Thanks," I said. "Anything we should know about the interview? Any questions? Any tips?"

"No, just, you know, be yourself, I guess!" she said. "Well, maybe Tuesday, then. I'll call you afterward to see how it went."

I hung up and turned off the TV. Violet objected at first; maybe she was an addict. But then when we got to her room and went to the bookshelf she delved in and was just as excited to read. When she fell asleep I checked the voice mail and found a message from Tate Hayes.

"Hannah, hello, it's Tate. A friend of mine is working on a show at the Met and said I could come next week and look at some of the pieces on loan in advance. Would you care you join me? We could have lunch and I can show you the museum archives, which is really a treat if you haven't seen them . . ."

Somehow the warm flickers of his voice, which sounded extra throaty today—did he have a cold?—made me take one hand and rub my arm. I must have had chills. I remembered how in college this often happened when listening to his lectures.

One time sophomore year, I was in Professor Hayes's office and we had been eating greasy Chinese food on his desk and talking for hours. This was around the time he was having slumber parties with Bianca Pratt, my modern art teacher, so it was pre-smooch by about two years. So there we were, not even discussing anything intellectual. It was more along the lines how eating MSG made me have sausage-fingers (à la Leigh's date) the next morning and my rings could not be budged on my normally thinnish digits until four P.M. out of total chicken fri-ri bloatfest. I was leaning back in my chair, chomping an eggroll, telling him about my insomnia (final essay, career, life choices, yawn yawn yawn) and how I basically played with my friends 'til all hours procrastinating because I simply *hated* school. He smiled and said that these were such magical times and that one day I'd be nostalgic for them.

"Noooo way," I said, defiantly. "Trust me, you could not pay me to relive this stress. All those people who say these are the best years of their lives are so pathetic. If that is true, then I'm leaping off the Transamerica Pyramid."

"You'll see," he said knowingly. "You never get times like these with everyone around you, every meal across from friends who are on call every night. You have a built-in support system." He took his feet off the desk and smiled at me, opening an F. T. Marinetti book from his shelf and flipping through the pages, 'til I saw warm recognition in his eyes as he cleared his throat. He looked at me for a second before reading. This was a momentary, key eye-lock.

Chopsticks in one hand, he read:

We stayed up all night, my friends and I, under hanging Mosque lamps with domes of filigreed brass, domes starred like our spirits, shining like them with the prisoned radiance of electric hearts.

Sitting in my apartment in New York, I snapped out of my reverie, realizing now that he was right. Though I did get stressed out at school and I wasn't going to whitewash those hard moments in gilded hindsight, I was nostalgic. Those times were stressful but always safe. A paper here, a quiz to cram for there, but in the end it was a system, and I worked well in a system. To so many people, school was a great big map of options and they were perpetually lost. But I was great with maps. I knew how to navigate and always get where I needed to be. But, of course, life post-school had no atlas, especially here. So I sometimes longed for the coziness of a calendar's locking grids, or a syllabus's directives, and hoped one day I could figure out what that might be. But when you're a grown-up, those directives have to come from yourself, and though what I wanted to do was still a blur, reconnecting with something that got me psyched up and feeling alive would be a step in the right direction.

Thirty-four

The weekend was nice and cozy. Joshie took Violet while I slept in 'til eleven, the first time since her birth I'd coma'd out like that. It was pouring cold rain, which my hermit-ass self actually guiltily reveled in—but I was just so happy to be at home and relaxed. I told Josh about my Brooklyn sojourn, which had him dying laughing, but he urged me once again to snap out of my doldrums. Just take Violet on some long walks and bag the whole playgroup thing.

Saturday night, afraid to leave the house in the gales of Hurricane Hermione, we decided to do a Time Warner On Demand instant movie. We scanned the endless choices. We were down by the Ts when I saw *Team America*, and remembered how my friend Trip in San Francisco was obsessed with it, declaring it the most genius, hi-fucking-larious movie of the year.

"And Joshie, it's perfect because it's puppets!" I said, selling my idea. "Violet will love that and it'll be operating on two levels, you know, like SpongeBob!" Josh relented, not particularly psyched to watch marionettes for two hours, but as a die-hard *South Park* fan he decided to give it a shot. Within minutes we were howling. It seemed to be a great selection—Violet was giggling hysterically and we were dying laughing about elements that went over her head, like a genius spoof of *Rent*. It was all peachy keen until an uncensored sex scene between puppets came on. We were laughing at first, but then it got so graphic, with so many insane contortionist sex positions (remember, puppets are bendy!) that even Kama Sutra devotees like Sting would have blushed. Worried we'd scar our daughter and probably have Bee dialing children's services should this get out, we decided to turn it off.

"Mommy, Daddy, look! Two bodies lying down!" Violet said, pointing at the television set as we tore through the couch pillows to retrieve the remote. *Click.* Phew. So much for movie night.

Sunday, Josh had to work all day to make up for his absence Monday when we'd be at our school interview, so I took Violet for a nice long walk. We trolled the perimeter of the park, up by the Harlem Meer and then down Central Park West with the beautiful but somewhat haunting Gothic buildings with impressive names. I remembered one of Josh's teachers died when a gargoyle fell off of a CPW building and killed her. Pancake, like the cartoons. Can you imagine some winged, beaked stone goblin taking you out like that? Talk about a New York death. With that in mind, we stayed on the park side of the avenue, as the thought of falling stone beasts made me shudder. When I got home, I talked to Leigh for an hour—she was in a hotel room in Dallas with another band, The Scratchy Throats, and said she had bumped into Parker at the airport on her way down there. They both had thirty or so minutes until their respective flights, so they plopped at a LaGuardia eatery and said "cheers" with four-dollar bottled waters.

"He is just a gem, Hannah," she sighed. "Alas. All the good ones are taken."

"It's so strange," I said, picturing Bee's beautiful but harsh face compared with Parker's ever-smiling one. "They just so don't *go* together. He is the sweetest, most nurturing guy and she's such a competitive ice queen. I don't get it."

"Love is weird that way," said Leigh, flipping through the channels on her in-room entertainment center. "Opposites attract. And you never know what happens behind closed doors."

"True. They just seem so suited on paper but not in real life. She's soulless."

"Ooh, gotta go, my room service is here and I just found that new Ewan McGregor movie on Spectravision. Good luck with your bigass mini-Harvard interview tomorrow!"

Monday morning, with Joshie looking so dapper and cute in his best suit, we settled Violet with Amber and hailed a cab uptown for Carnegie Nursery School. My heart was pounding through my blouse, Roger Rabbit–style. Josh laughed—he knew I was a wreck and he told me to chill out. It didn't matter that much but all I could think about was Bee's blithe pronouncement that rejection here meant a torpedoed chance for the Ivies.

We approached the stunning nine-story Beaux-Arts building, which had nannies in starched, pressed white uniforms waiting outside with a fleet of Bugaboos all in a row. Triple-parked Lincoln Navigators, Cadillac Escalades, and town cars literally blocked the entire avenue, inspiring a cacophonous orchestra of taxi and truck honks. Not that any of the expertly

coiffed moms emerging from said tinted-glass vehicles gave a
shit. In their Michael Kors and Zac Posen and Valentino garb,
they emerged from each SUV with the help of a uniformed
chauffeur, who aided their descent from the cars (their spike
Manolo Blahniks and Jimmy Choos hardly meshed with the
words "sport" or "utility"). Each walked up the stairs to the
school's grand revolving doors; the entrance might as well have
been a Paris runway, the fashion was so haute. Josh and I
looked at each other silently and followed them into the lavish
school, which had an airport-style security conveyor belt in the
lobby that the moms ran their Fendi bags through. I'd heard
that because there were so many children of billionaires, am-
bassadors, and celebs, security was quasi Quantico.

"Wow, this place is like a mini museum . . ." I said, looking
up at the jewel-box lobby complete with painted fresco ceiling
and marble staircase, after we passed through security. The
ornate façade was even more elaborate than Milford Prescott,
with a carved mahogany entryway, receptionist, sitting room
with upholstered furniture, and coffee table with leather-
bound books. A chipper assistant welcomed us and offered us
cappuccinos ("Skim or one percent? Cinnamon or cocoa on
that?"), then guided us to a waiting area with suede couches
and some class projects made by the kids. We looked at each
other and sat down, flipping through books that contained
such projects as "Froggie's Travels." The first page had a little
laminated frog encased in the plastic page protector and all the
following pages had pictures of the frog around the world.
Families took it on trips throughout the year during all the
school breaks, and there were tons: Rosh Hashanah, Colum-
bus Day, Yom Kippur, Thanksgiving, Christmas, Martin Luther

King Weekend, President's Day Weekend, Ash Wednesday, Easter Break, and Memorial Day. Despite the $20,000 tuition (for three-year-olds!), school was practically always out, leaving time for the students to go on very glamorous trips indeed. There was the 2D amphibian in a temple in Shanghai, at the Eiffel Tower in Paris, at Buckingham Palace in London being held by a guard, in the Coliseum in Rome, at an American resort in Bali, the needle in Seattle, the Sears Tower in Chicago, by a mountain in Gstaad, and on safari in Africa! With Abercrombie & Kent tents in the background, natch.

"Sweetie, maybe this school is too posh for us," I whispered as Josh lay back on the overstuffed couch and looked like he might fall asleep.

"It's cute," he shrugged.

"*Cute?* Babe, this fucking frog from these three-year-olds' class project has been to more places than I have."

Just then a tall, very attractive gray-haired woman in a Chanel suit came into the waiting room. "Mr. and Mrs. Josh Allen, I presume?"

We both stood up like a shot.

"I'm Mrs. Kincaid, the director of admissions. Please, do come in."

We followed her into a beautiful office overlooking the sunlit street. Orange leaves fluttered by. "Welcome to Carnegie Nursery School. Now, before I give you your tour, I'd like to tell you a bit about our philosophy. We believe children should enter kindergarten fully knowing how to read and write."

We sat quietly as she spoke for fifteen minutes about their methods—reading homework, the Chore Wheel (where each toddler has a responsibility for the day, i.e., help serve snack or clean up after crafts), and other elements of the curriculum (dinosaur species, geometry, ancient Greece). We peppered our attentive listening with nods in agreement and a few mm-hmms. It was semi-odd and surreal to me that it wasn't so much that we were choosing the school; they were deciding whether to choose us.

"And, lastly, on a personal note, I understand you're working with my husband looking for a new place. How nice."

"Yes! Troy— Mr. Kincaid has been so helpful and patient. I'm sure we'll find something soon, I hope."

"Now, before we take you to see the school, I'd like you to write a statement about Miss Violet, just about three hundred words is fine. I'll leave you for about ten minutes. We just want to see the first thoughts that flow about your daughter."

I was . . . stunned.

A surprise "statement"? Nice how Bee didn't mention that tidbit when I asked for tips. A little *Oh, you might wanna prepare for the pop essay* would have been nice. Mrs. Kincaid laid a crisp sheet of paper watermarked with the school crest and some pens in front of us, and exited.

"Sweetie, this is nuts," I said.

"Calm down. You can write, I read some of your school stuff. Okay, let's just calm down."

We exhaled together, and for the first time, I saw my usually calm, cool, and collected hubby actually seem slightly rattled. First we brainstormed about our daughter. She was too amazing and wonderful to jam into a page. No matter what we wrote, they could never see all the amazing things that we see in her. Everyone says his or her kids are smart, funny, energetic, spunky. We decided to go with the essence of Violet—

how loving she is—and how there has been no shortage of affection in our home. The girl hugs the supermarket checkout lady, the flower shop guy, any kid on the street. And in holding hands and connecting with people, her spirit and love of people is contagious to the point where even the most crotchety Scrooge seems to melt in her shiny-eyed gaze. Finally we finished, my wrist tired from jotting down our thoughts, and I felt that while it would be truly impossible to fully capture Violet, especially in ten minutes, we had at least showed Mrs. Kincaid that we were utterly devoted to our daughter. Mrs. Kincaid reentered her office, taking the piece of paper and sticking it into our file. "So, let's begin the tour, shall we?"

We rose and crossed the marble floors to a sweeping staircase, the only sounds the *click-clack*ing of Mrs. Kincaid's heels. Through the soundproofed doors we saw children at play, in the most beautiful outfits I'd ever seen.

"Pickup is right about now, so you'll be able to see some of the children," she said. We strolled all nine floors of the school, which was not only charming but also so beautiful it put most high schools to shame. It was truly a mansion. There was an Olympic-sized pool, a gilded library, and a state-of-the-art gymnasium.

Suddenly a little bell chimed and the doors opened in synchronized bursts. Streams of preened children spilled out.

"Hello, Cossima!" Mrs. Kincaid said to a little girl with two long braids. "Hello, India! Hi, McSorland! Good afternoon, Lorelei!"

Josh and I ended up back down in the foyer behind Mrs. Kincaid when her formerly chipper and now meek-looking assistant came out to meet us.

"Mrs. Kincaid? Mrs. Elliott, Weston Elliott's mother, is in your office, she says it's quite important."

"All right, Tracy," she said, then turned to us. "Josh, Hannah, it was a pleasure to meet you, and I look forward to meeting Miss Violet Grace next month when we commence our childrens' interviews. Good day."

She went into her office, and I then heard Bee's voice, in a very anger-infused tone.

"Mrs. Kincaid," she snapped. "I have a serious, *serious* problem."

"Yes, Mrs. Elliott, what is the issue?"

Josh's cell rang. He talked for a second then said he had to take the call and bolt to the office. He gave me a peck on the cheek and left the school. Curious about Bee's issue, I lingered, pretending to fix my boot on the sofa near the ajar door.

"Yesterday was the *third time* Weston was sent home with yellow watercolor on his sweater. His Ralph Lauren, three-hundred-ninety-five-dollar quadruple-ply-cashmere sweater!" Bee screamed. "I don't think I need to tell you again that Miss Glassman is doing an unacceptable job in keeping my son tidy."

"Mrs. Elliott," began Mrs. Kincaid, clearly used to dealing with women like this. "With all due respect, this is a nursery school. The children paint, they play outdoors, they get dirty. Perhaps you can send him in clothes that can be easily washed?"

"How I dress my son is my concern. I simply will not accept him coming home looking like he just finished a game of paintball."

Pause.

"Well, I shall let Miss Glassman know to put a smock on

him. As I recall, we tried, but Master Weston simply didn't want to wear one. We don't believe in forcing him."

"Well, make him. Or I can just send Miss Glassman our dry-cleaning bills."

I heard a chair pull out, scraping the floor. I quickly bolted outside so she wouldn't see me. Wow.

On my way home to see Violet, I realized what a beautiful day it was outside with the cool air and changing leaves. I paid Amber and packed Violet in her stroller for a long walk. Violet and I cut through the park, down by the old Plaza Hotel, where she studied all the horsies and their carriages. We walked down Fifth, past the Disney store (also a hit), all the way down to the Empire State Building. Before I knew it, we were crossing Houston Street into Soho. I looked at the hip kids and fashionistas. With models and students aplenty, it was just an overall younger scene.

"Mommy, my store!" Violet said suddenly.

I turned to see the most adorable kids' boutique, Makie, with a teeny tiny sign tied onto the door in twine. We went inside and the designer was there, and I gushed about how sweet and original her creations were. Violet ran around for about fifteen minutes as I selected some new clothes for winter. She didn't have any real coats and heavy sweaters, and everything uptown was so outrageously priced I couldn't bear to slap the plastic down. We tried on the cutest boots that looked circa 1928, fully Little Orphan Annie, and Violet looked beyond adorable in them.

We went to a little girls' lunch at KinKhao and shared dumplings (her fave) before saddling up for our walk back uptown. The little nugget passed out in the stroller en route, and it was chilly so I'd switched her little T-strap sandals to the shiny new brown boots we'd just bought at Makie. She looked like a little angel out cold, and I decided to take advantage of the zzz's and maybe try a little shopping for myself.

I went into Barneys and scoped the racks of beautiful things. I spied Kelly Osbourne with Richie Rich, the Heatherette designer I admired from afar, and ten minutes later I saw Liv Tyler delicately handing a saleswoman her purchases with her long fingers.

Suddenly, as I was waiting for a dressing room, I heard, "Oh my God!"

I turned to see one of the moms from Kidsplosion, who was on her cell. "Hold on," she said into her phone, turning to me. "Where did you get those adorable shoes?"

"Um, this place downtown . . ."

"Where? Name! Address!" She practically looked like she was breaking a sweat, her tone so urgent she may well have been on a vital nation-protecting fact-finding mission for the CIA.

"Um, this place called Makie? On Thompson between, I guess, Prince and Spring?"

"Milos, it's me," she barked into her cell. "I need you to go drive down to this place Makie. Ask for these brown leather boots in size 8 for Calliope. Yes . . . size 8. Then drive back uptown and pick us up at Via Quadronno. Bye."

She snapped her cell shut and walked away. No thank-you, no nothing. Just a dispatch to her driver to go get the same boots. Ugh.

Violet was asleep in her stroller when we got home, and I enjoyed a simple luxury I hadn't yet experienced in New York, a hot, late afternoon bath. Ahhh. My legs were killing from the long-ass walk, but I actually felt really good. And as I soaked in the lavender bubbles and looked out my window, the sun was starting to set into an electric blue, Maxfield Parrish sky.

Thirty-five

The next day, inspired from my marathon walk with Violet, we decided to hit the West Side and visit the Natural History Museum. Violet could name every dinosaur known to man, so I thought checking out dem bones would be fun. She was overjoyed and euphoric to say the least. The exhibit was truly incredible, and we wandered the halls looking at "buggies" and "wabbits" and "fishies," until Violet's little gams were about to give out.

Under the big whale, a cute mom and daughter with knitted scarves looked up in wonder.

"I love dis place, Mommy!" the little girl said in awe.

"Isn't it great?" the mom responded. "We can come here whenever you want."

Violet sauntered up to the little girl and gave her big hug.

"Awwww, she's so friendly!" the mom said to me sweetly. "Give her a hug, Amy!"

The girls hugged and we cooed at the cuteness factor of their embrace. The mother reminded me of a friend I'd had in grad school who had a baby and who was always very relaxed; she'd pass her baby around a party or I'd find her in the library with the baby hanging in the Baby Björn as she read. I remembered promising myself I'd be carefree and mellow like that. And this mom had that same chill vibe.

"You guys live around here?" she asked.

"Just across the park. It's not far, though. We had such a nice walk," I said.

"We take the cutest class ever, Broadway Babies, on the East Side. Do you guys do it?"

"No. What's that, like, making the kids into Macaulay Culkin child stars or something?"

"No," she laughed. "It's so cute you want to die. It's all Broadway actors and they do a different show every week, so it's like world-class entertainment for the parents."

"No way! I love the sound of that!" It sounded more rambunctious and alive than the sedate glockenspiels and triangles of Milford Prescott.

"You have to check it out. It's amazing how talented the teachers are, and it just makes you feel so lucky to live in New York."

"Mommy!" her daughter suddenly wailed.

"Okay, honey, we'll go to lunch now. I'm Holly Appleton, by the way. If you guys want to join our class, just ask for Heather Stone when you call, she's so sweet."

"Thanks so much for the tip."

"Your daughter's so cute—"

"So's yours!"

We left the museum and I called information for the Broadway Babies number and signed Violet up right then and there. They told me they had one spot left in Holly's section and that the next class would be the show *Chicago*. I wondered how they would perform a show about a sex-slaughter/double homicide with imprisonment and a crooked legal system for two-year-olds, but I did know one thing: I was psyched.

Thirty-six

The next day, I was reorganizing Violet's drawers (thanks to piles of outgrown clothes, sad!) when the doorman buzzed. Mrs. Dillingham was on her way up. Fuck, I looked like I had just come out of the ring with Mike Tyson. I tore off my grody Urban O tee and threw on a little white dress I hadn't ever worn, ripping the tag off just as the doorbell rang. It was so contrived, I mean, I would never be just lounging around the house in the dress but I knew Lila and her cronies always were decked out and probably never even let their staff see them in something as plebeian as blue jeans.

"Lila! Hi," I said, forcing a smile. "What a surprise." I hoped my highlighting of the ambush factor would make her think about barrel-assing into our apartment sans phone call, but no.

"Hannah, I'm concerned," she started, looking me over. I could detect a note of pleasant response to my outfit, though nothing was said of it. "I saw Bee this afternoon, and well, we got to talking about Violet."

Uh-oh. Didn't these people have better things to discuss than *my daughter*? Apparently not.

"And she mentioned that you . . . took her to the outer boroughs," Lila choked, practically near the point of vomiting. "On the subway train."

"Yes." I knew where this was going. "We had a playgroup there."

"Well, to be honest, she also mentioned Violet watches a lot of television and while I can't say I'm happy about that—Weston watches none, you know—I am extremely distressed that you took it upon yourself to bring my grandchild *underground* like that on those horrible cattle cars! They are all graffiti covered and dreadful. And the *people*! Why, it's the absolute dregs of society! God knows what could have happened to her. And it's a clear terrorist target, you know. What if these crazy bombers boarded your train? It's simply irresponsible!"

My blood boiled. I wished Josh had been there to dive in and stand up for me, but he was always at work and here I was yet again alone with his mother having to defend myself while trying to avoid confrontation.

"Lila, the trains are no longer graffiti covered—"

"No matter! I simply am not comfortable with that at all and if you truly *must* leave Manhattan, I will send my chauffeur."

I was livid. But I had to take a deep breath and exhale my need to club her over the head with a Big Bertha golf wedge. I felt the ire slowly seep away and I nodded calmly, not wanting to escalate the situation by saying, for example, that she was a nosy cow who should mind her own business. So I said nothing. She made fake small talk for the ten minutes afterward (asking "the latest" on our nursery school process, blah blah blah) then announced she had to go because she had the black-tie gala for Help Foreign Frescos Ball at the Burden Mansion in three hours and she had "not a thing to wear" (apparently there were painted ceilings abroad in dire need of our aid). Hmph. When she left I was desperate to get out of the house and I decided to take Violet outside to blow off my steam. We had walked a few blocks when I heard Violet say "Mommy, dat store!" and per her wish, we ended up at famed toy emporium F.A.O. Schwarz.

A mistake. Hordes of platinum-card-swiping moms lined up at the registers with bags full of big dollies and indoor cars, though we were nowhere near Christmas, and I felt like I was moving through the store as if watching everything through a fish-eye lens. In a distorted haze, the children's lollipops seemed warped bigger than their heads. The *vroom-vroom*s of the trucks seemed as noisy as the real rush hour outside, and Barbies seemed blonder than ever, and suddenly a huge clown seriously made me think it would lurch toward us and strangle me. I had to get out. I quickly took Violet and walked toward home. Maybe there would be a sweet message from Joshie, whom I was dying to talk to and regroup with.

Thirty-seven

Alas, no word from Josh save for a quick text message that he was in meetings " 'til late." But curiously, Troy Kincaid had called three times. There was a sudden private listing from a family who had to move back to Portugal in two months. The wife recently had a kidney transplant and was convalescing at home and didn't want people traipsing through the pad. She listed it under the radar with Troy Kincaid as the exclusive broker and because it was in our budget (just barely) I jumped at the chance to see it; he asked if we could come over right then.

Having looked at dozens of hovels with Troy, I walked through and looked around, and I knew. It's like with men: you kiss a ton of frogs and you frigging *know* when it's your husband. And this place was home.

I walked the hallway, seeing what would be Violet's room, and another little room adjacent that could be baby number two's room one day down the road. Everything was just perfect.

"Done," I said, resolutely. "This is it. This is home."

But naturally, it wasn't that easy. In New York City, the land of co-op apartments, you don't just plonk down the dough and get handed the key. No, no, no, in the land of vertical neighbors, where stacked upon each other are twelve New Yorkers with twelve opinions, we would have to go through the infamous co-op board.

Now, on top of Violet's schools, we also had to prep for our board package—a hundred-page application slash tome demanding all our IRS records, forms up the wazoo, and letters of recommendation—not just financial ones from Josh's boss and our accountants, but also social references to prove we were of good standing in the community, with friends in high places (i.e., other nice co-ops nearby).

It was a very tricky building to get into—very private with a lot of "nice" families, including a local NBC newscaster and a star trial lawyer. It wasn't some blingy fancy address, just a quiet tree-lined street, a true "preppy" building, complete with worn-in leather chairs in the lobby and old doormen who'd worked there for forty years.

The next day, after Violet and Josh came back to the apartment to see it and we formally gave our offer, we sat down with Troy at Payard nearby and made a list of who we could approach for our letters. The financial part was easy; Josh had a great pal who was a mortgage broker so that element was a slam dunk, as were his social letters from Parker Elliott and his other old pal, Milton McDermott.

"What about you, Hannah?" Troy said. "We need to have some social references written by your friends."

I looked at Josh nervously, not quite knowing how to tell Troy I didn't have any in the city yet. Leigh lived in a rental downtown, hardly a glossy reference for these kinds of people. Bee, who wasn't even my friend, wasn't eligible because her husband was writing for Josh. "Maybe I could ask . . . my friend Tate Hayes. He's a professor at Columbia, and taught me at Berkeley."

"Okay, that will do," Troy said. "Perfect. What about any other friends? You'll need another, maybe a female friend?"

Shit. Zilch. I thought for a minute and guessed maybe Maggie Sinclair would write for me? All these girls knew the drill, maybe she could bluff a little and say she'd known me since Bee's wedding? Ugh. "I think I can ask someone else, Maggie Sinclair?"

"Oh, yes, I know Maggie, she'd be perfect, just perfect."

Great. Now all I needed to do was ask her.

AND GOOD NEWS TRAVELS . . . INSTANTLY

Instant Message from: BeeElliott

> BeeElliott: I heard the Allens are bidding on a place.
>
> Maggs10021: Really? That's great!
>
> BeeElliott: Dunno, I heard it's—gasp—east of Third.
>
> Maggs10021: So?
>
> BeeElliott: Kind of a B building but whatev. Hey, did you hear about Tessa's kid?
>
> Maggs10021: No, what?
>
> BeeElliott: Supposedly did badly on ERBs—Lara told me he has Homework Resistance.
>
> Maggs10021: What's that? He doesn't wanna do homework?
>
> BeeElliott: School therapist says it's a big problem; Hallie says he'll get rejected everywhere—sucks.
>
> Maggs10021: Gotta sign—am feling v. tired today, baby's kicking like crazy + have been up all night . . .
>
> BeeElliott: 'K, bye!

Thirty-eight

Crazed with the newly added burden of our board package, I got Amber to play with Violet while I ran a bunch of errands (pick up tax returns, wait at Kinko's, yawnsville). When I was done I found myself on Ninety-sixth Street and began walking up Fifth Avenue to the north of the park in Harlem. Somehow my feet walked me to the Columbia campus. The buildings were so beautiful, and I thought of Barbara Hershey in *Hannah and Her Sisters* making her way across the quad with a bag full of books. While Tate's classes always excited me, I honestly loathed most of my classes, especially the piles of specific requirements, namely science, which I filled with guts like Rocks for Jocks and Nuts and Sluts. Beyond the classes in my major, which I loved, the rest just made me want to snag the sheepskin and bail, but as I walked around I suddenly found myself missing campus life terribly—not necessarily being a student cramming for a test, just being immersed in that environment. I missed the throngs of young people. I missed community. I missed belonging.

I asked a bearded crunchy dude where the art history building was, and headed where he directed me. It was different from my school—more East Coast, glam and grand, with a museumesque photo study of the images the students had to memorize for identification in exams. I peeked in a few windows—one had a lecturer with a big pointer explaining Etruscan vases, the next room a gray-haired woman discussing a flowery French Rococo painting, the next was a seminar with violent 1980s art on the screen.

And then I saw Tate through his lecture hall window. He was waving his hands while explicating the image in front of the class, a Dutch landscape. I quietly opened the door and darted into a spare seat in the back of the crowded auditorium.

"Here we have the dusty, muted topography of a plain, almost grisaille road with a simple figure walking. But look at the sky. It is alive with vigor and forcefulness; the figure is devoid of emotion, but consider this tree. It's anthropomorphized, twisting as if agonized, screaming out of its anchoring roots."

Forget crack: nostalgia is a true drug. Over the past months I had been dipping into the vats of memories on purpose, because they were a safe place. It was weird: before I met Josh, when I was between relationships and wallowing in loneliness, I always mentally wandered back to Tate Hayes. I used to imagine what it would be like to fully make out with him. What would have happened if he hadn't put the brakes on our kiss? But all those reveries always took place in the past, like I was mourning something that never happened to my twenty-one-year-old self. It was like a sex dream I had once starring the actor Jim Caviezel from *The Count of Monte Cristo*. In my visions of him ripping my clothes off, it wasn't about my bumping into him buying Tylenol at Duane Reade and bringing him back to my apartment. It was me in the lavish ballgown the actress opposite him wore. The fantasy existed on a plane that could never occur: we were running through the foggy moors, and he laid me down in the grass, unlacing my ribboned bodice. I wasn't cutting and pasting him, my fantasy, into *my reality*, I was cutting and pasting myself into his costumed realm. And that was the scope of my scenarios.

In the single days of my mid-twenties, my thoughts of Professor Hayes involved a schoolgirl version of myself, back in time, if he hadn't stopped kissing me that rainy afternoon. The dream was that we were lovers and traveled together and he would show me the whole world. I would be his coltish, adoring pupil who made him feel young and reborn.

"Next slide, please. Oh. This . . . this is a favorite." He looked at the image as if it were an old flame that he'd bumped into in the grocery store. He had that nervous excitement of seeing something so familiar that he knew intimately but had not laid eyes on for a long time. He sounded almost turned on as he spoke. He offered the class the historical background of Vermeer's Delft, what it had been like when the artist raised his brush to make the pearls in the picture.

"In this work by Vermeer we can feel the delicate quiet of this room as the maiden weighs the pearls in the balance. The rigidity of the moral codes reflected the essential anxiety of a culture that cherished virtue and shunned vanities, yet was swimming in spices and silks. Weighing upon every head was this burden of privilege and the quest for equilibrium in the face of a harsh dichotomy of luxuriant pleasures versus a determined lack of absorption in material things."

I was amused to think that though centuries separated us, the Dutch and I seemed to have a bit in common, as I was also thrust into this world of material things and trying to swim upstream to groundedness. Only the terrain was chockablock with Bugaboos, not overvalued tulips.

As he continued, I became lost in his swirling words, which

washed over me in the colored light of the slide. Suddenly the class was done and the bright overheads came on. While Hayes was giving instructions for finals the following week, the students were hurriedly loading their notebooks into bags and darting off in a whirl of zipping knapsacks and shuffling sneakers. I sat quietly and watched him as he gathered his notes and ran his hand through his hair. The projectionist came out from the booth, carrying the carousel of slides.

"Professor Hayes—Tate," I called, as the last straggling lass slung her Jansport over her shoulder to leave.

"Hannah, what a lovely surprise! What are you doing here?"

"I have a favor to ask."

"Anything you need. Shall we go sit down and get a coffee?"

Ten minutes later we were seated in an old coffee bar with dark booths and little café tables. He was stirring his espresso as I returned with my giant frothy drink.

"What's that?" he asked, eyeballing the enormous mug that I proceeded to douse with so much sugar it was as if the cup was on fire and the sugar dispenser was a hose. I was a total seven-year-old with my sweet vat next to his tiny cup of bitter, grown-up espresso.

"It's a mochaccino. Grandissssssimo."

"I suspected you'd get something foamy and fancy," he said. "I suppose now it's obvious—the chocolate is very you. I seem to recall scores of small foil balls amassed on my desk as you made you way through my Hershey Kiss bowl."

Fucking great memory.

"Well, I hear there's an enzyme in chocolate that is clinically proven to make you happier," I said. "Nothing I didn't already know, naturally. From my extensive research."

"So, my dear, what big wish can I grant?"

"Ugh, this is so crazy, but we're actually buying—well, trying to buy an apartment, and we need these, like, social recommendations—"

"Done. I do this all the time, no problem."

Yayyyy. I was so thrilled. "Really?"

"Of course, everyone has to deal with that. I know the drill. I can get it to you by next week? Why don't you pop by Friday after my office hours and I'll have it ready for you."

"Perfect, thanks so much. You are a total godsend."

Thirty-nine

There I was the following day, happily stirring Violet's Quaker Instant Maple n' Brown Sugar over chants of "Oatmeal! Oatmeal! Oatmeal!" when the phone rang. I was smiling at Violet's breakfast excitement, when I heard the sharp cut of an anger-infused voice through the receiver. Giggles turned to goose bumps.

"Mrs. Allen, please."

"Oh, hi, um, this is Hannah Allen."

"Nelly Abercrombie. Registrar for the Fifth Avenue School."

"Yes, hello!" Heart racing.

"You and your husband failed to show up for your interview this morning."

Huh? I never had heard from them! I assumed I didn't win

the drawing for a coveted application. The Web site said in huge bold letters that we would be notified in writing and *not to call* the school.

"Oh my gosh, Mrs. Abercrombie, we never got anything about it. I am so sorry."

"Well, we never got anything returned to us at the school, so . . ."

Beat. Was she accusing me of lying? "I swear, I am the most organized person. We would never, ever miss something like this—"

"Then why didn't you call?"

"Well, both the Web site and the woman on the phone on dialing day said not to. I didn't want to be pushy."

"Didn't you suspect something was amiss when all your friends had already been notified of tour dates?" she huffed.

I stuttered something humiliating about how we just moved here and I didn't know anyone else applying. She snorted in reply, then added, "I don't know what to tell you."

Now our school options were officially swirling down the toilet bowl. "So that's it, we've missed the boat?"

She took a pause so pregnant quadruplets could have been born. "Okay then, I'll give you a second chance. We have one last tour tomorrow at nine A.M.," she said, ordering, not asking. "Promptly."

"Done, we will be there. Thank you, and again, I'm—" *Click.* Beeyotch. My palms were sweating so much the phone almost slid from my hand. I speed-dialed Josh at the office, panting and hysterical.

"He's in a meeting."

"It's very important—can he talk for one minute?"

"Sorry, he's with clients in the conference room."

I was in a panic. "Can you just tell him his wife called, please? We have to go to a school tour tomorrow at nine."

"Tomorrow? Let me check his schedule . . ."

My forehead was shvitzing and I could feel my pits burning with sweat-on-deck.

"Nope, he has a meeting at nine thirty downtown."

"Listen. Cancel it. This is very important. It's an emergency. Just tell him to do it, please." I had never heard myself sound so forceful, but I knew I had to throw down the gauntlet.

I looked at Violet and exhaled, my eyes filling with tears. Did I somehow fuck up and mistakenly toss the letter? No, hell no, that is so not me. Maybe it just was plain old lost. Fuck! Nightmare.

That night, Josh came home at eleven P.M. to find me passed out. I tried to revive quickly and give him kisses, but he was exhausted and said the school tour the next day had fully ruined his morning.

"Sweetie, I am so sorry, I know it's such a hassle—"

"It's okay, Han. I know it's not your fault. That woman sounds like a nightmare."

Little did we know.

We arrived to the Fifth Avenue School's grand entrance, complete with a drive-in court for the chauffeurs and nine security guards because "lots of prominent families send their children here." Just like Carnegie, there were lavish rooms with moldings, carpeted halls, and a state-of-the-art kitchen. Weirdly, there were not one or two but ten couples on the tour, so everyone was pushing one another to get into the rooms, craning their necks, and fighting to talk with Mrs. Abercrombie to get brownie points for seeming interested. The parents all were older and seemed very controlling and pushy. Once the tour was over, we filed into a marble drawing room with leather chairs lined up for a question-and-answer session, which began with attendance.

"The Horowitzes?" she asked. A meek woman and her bespectacled husband raised their hands.

"The Whitneys?" Two blondies raised their hands.

"The Allens?" We raised our hands.

"Well," she sniffed, looking us over. "How nice of you to actually show up this time."

I felt like Thor had just chucked a lightning bolt at me. My whole body felt walloped by her acidic tone as I looked at my lap and then at Josh, who sat poised, giving me a tight smile. *Fuck this fucking school!* I hated her already. And if she's the director—for three decades no less—the environment would be sculpted from the top down, i.e., a bitchfest run by this toad.

"Let us begin," she said, after finishing the list of halo-covered parents who had actually shown up. She talked about the school's philosophy (I loved how every school thought theirs was so original and unique. I mean, the kids are fucking tots), discussed parent involvement (from chaperoning field trips to chairing the annual black-tie gala fund-raiser), and then opened the floor for questions.

One woman raised her hand.

"Yes, you in the tweed," Mrs. Abercrombie acknowledged.

"Um, you said all your students leave here for kindergarten fully knowing how to read and write—"

"Correct." She beamed.

"Well, um, what if there's a child in the class who's . . . lagging a little. Will the teachers stop to help him or her?"

I kind of thought it a weird question, she might as well have worn a T-shirt that read "Hey, my kid's kinda slow."

But Mrs. Abercrombie nodded, explaining that this happens all the time. "You see, we know what it is to have lagging students," she began. "Because we have many, many in vitro families."

Huh? Josh looked at me. I was in shock. What was she getting at?

"You see, in vitro just isn't Darwinian, people!" she said as I spied at least two women looking at the floor. "The most tenacious sperm isn't the one that's getting there, so as a result we have all these kids who are way behind!"

Ew! I was so offended by her uncouth, un-PC, and probably untruthful "research" that I almost stormed out, but was too surprised to move.

"We have seven sets of techno twins here at the Fifth Avenue School. Seven sets! And in every single one of those pairs, one of the children is behind. That's just the way it goes. As I said, not the fittest sperm gets there, the one chosen by the lab technician does! Not Darwinian, people, not Darwinian."

"We are withdrawing our application!" I seethed out on the street, walking a mile a minute.

"Calm down, sweets. Don't get so emotional."

"*Emotional?* That *bitch* is evil, Joshie, *evil*. I hate that school and I hate that place. We are yanking our application."

"Don't be so upset," he laughed, more amused than horrified. "She's a freak, so what? The school seemed fine."

"I don't know what we're going to do, Josh. We only have one school left, Browne-Madison School, and if that blows, poor Violet is going to either be with snobby couture kids or Darwin's finest pressure-cooked offspring under that bitch's tutelage."

"Deep breaths, my love," he said, laughing and patting my head.

Forty

With one co-op board letter under my belt from Tate Hayes, I had the courage to call Maggie. I asked her if she wanted to grab lunch and she said suggested we stroll with the kids in the park. When I got there, she was saying good-bye to Hallie—in full track suit with personal trainer—who barely greeted me while looking Violet over.

"Well, hello there. Violet!" Hallie cooed with saccharine coursing through every word. "Aren't you sweet! Oh, I wish Julia Charlotte were here, but she's at school, darn!"

Awash in Adidas by Stella McCartney workout togs, Hallie and trainer jogged off, leaving me with Maggie. I filled her in on my apartment quest thus far.

"That's great, Hannah! Bee had told me you guys couldn't find anything in your budget, so that's great news!" Nice, thanks, Bee. Wait, how the hell would she know that? Ugh.

"Yeah, well, that's the good news. That bad news is we need some, um, social letters or whatever? And I was wondering if you'd mind writing one for me. I know that it must be such a pain and I am so embarrassed to have to ask, I'm just . . . desperate. I'd be forever in your debt."

"Sure, of course!" she said, smiling brightly. She seemed almost touched I'd even ask her, seeing as how we both knew deep down that we weren't close, but she was happy to oblige. "I'll drop it off next week. I know these things have to happen quickly."

"Thanks, Maggie. I really appreciate it, I really do."

We then sat in silence for a beat as we watched the kids run around in the meadow.

"You know, Maggie," I started. "I . . . don't have many friends here, and to be honest it's been pretty hard for me. I don't know, it's . . . been an adjustment." All of a sudden I felt this heinous, uncontrollable wave of tears burn its way to my eyes. I barely knew this woman, and what I did know, I wasn't crazy about (mostly 'cause of Bee, Hallie, and Lara, her Momzilla friends), but something in her tone one-on-one suggested she was actually probably a good person. "It's just, my husband has been working nonstop for two months and . . . I miss him," full-on tears now streaming. "I miss my husband and I'm so lonely. I mean, I live for Violet, and she's the most loving, amazing daughter, but I just . . . am always alone."

And then something amazing happened: Maggie hugged me. Her friends were all total Momsicles who barely hugged their own children let alone their friends—an air-kiss, maybe, at an event—but somehow it was just what I needed.

"Listen," she said. "I know it can be hard. Everyone's worrying about their own lives, and it's easy to get caught up in the stress, but you just got here! Don't worry. Josh just probably has to prove himself since he's new on the job."

"It's just hard. I feel so clueless so much of the time. I feel like a Martian. Maybe it would be different if I were native born."

"You know, nearly everyone you've met isn't from here, either," Maggie said comfortingly. "Hallie's from Ohio. And Lara literally came from a Portuguese fishing town, population five hundred seventy-six."

No. Way. "What? You're joking," I said, stunned, wiping my face.

"No! That's the funniest part! Bee's from Manhattan and she's sort of the ringleader. But Lara, Hallie, no way! They're so hung up about the scene here that they overcompensate by stressing out ten times more about getting their kids in everywhere and competing nonstop."

"Gosh, I thought I was this hick—"

"Not at all, Hannah. You're hip! And edgy and . . . yourself. Those women are so worried about fitting in and keeping up they lose that."

"Wow . . ." I said, wiping a last tear.

"Don't worry," Maggie said, with a pat on my back. "And please: don't change."

"My mother-in-law would probably not like to hear you say that. She's dying for me to have a Tess McGill–style makeover," I confessed. "I think she'd much prefer it if Josh had married someone like Bee."

Maggie sat quietly and didn't really respond.

"Don't worry," she finally said. "It's all about your family and what you guys have. Don't let the outside world get you down."

I knew she was right and it actually felt good to open up. Leigh was like my sister, but it was hard to complain to her when all she really wanted—a husband and a child—I already had. Maggie seemed to understand the pressures I was facing, and I realized that even though she was in the thick of the supposed golden circle, she probably felt pressure to keep up, too.

After we said good-bye I realized I felt a bit better. And luckily the next day would bring some structure—Broadway Babies—since all my days were like a vast open field that needed to be filled. I had been at a point where I was almost psyched when the toilet paper ran out because it meant I had to go get some more; it was a purposeful errand, a task, and I could be useful and try to fill a void. Not just in the empty toilet paper holder but in myself. Now I felt a turn. I was officially convinced that I had to throw myself into my life here, and little by little, hopefully, it would feel like home.

Forty-one

I am in the Metropolitan Museum of Art with Tate Hayes walking in the Temple of Dendur, looking through the windowed wall. We watch the breeze whip the last of the crispy leaves from the naked treetops through the massive vitrine.

"It looks so beautiful out there. Those leaves are all gone. I can't believe fall's almost over," I say.

He stares out the glass and says, "I have an idea."

"What?"

"Do you want to see the archives? You know they only display under ten percent of their inventory holdings? We can go down and I'll show you some real treasures."

"Oh my God, that would be incredible."

I follow him past hallway after hallway of sarcofagi, through carpeted atriums and down more marble stairs to one of those camouflaged doors you never really notice in a museum. Security cameras and checkpoints are everywhere, but he has the special electronic pass that has kept clicking us deeper and deeper into the inner sanctums of the museum's maze.

Tate gives a glance up at a camera and we walk by as if I was supposed to be there. He punches a code on a keypad by a massive reinforced door. The light turns green. We walk into a fireproof vault room, which holds the vast collection of works on paper. There are rows after rows of drawings and prints in long, shallow flat drawers. In a private print study, he sits me down, puts on some gloves, unlocks a flat drawer, and carefully places a piece of paper in front of me.

It is Dürer's *Adam and Eve*. The lines are so intimate, I feel unbelievably close to the wrist that had flicked back and forth to create it. Every notch of the needle is there; it is as if you could see every flash of thought in each micromillimeter of black.

Next comes Rembrandt's *Hundred Guilder* print. Next a Lucas van Leyden. The crosshatches of a windmill. The light made from the whiteness of the paper peering from scores of gray pin-sized lines. I can't believe what I am looking at.

"This is . . . the most miraculous experience. These are too much to see so close up. *I'm not worthy!*"

He doesn't get my *Wayne's World* reference and I suddenly feel like a massive dope.

"This is how prints were meant to be seen. They were disseminated to achieve fame, to be held up just as you're holding them."

"These lines," I marvel, reeling. "You feel so close to the artist."

"He etched like he breathed."

I look up at him. His eyes seem genuinely moved by my appreciation of what he has revealed to me in this secret trove. He glances down at me in my chair, at the former pupil saying nothing, and lightly brushes his fingers on my hair.

"Come." He turns and walks out, and chills engulf me as I follow him obediently.

We walk farther down the hallway and enter a huge, cavernous cement room with high ceilings and metal slats next to next, like in a poster shop, but with steel casing and locks on

each. He takes out his keys and unlocks them, walking his fingers across the racks, settling on one, then smiles at me and
pulls it out. It is a Pieter de Hooch, a quiet interior with check-
ered floor and mother and child. I gasp; I can't believe my
proximity to the work, I can see the paint sitting on the panel.

"Oh," I sigh—almost sexually, I realize, after it comes out.

"Look at this." He pulls out another grate, a slat with two
Caravaggios. Across the room, another has a soft Whistler, and
then a Robert Henri. I am overwhelmed by the moment, the
art surrounding us, the pricelessness of a dream come to life,
a dream actually transcended by reality.

"He painted children in this way that sort of reminds me
of you."

"Thanks. I'm, like, a toddler?"

He looks right into me, probably through me. The room is
ice-cold cement, metal grates, and locks. But the emotions
and colors in the sealed slats are boiling, bursting beneath the
chilled metallic coverings. So are we; the room is now, in this
instant, an echo of our past—a dry interaction of teacher and
student, on a campus, in an office. Cement. Patterned, like the
orders and formulae for storing the works around us. But under it, for me at least, beneath the college-girl jeans and
turtleneck, through the textbook-filled backpack, are heat and
color: portraits of intimacy, still lifes of bounty, restless
oceans of longing.

"No," he responds, as if I am, indeed, a toddler. "You are
not a child. But you have the same liquid eyes."

He reaches toward me, runs a hand through my hair, and
pulls me to him in one full motion. He puts his hands on my
face, holding my head as if it were a precious object, and leans

in for a lightning-charged, all-enveloping, electric kiss, like the one in his office years ago. He presses his mouth against me, and it is sweet and hot, like cider. His hands move down from my face to my shoulder and back, squeezing me harder for a deeper part of the kiss. My hands are around him, then in his hair, on his neck. I gasp for breath as if underwater. It's now way further and longer than that kiss in his office, we are surpassing the past into uncharted, scary territory. I am submerged with him, sucking in my lust for him like air I need to breathe, treading with every muscle in a submarine blur, and now, through his warm mouth, my lungs can finally open. I put my hand down the back of his collar to feel the first inches of skin down his back. He lifts me off the cold gray floor in his arms, as the kiss grows more fevered and desperate.

He takes his glasses off and tries to put them on the desk but they clatter to the floor. He comes back to me, smiling, and kisses me so hard my whole body is swept up in him. I have to have him. His hands move over my clothed breasts, then under my shirt to the flesh. He pants for the first time, then brings me to the side of the last grate in the row, which has been pulled out. We are blocked from view, hidden in a corner, and his hands move across my chest, then down my thighs. He pushes up my skirt and lifts me onto the cement ledge at the end of the cabinet. It is cold, but a meat locker could not bring down my body temperature by a tenth of a degree. Face to face now on my perch, I kiss him with my hands on his back, almost grabbing him to make sure he is real. His hand slides up my thigh and rips down my panties. I almost scream with surprise and pleasure, and he covers my mouth with his hand as he pushes inside in a way that made my eyes close each time.

My head rolls back and he kisses my neck and I stifle a growing whimper of abandon as he covers my mouth with more violence and protection. Around us are the paintings, skyward bursts of Italianate cherubs, trumpets heralding us, the lute strings in every Spanish still life vibrate with me, and every Rococo picnic-scene concerto resonates in our movement. The genre pictures of Falstaffian merrymaking toast us, the glistening leaves of every landscape flutter a bit in our honor with the gasps from our mouths. The coy smiles of painted maids are for me right now, through the very wall he presses me against, through the cinder blockade he pushed me into, until he holds his breath for a few desperate, charged moments. "Oh, Hannah!"

"Mommy? Mooomieeeeeee!"

What?

"Mom!"

Is Violet in the Metropolitan Museum of Art? Now swimming in confusion, I feel I am at the bottom of the ocean and the light of the sky far above is Violet's voice, summoning me from my breathlessness of leagues below sea level to the surface of reality, of life. I burst up like a water-deprived fish, gills gasping, from submarine levels into the sharp air of consciousness.

I wake up. And get out of bed to go get my daughter.

Forty-two

"This is normal."

"No, it's not, Leigh. I am a married woman!" I said, shaking my head that afternoon as Violet played with her blocks. "I love Josh. I never fantasize about other people."

I twisted the phone cord in my fingers, guiltily recalling an Adrian Grenier cameo one night, or two.

"Then you're a freak!" she exclaimed. "Fantasy is healthy, Hannah! It's okay, you just feel guilty 'cause it's someone you know and not Orlando Bloom like every other woman."

"I guess."

"Remember in school you once had that crazy sex dream about that nerdy lab partner of yours where you guys smash all the test tubes onto the lab floor and fuck on the counter next to the Bunsen burners?"

"Thanks for bringing that up."

"No, but what I'm saying is, it's all meaningless! It's not like you secretly wanted that loser! Don't overanalyze. It's your dream, that's all! It's not some betrayal."

"I think I haven't slept that soundly in a while. I was in shock for the first ten minutes. I never even remember my dreams. It wasn't until I felt the cold refrigerator air on me getting Violet's bottle that I realized it was all fake."

"It's a good thing, Hannah! The science geek, you wanted to boil yourself after. This is at least a hot guy. I wish I could have a dream like that."

"Gosh, I can't even think about this. All right, I'll see you tonight, I gotta go."

I hung up and got on the floor with Violet. As I built the tower of blocks higher and higher and she stood on her tippy toes to carefully place the next one, I thought it would topple. I felt as off-kilter as her blocks. And just as I was starting to take a deep breath to calm myself, they all fell down.

Forty-three

Still oddly groggy from my unsettling X-rated dream, I took Violet to scope our would-be apartment and take some measurements. Troy had told us the board would be convening that very week and then not again for two months, so they agreed to meet us based on our financial package, even though our social letters weren't in. A response would be forthcoming, pending our complete file. I was relieved to be a step closer to turning the key on a real home, but it still seemed a remote possibility. Nevertheless, I already felt a connection to the building. The doorman, Tony, was so nice, and the place seemed warm and homey. The super was in the lobby and told me Tony had just stepped out, but he managed to find the key in a lockbox in the lobby, and since we'd plonked down 10 percent already and the family had cleared out of there for Europe a week before, I felt entitled to wander and imagine our roots there and life beyond a tragic white-box corporate apartment. The super patted Violet's head and said, "This is going to be your new home!" I just prayed that was true—that we would survive the board's grilling.

When we got upstairs I was fumbling with a key ring that had ten keys on it. As I opened the door, I heard a laugh and was surprised to see Troy in the living room. Could he still be showing the place? I was stunned. Then I saw his "client" was none other than Bee.

"Oh, hi . . ." I said, coolly. What the *eff* were they doing here? I knew she was not a threat to buy it out from under us because she would only leave her palatial spread for something grander, and this joint was half the size. Violet hopped out of the stroller and ran around them as I stood still.

"Hannah, hi," Troy said nervously, with his British accent extra clipped. "I just wanted to show Bee your apartment, since I had the key . . ."

"Uh-huh."

"It's really nice," said Bee. "I didn't know the apartments in here were so spacious. I mean, it's such a random building."

I wasn't quite sure what *random* meant but it didn't sound good. "Well, I just needed to get some measurements . . ." I said, and walked by them to the bedroom.

"Okeydokey then, Hannah, I'll call you before your board meeting in a couple days," said Troy as the two of them walked out and closed the door behind them. Wow. I did not appreciate my broker sneaking in Bee. I know there was no lawyer or doctor-patient privilege but it somehow felt creepy and un-kosher to me. She had probably begged him so she could scope out the digs—I knew she was obsessed with how people

lived since she always seemed to be making editorial comments about people's apartments, taste, bank accounts, etc.
Hmph.

Troy and I never did connect before the board meeting.
We traded calls and I grew more and more frantic, literally asking him on his voice mail to leave me any tips I
should know. I still was bitter that he'd showed Bee our
apartment; the more I thought about it, the weirder it
seemed, and I was pissed he didn't seem to be making an effort to reach me.

I had read Josh the riot act about not being late for our interview, and he thankfully showed up on time, kissing me on
the cheek as we entered the lobby with twenty seconds to
spare.

Maggie had told me the interview was really more of a
welcome-to-the-building cocktail party. That simply was not
the case.

We walked in to find five men, all in pressed suits. All were
bankers. Sorry, one was a real-estate lawyer: the host and
chairman of the board, who had basically told his wife to
skedaddle so he could have the meeting in their living room,
which was all white. I mean everything. I thought I was either
in an Ian Schrager hotel or a mental institution. I'd worn my
cool knee-high leather boots (which Leigh called my "Fuck

You Boots") 'cause they were so badass. Plus, I was a full four inches taller and I felt very confident and put together compared with my usual sweatpants/mom-bun self. Not so fast, Hannah.

"Excuse me, Mrs. Allen," the host, Wynn Sutherland, said, looking me over. "Can you both please take off your boots? This is a shoe-free household."

I took a deep breath and exhaled my rage. Josh clearly sensed this and smiled.

"I hope you don't have a run in your stocking," joked another suit. And just as the words came out of his Locust Valley lockjaw, I remembered. I realized that, yes, in fact I did have a fucking inch-long run. Right down the front of my calf. I'd kept a stash of messed up Pat Benatar–esque pantyhose to wear specifically with pants and these boots. Naturally I didn't think I would be asked to de-shoe, as this is not Osaka.

I calmly unzipped my boots, revealing the gaping punk-rock run, and quietly sat down. Josh smiled; I thought he would lose it. I flared my nostrils.

The five board members reclined on an overstuffed white couch and two flanking white armchairs. We were offered a bench. Yes, a hemorrhoid-inducing modern, cushionless wooden bench. I don't care what fancy designer fashioned it, the thing was painful.

"So," Wynn began, sipping his seltzer (we weren't offered any). "Hannah, you're just a mom, right?"

Just a mom. Words of death. "Yes, well, I have a deg—"

"Uh-huh. And Josh, you're down at Jupiter Capital?"

The next forty-five minutes involved Josh talking and me nodding like the good wife. And trying to cover up the flesh showing through my ripped tights. I felt invisible. Fuck these people. Did I even want to be in a building with them anyway? I'd never seen anyone before when I'd visited. I guess even though they're on top of one another, neighbors don't really hang. In fact, they don't even seem to see each other in the elevator.

Finally, as everything wound down to a close, one of the interviewers asked about Violet. Where did she go to school? When Josh mentioned Milford Prescott, well, he gushed.

"Our little Wynn the fourth—Quattro we call him—just loved it there. Great place." He winked at me. Was that a sign that we were in the building? I was starting to see how all these parents use these schools as a club of sorts to seal people in as their "kind."

Out on the street, Josh razzed me, laughing about my tights.

"I'm sorry, but this isn't fucking Japan!" I ranted as he giggled, trying to console me.

"Sweets, it wasn't a big deal."

"Yes it was! I studied art history. And taking one's shoes off is a sign of humility. I was humiliated!"

"Oh please, can it with the iconography," he teased, hugging me.

"I'm serious! Don't laugh! It was all about you in there. I was frigging cellophane. You heard him, 'just' a mom."

"Don't let this get to you. It's just part of the game to get the apartment we love."

"There's a game here for everything, isn't there?"

AND SO MUCH FOR BOARD CONFIDENTIALITY . . .

Instant Message from: BeeElliott

> BeeElliott: So I heard you wrote a board
> letter for Hannah and Josh Allen?
> Maggs10021: Yes!
> BeeElliott: How did that happen? God she's so
> aggro to ask you!
> Maggs10021: I didn't mind, no trouble at all—
> BeeElliott: That building is nice but no
> great shakes.
> Maggs10021: I like it! Clara Peacock lived
> there before they moved to Greenwich.
> BeeElliott: Whatever. Poor Josh. He's buying
> her this pad and doesn't even know she's fully
> cheating.
> Maggs10021: Are you sure? I can't see that.
> BeeElliott: I'm going to tell Park about when
> I saw her with that guy. I hadn't told him. But
> the more I think about it, the more I think Josh
> should know.
> Maggs10021: Bee, don't do it—it's none of
> your biz.
> BeeElliott: Josh is our friend. What if she
> gives him some disease? It's his best friend,
> Parker needs to know.

Forty-four

Once again, at the worst time ever, Lila popped by to see Violet, toting a bag with an impossibly impractical smocked silk dress for her to wear.

"Hello," she said, waltzing by me, surveying the room, which, naturally as it was first thing in the morning, looked not unlike Afghanistan.

"Lila!" Violet said, running to give her a hug. Her fingers still sticky with oatmeal, her embrace made her grandmother practically recoil in horror, lest her linen suit be tarnished with stray oats.

"Can I get you anything to drink?" I offered.

"Some San Pellegrino would be lovely," she said.

Um . . . no Pellegrino. How about . . . tap water or tap water? "Oh, we just ran out," I lied. "We have some flat water? Or juice? We have apple and orange—"

"Juice? Heavens no, thank you. That is simply loaded with sugar! Please tell me you don't give Violet that garbage. It's full of high-fructose corn syrup. Bee said when they give out the apple juice during snack time at Carnegie she has the teacher get Weston's thermos of ice water. *Much* healthier."

Rage was boiling up inside my veins. "You know, Lila," I said, with my utmost restraint. "A little juice never killed anyone. I practically chugged Red Cheek as a child and I'm fine."

She sneered, looking me over, saying nothing. And in that moment, I knew. I knew she thought I was a big fat juice-

guzzling bovine unworthy of Josh, unworthy of this neighborhood.

"On another topic," she said, abruptly switching gears. "I
saw Bee and her mother yesterday and she mentioned that
these days it is absolutely necessary to write a first-choice
letter."

"For the schools, you mean?"

"Yes. You must write Carnegie and let them know at once
that it is without a doubt your first choice."

"But . . . I don't know if it is—"

"Listen, *Hannah*," she said, as if the letters of my name
spelled D-O-O-D-Y. "You can't waste time on this. We are
talking about Violet's education and this process is not to be
taken lightly!"

"I'm not taking it lightly! I'm just not sure it's our first
choice. It's something for me to discuss with Josh when he gets
back."

Now she was furious. "The women are customarily in
charge of such things. It is to be written on your stationery,
which I am happy to order for you since I recall your foldover
monogrammed cards to be of flimsy cardstock. It must be engraved, a nice card. I'll take care of it."

I couldn't believe this bitch. Marching into my house,
telling me I had crappyass grade-D paper, taste, body weight,
and mothering skills.

"Lila," I said, near the point of literally bludgeoning her.
"I'm so sorry but Violet and I have to go, we have class and can
discuss this later."

"Yes, we will," she said, rising to leave. "When Josh has
some free time this weekend, I think we should all sit down."

Forty-five

The next day was a frenzy of class uptown at Milford Prescott, dry-cleaning, and grocery shopping—Violet loved the Food Emporium because they had teeny tiny shopping carts with flags that said "Customer in Training." The good news was, she was elated. The bad news was, it took two hours to get out of there since she was charging down the aisles, almost steam-rollering over old ladies and nannies with two-page shopping lists. We got home and I started unpacking the food, deciding what to cook. I hadn't heard from Josh all afternoon. I had left him two messages and was making a nice dinner—well, to the best of my abilities—and was dialing his cell when I heard him come in. It was eight o'clock, which was very early for Josh to come home, and I was thrilled.

"Joshie, is that you?" I called. "Miracle!"

I ran up to him and his face was wet from the rain outside.

"Hi sweets! This is so great you're home!" I said, going to give him a hug. But just as I was leaning in, I noticed his face was stone-still and cold. He put his arm out to stop me from embracing him.

"Don't."

"What's wrong?"

He inhaled sharply, looking very angry. I started to worry something bad had happened at work. But I had no idea what was about to go down.

"Hannah," he started. "I know about you and Tate Hayes."

"What about him?"

"That you're . . . seeing each other."

What? My blood froze in every artery.

"That's crazy, we're not ha—"

"Don't say that. Hannah, I *know.* Don't you understand? I know for a fact."

"Well, you're wrong! Sweetie, I *swear* I didn't touch him—"

"First you're going to museums, then you're so close he's suddenly writing a board letter, then I find out you see him outside of museums, you kiss—"

"*Kiss?* Josh, it never happened! I mean, yes, we've been spending time together but it's chaste—what was I supposed to do? I move here because of you and you work 'til midnight! I'm alone all the time."

"So you fuck your old professor?" He looked as if he might cry.

"I didn't!" I now had full tears pouring down my face because I felt so horribly guilty about my dream.

"You were my best friend," he said, shaking his head. "We used to be like a team, and over the last few months, you've . . . pulled away. Don't deny it, Hannah. We speak less and less during the day—"

"Because you're in meetings! I can never get you on the phone!"

"And now I know you are spending time with this guy you told me you used to idolize. Turn the tables, Hannah! How would you like it if I were doing that? While you were working sixteen-hour days?"

I stood shaking, my world caving in. I was traumatized on

so many levels but my core, my rock, was always Josh and to see that cracking was too much to bear.

"I have to go to Switzerland tonight, I have to pack. They needed someone to go and I volunteered since I can't even look at you right now."

"What? *Tonight?*"

"I'm on the eleven fifty-five P.M. flight."

"You can't leave now. We need to talk about this. Sweetie, you are my life! I swear nothing ever happened with Tate!"

"Right, it's *Tate* now. I can't talk to you right now, I'm beyond exhausted."

"Sweetie." I reached out, sobbing.

"I'll be back in two days and we can discuss it then."

I was now seriously bawling, crying as I followed him around begging him not to go.

In a whirl of zipping bags and buttoned coat, my husband kissed Violet and walked to the door.

"Josh, I love you" was all my sobbing, fatigued, eyebagged self could muster.

He exhaled, his face weary with sadness. "I love you, too," he said. As the elevator doors closed, we shared a look into each other's eyes but it was weighty with regret and fear and doubt. I doubted he believed me. I doubted my own status as a good wife. I doubted I could ever live without Josh.

Forty-six

I picked myself up the next morning when Violet woke up and after breakfast I staggered along Lexington Avenue with the surreal feeling that I was watching a door close in slow motion. And of course, it is only after it's closed that you freak. I crossed the street and the flashing orange Don't Walk was hypnotic and silent, and the sirens, screeching cabs, and pedestrians faded into a blur as if I'd pressed a giant mute button on the world around me. The only sounds were my racing pulse and heavy breath. When I said I couldn't remember my life before Josh, I wasn't exaggerating.

Josh and I had met at a party as the dot-com bubble was about to burst and people were still throwing insane over-the-top ragers all around San Francisco. Bands would play 'til the wee hours, there was booze aplenty, and everyone was wearing T-shirts or hats with their company's Web site on it. Basically it had been nerds on parade, partying to make up the time they'd lost with their noses in books. Now they were rocking out, pinching themselves that their IPOs were imminent and the geek would inherit the earth, short of a few golden handcuffs due to rules on vesting stock.

In a room in the Marina jammed with fleece, where I truly thought that if someone coughed a Teva might fly out of his throat, I sat on a Crate and Barrel couch watching a crowd that had no shortage of white baseball hats and khaki.

I remember I was party-locked talking to this one girl who

was a designer of Swiss Army knives. Weird. I mean, aren't they all the same? What, does she decide to add letter openers this year or make them blue instead of red? It was like saying "I design Birkenstocks" or "scissors." What's to design? She was droning on and on about the different sizes when I saw Josh walk in. He had a smile as long as the Golden Gate bridge, minus the Don't Jump signs.

We made fleeting eye contact a few times but I would never have had the balls to just go up to him, particularly when he was talking to a couple giggly blondes who had seemed to master the laugh with head thrown back slash hairflip all in one. I could tell even from fifteen feet that his charisma and charm were infectious.

The food at the party sucked (naturally there were way more cocktails than snackables), so I had my fingers in a tiny box of raisins that I always carried around like a six-year-old. I still credit those raisins to this day, because before I knew it, Josh had crossed the room and introduced himself to me and Swiss Army knife designer girl.

"A raisin eater," he said, smiling. "A gal after my own heart."

"Yes, I'm kind of a raisin addict," I said, semi-mortified at my own uncoolness, though psyched he was a co-lover of the grape, meaning raisins not wine. "I always have these little red boxes strewn around."

"Sun-Maid is super nineteen hundreds, though," he said curiously. "Haven't you ever had Pavich raisins?"

"What? No. What are those?"

Swiss Army girl, finding the line of convo clearly way too loserish for words, got up to go bore someone else.

"You're kidding. You love raisins and haven't had Pavich? You're crazy. They kick those red boxes' ass."

"Well, I love Sun-Maid. I'm really into brand loyalty."

After an hour of convo with him, I got that sudden fevered buzz when you realize, *Wow, I've been talking to this guy for a while now.* There was mucho ST (sexual tension) and I was nervously pumped; I even remember my friend Eliza and her boyfriend giving me a sly thumbs-up behind Josh's fluffy head. But damn, I was always the worst flirt on the planet. I am incapable of the head thrown back with laughter, the eyelids at half-mast/come-hither special, or the hair flip slash smile. No games, no *The Rules* horseshit, no strategy. Which is why I often screwed up, letting the floodgates open too early, scaring some guys away with my affectionate ways. Because I'd spied Josh talking to the Muffies across the party, I suddenly had visions of him limboing with Hawaiian Tropics contest winners with golden tans and ass-length platinum corn-silk locks, and convinced myself he'd never be into me.

When the party was winding down he asked me for my e-mail, and when he heard I was at Berkeley, he said he was up there often and that maybe we could get coffee.

By this point, Tate Hayes had already left for New York, and my love life had been rocky ever since. Until Josh. On Monday, after gliding through a class flickered with thoughts about him, I went to my mailbox and saw a can of Pavich raisins sitting in it. A small note was affixed that said "Time to try the real thing, The Raisin Tsar." I turned over the card and the other side was Josh's business card with all his info. Nervous and excited, I opened the can. The sweetness of the natural

confection made me shiver with crush—I prayed it was a por-
tent of more deliciousness with him to come. I went home and
turned on my computer to e-mail him.

> Raisin Tsar,
> Your noble shriveled-grape highness, I humbly retract
> my statement praising the virtues of shabby-ass Sun-
> Maids. Long-live plump Pavich perfection.
> Your loyal subject, ever in gratitude, Hannah Greene

I hit send and worked the morning away until my stomach
started giving me a shoutout. As I was reaching for the raisin
can for another handful, my e-mail chimed with the familiar
happy sound of "shwing!"

> His Majesty would like to see if thou art hungry for dinner.

I wrote back "Absosmurfly," suspecting that as a child of
the eighties he'd get it, and sat waiting for a response, squirm-
ing in my seat with *Rocky Horror*—style antici . . . pation.

We met two hours later and seconds after we'd said hello on
a street corner, a thundercloud burst, and like a cartoon, I literally saw the jagged lightning line and it started pouring tor-
rential, flooding rain. We were closer to a gross deli than
anywhere else, so we bolted toward the teal neon sign in the
distance, screaming. We arrived soaked and panting from the
Carl Lewis sprint.

"Holy shit!" bleated a wet Josh. "I feel like Dan Aykroyd in
Trading Places in the wet Santa suit!"

I paused. *He likes movies*. "I was thinking John Cusack in *The Sure Thing* when they're stranded on the side of the road," I said.

"Good one," he smiled. His wet hair flopped on his face and his eyes looked greener against his red cheeks splattered by cold rain.

I was so freezing I grabbed a styro cup and went over to the hot chocolate machine. "Oh, yes!" said Josh. "Machine hot chocolate is the best thing."

"I know it—machine ho-cho is nectar of the gods." This guy seemingly had my identical taste buds grafted onto his tongue.

"My friends and I were so addicted to this shit at Stanford that we made friends with a dude in the kitchen and during the summer he smuggled us a machine and we had it in our house."

"Oh my God, that's my dream! Except I'd probably drink myself into a Roseanne Barr state."

"Like you have anything to worry about," said Josh, looking at me.

I looked down, bashful and now officially in crush mode. We walked to a cute café and plopped and talked for three hours, with topics ranging from movies (a shared love of everything from Woody Allen to *Goodfellas*), to childhood pets (me: a goldfish named Billy Ocean, him: a golden retriever named Topaz), to work, ex-flames, family, friends, New York, skiing, and ethnic food (the spicier, the better). He drove me home, leaning in for a peck on the cheek before saying bye. I hopped upstairs, went through my mail, and curled up in bed with a Pottery Barn catalog. I was looking at the monogrammed towels when the phone rang at eleven forty-five P.M., startling me since it was way after anyone ever called.

"Sorry to call late," said Josh. "I just wanted to . . . make sure you got upstairs okay. No monsters in the closet."

"Oh, you are so cute. No monsters so far." I could feel myself blushing.

"Oh good. So . . . whatcha doing?" he asked.

"Oh, nothing," I lied. I had been fully thinking about what my married-to-Josh monogram would be on those towels. "How about you?"

"Channel 11, *Star Wars*." He had clearly found his late-night viewing pleasure.

"I never got into that."

"What? Are you American? You sinner. Who isn't into *Star Wars*? You should be arrested."

"I'm sorry," I said. "I hate space. That's one of my rules, no space."

"My heart is breaking. Carrie Fisher was my first love."

"Sorry," I said, wondering if my hair was long enough to put into those braids. "I hate the future, I hate animals that talk, I hate sci-fi, I hate magic, I hate flying things, I hate spells—"

"You are missing out."

"Well, I will leave you to spank it to Princess Leia, then."

He laughed. "Oh come on, watch it with me a little . . ."

I reluctantly tuned in and watched a little. Okay: Harrison Ford was so cute.

"How weird that he was a carpenter before this," I mused.

"So weird. And he's been in so many amazing movies."

I watched for fifteen minutes. Chewbacca roared, R2D2 squealed out some whirrs and beep-beeps, C3PO unleashed some computer British accent, and I . . . dozed off.

"Are you there?" asked Josh.

"Oh yeah, sorry, I'm drifting. I might have to go snooze."

"Okay, well, we tried, didn't we, Chewy?"

I laughed and said good night.

"Good night, Hannah."

Forty-seven

The next day, I walked with Violet to meet Bee and Maggie and within minutes they asked me what was wrong.

"Oh, I don't know," I lied; I would never tell them I was panicking that Josh would leave me and that my whole life was swirling down the toilet bowl. "Just stressed, I guess."

"You know, Hannah, not that it's any of my business," said Bee, a statement that is always followed by the word *but*. "But maybe you should consider working out sometimes. I mean, Maggie and I have our Pilates and yoga twice a week and it seriously helps with all the pressures we face."

"It really does," attested Maggie. "Come with us!"

I shrugged, saying maybe, when the truth was I knew I wasn't into it. There was no way I'd hook my ass up to one of those *Star 80* creepy Frankenstein machines for a hundred smacks an hour, no thank you.

Lara and Hallie strolled up a few minutes later, Hallie announcing her in-laws had bought Julia Charlotte two ponies for her to play with at their weekend house in Millbrook. As I was about to gag, Lara said that her son had taken up violin and was loving it, already learning some complicated sonata. It was kind of weird to picture a three-year-old toting a violin case, but whatever floats your yacht.

"Oh, and we just got this stunning pure-bred Cavalier King Charles spaniel," Lara excitedly reported. "It's a Christmas present. We named him Jeter. My husband loves to walk him at night. It's so funny—I hired a dog-walker but he just walks alongside her—he holds Jeter's leash and the gal scoops the poop! So funny."

Luckily, sparing me any more reports about Lara's and Hallie's prodigies and their bratty gifts, Violet started asking for lunch, which made for a graceful exit. I walked her home to Amber and read her some books before she fell asleep for her afternoon nap. I snuck out so I could get a manicure and some personal maintenance stuff (read: pit wax). But as I walked by the manicure place on Lexington, I saw that Hallie and Lara were in there gabbing away and I simply couldn't face it. I felt so down and depressed, and the last thing I needed were tales of Julia Charlotte's perfect use of chopsticks or discussions of how clever the new documentary on Saudi weaponmakers was. So I just kept walking. My feet just moved in a straight line until I stopped when I saw some women holding yoga mats opening the door to a studio. I figured it wasn't possible for me to be more stressed than I was at that moment, so I peered through the window and saw Nuala-clad women cheerily bouncing up a flight of stairs to the yoga center.

I was wearing sweats and a hooded zipper sweatshirt anyway, and Bee and Maggie had planted the seed about working out, which kind of did make sense. I thought that maybe I should see what the goddamn fuss was all about. While my initial inclination was to bash yoga, I knew that all those millions of skinny chicks couldn't be wrong, so I spontaneously entered the two fifteen class. I felt nervously excited as I watched everyone spread out their mats and the instructor, Raven, took the front of the room. She had a soothing way about her and I knew I'd done the right thing by coming to this class. Lots of women, strong urban women, and I was part of the group. Anyone was welcome, it was all about open arms and accepting hearts. Let the *om*s begin!

After about fifteen minutes I wanted to kill myself. Raven cooed her instructions and softly whispered for us to "get into the moment" and find ourselves "in the space between the inhalation and the exhalation" and "surrender to the forces that inhibit our bodies from being what they can be."

Garbage. Raven turned the temperature of the room up to like a hundred degrees and I was literally in a steamy jungle of feet and ass. It was a fucking sauna and the one man in the class was next to me, grunting and moaning the whole time like a wuss loser. I felt the germs of every rectum in my face and the sticky toes of the butch woman with pigtails on the other side of me. I sat there in my poses thinking that my thighs were killing me and my butt was aching and my back was about to die and my life's in shambles and this sucks ass and all I want to do is sneak out and go to Häagen-Dazs.

What did Raven mean when she said to find my inner being? My inner being wanted to get the fuck out of here. So I left after a half hour, figuring I'd already wasted my thirty bucks and I didn't also need to waste my time. The teaching assistant followed me out of the studio, stomping in her crocheted leg warmers, enraged.

"You know, leaving early like that really disturbs the peace of the class. It's just quite selfish, really."

"Oh my God, I am so sorry," I said, feeling embarrassed. "I just couldn't get into it. I'm sorry." Oops.

"Well maybe if you gave it a full chance it would have worked for you." She gave me an evil look-over. I felt like telling her to go fuck off and do some chants but I just smiled knowing I wasn't going back to her flakey shithole sauna anyway.

I walked home, sweaty and disgusting, feeling even worse than before. I was so mortified from the run-in with the yoga TA, I felt my cheeks heat up and I started to cry. I knew my period was around the corner and hoped it was just PMS, but I knew deep down this was way heavier than that: my marriage, my perfect marriage, was on the rocks, and it was my fault. Josh was right, I would be pissed if he was romping in museums with some old flame–type. I would be horrified and beyond devastated if he had a sex dream about her, no matter what Leigh said about it being normal. And I shook with the thought of him upset—and alone—in Switzerland. Hysterically crying, I hailed a cab. I had to tell Tate Hayes that we couldn't spend time together anymore.

Forty-eight

Still in my disgusting sweats, I paid the cab driver and ran up the steps to the art history department. I wandered by a classroom, thinking Tate might still be in class, but the lecture hall was empty. I walked to his office and the door was ajar. I knocked as I opened it to find Tate sitting in his cognac leather chair.

"Ahhh, Hannah! Here, I have your co-op board letter."

I took it and nodded quietly, putting it in my bag.

"Are you okay?" he asked, noticing my stressed face. "Sit, sit."

But I couldn't sit. I was too revved up and paced his office like an inmate in Bellevue. "Thank you for this. I'm kind of . . . going through . . . a bad moment, I guess. Sorry."

"What's wrong?" he asked, looking concerned and upset to see me upset.

"I'm just so depressed! I'm going through a lot, and Josh and I are . . . having issues and I'm just so down!" I started to cry. Not just one or two tears but streams. I wanted him to be my shrink so I could get out all my problems: Lila, the Momzillas, the pressure.

He got up with a tissue. I was so grateful to have him there, a safe place with a wise soul to help me.

And then, as I reached for the tissue to wipe my eyes, he grabbed me and kissed me.

I pushed him off, stunned. "Tate, no! That's not why I'm here—"

"I know you've thought about it. All those years ago? Is that a distant memory for you now?" he asked, touching my hair.

But as much as I felt broken and alone and desperate for human connection at that moment, as much as he had always been this fantasy for me, I was repulsed. Not because he wasn't gorgeous or brilliant. But because he wasn't Josh. Here he was, trying to cheat on his wife. And I could never do the same. I just wasn't wired that way.

"No, I just . . . can't. I can't see you anymore," I said firmly. And as the words came out of my mouth, even though I had recently lived for our time together, I truly didn't want to see him anymore. "But thank you for everything. Our time together has been very fulfilling to me, and I'm grateful, but . . . I love my husband," I said, tears pouring out. "I love Josh."

"Oh come on, Hannah. Don't tell you subscribe to this bourgeois notion of a perfect marriage."

"I do," I said, realizing suddenly that he'd obviously strayed during his wife's frequent trips to Italy.

"Well then, I'm sorry—"

"Me, too," I said. I turned and left, closing the door on Tate Hayes.

I opened my cell phone, panting, dialing Leigh to fill her in. On everything. Within an hour she was at my apartment and we spoke in hushed tones as Violet played with her dollhouse on the floor.

"Okay, let's just calm down," she said, putting a hand on my quivering knee, as I not-so-expertly tried to cry covertly. "You didn't *do* anything, right? You know you can tell me."

"*Leigh!*" I snapped. "Of course not. But Josh doesn't know that—he clearly thinks something happened. I mean, I told him we kissed way back when. What was I thinking spending time with Hayes? To the point where I even fantasized? I feel horrible. I am just a wr-wr-wreck," I stuttered.

"Don't worry. You guys are rock solid," she comforted.

She sat beside me and hugged me. "I have no idea where he got this," I said breathlessly. "I mean, where would a rumor like this start? I am just so angry. What makes me more angry is that while I did nothing I still feel guilty because if Josh hung out with some chick and went to museums and stuff I'd chop her head off."

"It's different with guys. For them proximity breeds intimacy. Guys don't hang out with some chick and not want to fuck them."

"I just have been so lonely. I would never cheat, I just . . . need the stimulation, you know? I was feeling so adrift."

The phone rang. Normally I would just let it go to voice mail, but I was praying it was Josh and leaped to answer.

"Hannah, hi, it's Maggie!" she said. "I just gave birth to Talbott Xavier Sinclair! Seven pounds ten ounces."

"Oh Maggie! That's so great, congrats!" I was touched she'd called me from the hospital.

"We're coming home tomorrow morning and having a sip 'n' see in the afternoon from four to six if you and Violet want to stop by."

"I'd love that," I said. "I'll see you then tomorrow at the sip 'n' see. Bye!"

"What the fuck is a sip 'n' see?" asked Leigh when I'd hung up.

"Well, most peeps don't have another baby shower for the second kid, so you go over when they're home and you *sip* tea and *see* the baby and bring presents and stuff."

"So it's basically a way for these rich moms with way too much money already to get even more loot."

"Basically."

Leigh sat with me all night and we talked about my darkest fear, of Josh leaving me. I told her that from the moment he'd entered my life, I'd felt so safe and lucky. She asked me to retell her about that moment, how Josh and I met and fell in love, to walk her through our past to help me think of a way to seal in our future. And when I finished retelling her our story, I had a lightbulb.

Forty-nine

When Josh and I had our second date a week after meeting, we ate, talked for hours, and did full A&E biographies. I learned that he had been devastated by losing his father when he was very young and that his mom, Lila, emotionally drained from the loss, was very shut off to Josh and moved him abruptly from the suburbs back to New York City at age eight.

"That's so terrible—losing your dad and leaving home, suddenly in the city?" I asked, unable to imagine.

"It was terrifying. But I almost, at that point, was numb, like nothing could get worse. And then my mom came in my room and said, 'It's time to pack up. You can take whatever you want, but it has to fit in these two suitcases.' "

"No—" I was so traumatized.

"Yeah, so I took one and filled it up with my clothes and some picture frames of us from around the house. And then I took the other suitcase and just filled it up all the way with Legos."

"Legos?"

"My dad and I would always be building weird fantasy skyscrapers. We'd commandeer the whole living room and the mess drove my mom crazy," he laughed. "But Legos have always reminded me of my dad, we'd always make these colossal projects. I guess I just thought if I brought all those little bricks with me I could rebuild my life wherever I was going." Josh stopped abruptly as he noticed that I'd let a single tear escape down my cheek, despite my valiant quest to hold it back.

"C'mon, it's okay!" he said, seemingly touched by my emotion. His cell phone rang and he turned it off.

"You can get it," I sniffed, wiping another errant tear.

"No, no, it's okay." Changing the subject, he looked at me and said, "Hannah, I really can't believe you are anti–cell phones so much. How can you survive without one? What if you needed to get ahold of someone?"

Yes, it's true: I was a cell phone holdout. I just didn't want another bill, nor did I want a Nokia-shaped tumor in my brain.

Plus, I was oddly a fan of pay phones, despite the risk of contracting Hepatitis D. "I don't know. I don't think I need one."

"Once you get one you can't imagine how you lived without it."

"So I hear."

Our next date, a few nights later, we had tickets for Nine Inch Nails, my favorite band. Seriously. Trent Reznor got me through high school, and when Josh wore an old NIN T-shirt on our second date I gushed incessantly and he said he just so happened to have a connection for hot tix. So we were going together; I was elated and took forty-five minutes to get ready, even though I still emerged looking like I'd thrown on my black jeans and blouse. He was waiting on my doorstep when I skipped down after hearing the magical sound of my buzzer, which was cacophonous torture when anyone else rang it but music when I knew it was Josh downstairs. He stood there, smiling, looking gorgeous. He somehow already felt so familiar to me; I swear I was in love with him as early as that moment.

"I have a present for you," he said mischievously.

"You do? Why?"

"Because it's time you enter our lovely millennium."

He handed me a small package with gift wrap and a bow, and I opened it to find a Virgin Mobile cell phone.

"What?" I laughed. "I can't let you get me a cell phone!"

"Why not? It's pay-as-you-go. I got you the first three months. If you hate it after ninety days, you can chuck it in the Bay."

"This is so cool and newfangled-looking. Thanks, Josh." I gave him a big hug and we started walking to the concert. "Now you have to show me how to use it, I am such a dope with techie shit."

"Right, the girl who's never had a microwave."

"My mom didn't want me to have babies with six heads."

"The phone will not send messages to your womb for extra noggins on the kiddies. Now here's what you do . . ."

He showed me how to enter my friends' numbers and I asked him to put his cell in there as well.

"Okay, you do it, then. Now press here—" He showed me.

"Okay, and then J-O-S-H, okay . . ."

I did it! I looked at the screen, proudly. "I have a phone!"

"Also, here's how you do text messaging, which is great if you can't hear your phone or you need to meet someone in a noisy place."

He typed in "Hi Hannah" on his phone and hit send. Suddenly my phone vibrated.

"Ahh!" I yelped, not feeling used to something shaking in my pocket. I thought I was being assaulted. "It's shaking! It works! How do I answer it?" I was such a raging, bumbling, incompetent idiot.

"Press the green button."

I obeyed. My face lit up with the joys of technology. "Yay, there it is, 'Hi Hannah.' That is so cool!"

"Magic."

"I am so into this!"

"See?"

We started talking about our shared excitement for the concert and then on to other affinities, which I had to remark was all very *High Fidelity*.

"Well, he was right," said Josh, smiling at me. "It's not what you're like, it's what you like that matters." I felt the same way.

What you like defines what you're like. I didn't like to get wasted every night. I liked long walks. I liked live music. I didn't like sports, except skiing. Ditto on every front with the fresh-faced boy walking next to me. And I knew I could go flying down the double-black-diamond slope of falling in desperate love with him. I needed to hold myself back so as not to smother him with worship. He was confident but so real. He spoke eloquently and yet he wasn't an uptight academic. He was strong and funny and just about the coolest human ever. I had been convinced Tate Hayes was the only man I'd ever be obsessed with but he was quickly being eclipsed.

We arrived at the venue and when the band came on, I had the exhilarated rush of seeing them live, and the hard-edged sexy grit of Reznor's voice made me feel so invigorated. And alive and sexy. As the chorus broke on the first song, the crowd cheered rowdily and I started to move to the drums. Josh was next to me and smiled brightly and I patted his arm as a blissful thank-you for taking me there, and I got lost in the grinding music and the stellar people-watching.

At the end of the song, the place went berserk. I could not have more thrilled. As the bass sounded, marking the beginning of another song, "Something I Could Never Have," I screamed with excitement and looked at Josh, who looked at me Cheshire Cat–style.

"What?" I said, but could barely hear myself. He just looked at me with his little grin.

"Nothing," he said, inaudibly over the drums, and just smiled.

I started to dance and get really into the music, and with everyone else thrashing around me, I felt totally uninhibited and electrified. As I was thinking the bliss of the moment was opium for the crowd, because I sure as hell felt high and felt like I was seventeen, I was suddenly alarmed to feel my pocket vibrating. I stopped dancing abruptly and was totally freaked out at first, like some schmuck behind me had groped me. I then remembered that I was now the proud owner of a cell phone, and I calmed down. I looked at Josh, who was looking ahead at the stage, singing. I took out my phone, which no one knew the number to yet; it must have been a wrong number. I pressed the on button, and it said "New text message." What? I hit the display button and five words came up on my little lit screen:

"I want to kiss you."

I looked up at Josh, who looked at me. He had sent it while I was thrashing around dancing in front of him. I breathed out a sigh of relief, relief that it was not all in my head, relief that love could, in fact, be that easy.

As the crowd bounced and moshed around us, we stepped toward each other, as if in slow motion. Josh took me in his arms and kissed me slowly as the world around us blurred with dark booming chords and waving limbs. We kissed and kissed through the chorus of a song and the collective pulsating of the goth crowd.

The twisting thick guitars filled the cavernous room and we

just kept kissing. There was no fear, like I'd had with Tate, no nervous, nauseous energy, just a muted elated thrill. The thrill of the best kiss I had ever had. Number one. I felt like it was what I had always wanted. It was brand spanking new and yet it felt like I was finally home.

When the concert emptied out, we could barely walk, we were macking so much. I laughed so hard at one point because one woman walked by and said, "They're sure not married!" and we burst out laughing.

"Maybe one day!" Josh yelled back to her. My insides burned with love for him and excitement over his comment (like Sloane in *Ferris Bueller*, "He's going to marry me!"). I wished I could know him all right now, download his whole life, his memories and Legos and conversations, *Matrix*-style. He was so familiar to me and it wasn't the crazy smitten melt-down of a crush, it was the mellowed bliss of finding another half. It was like: "of course."

We arrived at my door and I assumed we would go upstairs and fool around, since we were such a walking cuddlefest, but Josh stopped at the front door, holding my hand.

"Beautiful girl," he said, putting his hands on my face. I wanted to have sex that instant. "I will leave you here to get some sleep. But can I take you out Friday?"

A whole forty-eight hours! No!

"Okay, sure."

We kissed again for like fifteen minutes and I finally turned to go upstairs. I was smitten. I had to pry Cupid's arrow out of my ass cheek. I flew to my stereo to put in the song we first kissed to, so I could relive the experience. Memories are like money in a bank that you can draw upon, and I had just received a huge deposit. I had to keep revisiting the memory all night and couldn't wait to make a new addition to my vault on Friday.

It was two A.M. and I wanted to call Leigh but I knew she had work in the morning. I washed my face—though no apricot scrub could scour off my smile—and got in bed. I thought I saw stars on my ceiling. I took a deep breath and started to close my eyes, but then I suddenly heard a weird buzzing outside my bedroom.

Holy fucking shit—there was someone in my apartment! I sat up startled, my whole body frozen, thinking there was a masked burglar breaking my lock. I tiptoed out into the living room and saw the culprit. My phone was jumping on the floor, vibrating its way across the rug. Thank God. I picked it up. A text message.

"I want to kiss you more."

My whole body brightened, I was so in love with him. And I knew, to my bone marrow, that Josh would later become my husband. I smiled with excitement and was so exhilarated I could barely put the heart palpitations aside to sleep, but when I finally did, I slept soundly for the first time in over a year.

Fifty

Since I was feeling miserable and uggles, I decided to treat myself to a manicure before going to Maggie's tea party. I walked in to Trevi Nail and after the topcoat was applied to my coat of feminine Mademoiselle polish, I opted for a mini back massage. I figured I had extra time and my nails would dry as Kiki pummeled my hard-as-rock stressed back into submission as I sat facedown in the massage chair, my head in that toilet-bowl-shaped teal pillow ring. But if I thought I would get a dose of relaxation, I was sorely mistaken.

Two minutes into my massage, which felt good but had lent little relief to my situation, I heard a familiar voice enter and then get louder as it approached the manicure stations near me.

"She's just so̕oo nothing special. She and Josh are fine, but for your co-op I would want nicer families. More polished. You know, Josh's mom, Lila Allen Dillingham, is such a class act; I think she was hoping Josh would do better. She actually once told me she thought I would be perfect for Josh and that it was too bad I was taken! Isn't that funny?"

Fuck. The voice belonged to none other than Bee Elliott.

But what could I do? I was trapped with my head in the toilet bowl. My heart was racing through my chest. Sweat began to pour from each and every pore. So Lila *did* think I wasn't good enough. And not only that, she thought Bee would have been perfect for Josh. I thought I was going to have a coronary.

"Also, quite frankly," she continued with the loudest whisper I'd ever heard, "I think their marriage is on the rocks."

"Really?" asked the other woman, probably a board member's wife in our would-be building.

"I mean, he could do a lot better. You should see how she dresses her child. I mean, sweatpants! The little girls in Weston's class at Carnegie all have beautiful dresses and their hair is groomed with cute big bows. It's as if she doesn't care about her daughter's appearance! Well, she hardly cares about her own! She wears black jeans and gross T-shirts. I mean, hello? You're not in California anymore!"

I was in clinical shock. I mean, get the defibrillators pronto. If death does indeed greet one with a dizzied blur of white light, then I was certain the grim reaper was near.

"But why is the marriage on the rocks?" the woman inquired. I myself was dying to know.

"We finished," Kiki whispered to me, patting me on the back.

Without taking my head up, I said, "Keep going. Just keep going, twenty more minutes, please."

Kiki, psyched with her score of more time at a buck-a-minute, went back to her chop-chops and muscle grinding. Which were amplified within my body, as Bee's each word reverberated through my system and karate-chopped my heart.

"Well, I happened to see her with this guy," said Bee. "On Fifth Avenue. It was this tall guy with longish brown hair and a tweed jacket. They looked very much in tryst mode. I told Parker and he didn't believe me, but he said since Josh was his best friend he might let him know. I mean, how humiliating?"

So that was the answer. That lying bitch had poisoned Josh against me, that fucking evil whore.

I was sweating so much you could wring my clothes out and fill a bathtub, but I fought my own desire to stand up and ambush her. I wanted to take the metal nail file and gouge her blue eyes out and throw polish remover in the sockets. But I took a deep breath and channeled Josh. What did he always say? Don't do anything rash when you're upset. Stay calm. And what did the Godfather say? *Keep your friends close, but your enemies closer.*

Fifty-one

The doorman under the antique steel canopy of the Sinclairs' Fifth Avenue building buzzed Violet and me up to the tea party, which was packed with not only beautiful children and their Chanel-suited moms but also an explosion of presents. Tiffany blue and Cartier red packed the Colefax-and-Fowler-papered foyer. In the living room, there was a double stroller with a huge bow, shrink-wrapped baskets of pale blue onesies, and a huge teddy bear wearing a cashmere sweater that had "Talbott" embroidered on it.

Clearly the tiny Lacoste shirt I'd brought was very Little League in comparison. So many New York women (like the ones at this party) dressed their boys in kinda pansy-ass ruffles and bows. If I had a boy, I'd do long-sleeved T-shirts, cords, sneaks, not Little Lord Fauntleroy explosions of lace and velvet-covered buttons.

Violet was overjoyed at the scene and immediately went up to one of the little girls; luckily she was unable to read the bubbling lava pit of rage that was locked inside me. She took the girl's hand and they played on the mat as a balloon blower made them hats. I watched her play and interact with the children; she was so loving, always hugging the other kids, wanting to hold their hands. I noticed that none of the other moms seemed to even look at their kids at all; most had nannies in starched uniforms watching over them anyway so they could socialize—and sip 'n' see—but even the ones who just were (gasp!) solo with their kids barely glanced in their direction. I was scanning the room—it was mostly women I didn't know—when I saw Hallie.

"Hi, Hannah," she said looking me over. "So, how're pre-school interviews?"

Naturally it was her first question, before, say, *How are you?*

"Oh, fine," I said. "You know."

"How many letters do you have for each school? Like Carnegie, how many letters?" I had gathered people generally got recommendations from current parents. Naturally, since I didn't have friends close enough to ask (plus I'd already asked Maggie for our co-op board) my file contained exactly zero.

"Um, not many . . ." I said, meaning none.

"So is Carnegie your first choice? The second I saw it, I knew Julia Charlotte had to go there. Are you going to write a first-choice letter?"

"I'm not sure."

Lara approached, hearing the convo. "Ooooh, Hannah," she interjected, holding a glass of chardonnay. "You must must must write a first-choice letter to Carnegie, it will totally up your chances."

"But . . . I don't know if it is my first choice. I loved the other schools, too—especially Browne-Madison. It seemed very Violet—warm, nurturing, even more than Carnegie. I mean, the building's not as grand but it's still cute."

"*Browne-Madison?*" Hallie said with disbelief. "Hannah, they may be all artsy and loosey-goosey and whatever, but their kindergarten placement is really B."

"Well, you simply cannot send your child to Browne-Madison over Carnegie," Lara said. "It's, like, against the law, that's like turning down Harvard for Hamilton."

I was quiet.

"Seriously, Hannah," Hallie said. "First-choice letters are *key*. You have to let Mrs. Kincaid know without a doubt that you will matriculate should she offer you a place."

"Okay, thanks," I said, not listening and just looking for Maggie, who I seriously needed to sit down with.

"Browne-Madison is a total level down," said Lara. "Don't you want Violet at a top-notch school so she can sail into the continuing school of your choice?"

"I guess."

"So Hal," Lara said abruptly, looking at Hallie. "Are you so excited for Christmas vacation? Where are you guys going again, Cap Juluca?"

"You know, we did that last year, so we decided on Mill Reef this year," Hallie said, squeezing her lemon wedge into her Perrier. "Ugh, I have been so stressed out over this trip! I was late because I've been FedExing color samples and fabric swatches to JetSet Baby all morning."

"Oh, aren't they the best?" Lara exclaimed. "We live for JetSet Baby—that company is truly a godsend. Hannah, you must use them when you travel next."

"What do they do?" I wondered.

"It's brilliant," Hallie pronounced. "It's a service that helps you with child adjustment when you travel. Dr. Poundschlosser recommended them. It's a truly gifted team of designers who come to your house and take a hundred photographs of your child's nusery. Then they repaint your hotel room the color of your child's room at home and make slipcovers for all the furniture in your fabrics, so your child feels at home and isn't alarmed."

In a word: *Ew*.

I was stunned. They would die if they saw Violet's unpainted makeshift "nursery," which was basically a crib in a room. "How much does that cost?" I thought, immediately feeling tacky for asking—reminded of that expression that if you have to even ask, you can't afford it. But hey, I simply had to know what these women shelled out for "child adjustment" on a ten-day vaycay.

"It's not bad," shrugged Lara. "Ten thousand, give or take, depending on your fabrics."

My face belied my disgust. I didn't even have to say *yikes*, but I did.

"Well, I'm sorry—but they do sleep better because of it," Hallie said defensively, possibly understanding how insane this was. Or not. "One simply cannot put a price tag on sleep."

"Oh, I know it!" added Lara. "When my son was little, we paid the baby nurse extra to walk with him in the Baby Björn on the treadmill in our gym so that he'd fall asleep! Money well spent, I say."

As I pictured some poor exhausted Malaysian woman hoofing it in her white uniform on their treadmill, I spied Maggie coming over. Thank goodness.

"There you are!" said Maggie, walking over in a Diane Von Furstenberg wrap dress. Save for a little bump, she looked so thin it was hardly as if she'd just borne fruit forty-eight hours before.

"You looking amazing, Maggie. Wow," I said. "I hope I look like that when I've had two kids."

"Doesn't she look stickish? You'll definitely be KMBC, Kate Moss by Christmas," said Lara, waving to a new party entrant.

She and Hallie ran off to hug the woman who entered and Maggie smiled at me, seeming to sense I was relieved to see her. "Congratulations," I said, hugging her.

"How're you doing?" she asked me.

"Um, okay, I guess," I shrugged. "Aside from the fact that Hallie and Lara just ambushed me about preschools. We are so getting shut out. We have no letters! They made it sound as if I needed recommendations from the entire Verizon white pages!"

"Please, they are freaks," Maggie whispered, shaking her head. "Tune them out. Plus, maybe these preschools care about social connections now. But the kindergartens won't. And if they try their mob strategy, it will fail; I always think the thicker the file, the thicker the kid."

I smiled, but then the chill that had been plaguing me set in once again. "Where's Bee?" I asked, looking around the room.

"Hannah," she said, looking both ways spylike. "Let's camp out in my room for a sec."

"Yes! I really need to talk to you—"

I got the nervous energy bolt through my body as I followed her past the crowd, which included pearl-stud-wearing blondes and a Malaysian baby nurse holding tiny Talbott, into her bedroom, which was a lavish pale-blue-and-beige confection of toile fabrics, soft carpets, and a dreamyland princess canopy bed.

"I've been dying to call you but I know you just had a baby and are swamped," I said, heart racing. "But I have to talk to you. Something happened."

"What?"

I relayed my manicure story, and, while horrified, Maggie

didn't seem surprised. That was because she'd heard it all already.

"Listen, Hannah," she said, putting a hand on my knee as I wiped errant tears I'd vowed not to cry. "I know. I know everything. Bee is a mean, mean girl. I guess I've known it all along and secretly hated her, but I was always too scared of her to do anything about it."

"Can you imagine being so psycho and evil?" I said, still in shock.

"It's not you. It's her. She's a miserable person," said Maggie. "She's always been perfect and wants to be the only one with the good life, but it's all a lie. Hannah, *she's* the one who's cheating."

What?

"She's been sleeping with Troy Kincaid for over nine months."

"She has?" I was stunned; a JetSet Baby fabric swatch could have knocked me to the floor. Incredulous. In shock. So, the flawless Ralph Lauren family wasn't so picture perfect. "Poor Park! Oh my God! Maggie, I walked in on Troy quote 'showing her my apartment': God how dumb am I?" I was reeling. They fucking did it on my floor, those jerks.

I was literally about to keel over.

"Wait, it gets worse," she said quietly.

"What could be worse than being a compulsive liar who screwed someone else's husband?" I asked.

"She tried to screw yours as well."

Beat. Times ten. She *what*? Josh?

"It was before you were technically married, though," Maggie said. "When he was home once for some meeting and you were out west, she was hammered and totally made a pass at

Josh. I actually thought she had harbored a crush on him from grade school or something," she continued. "But he fully shut her down. I think that's why she kind of had it out for you from the moment you got here."

"Bee had it out for me from day one?" My heart was pounding through my chest as I began to crumble to pieces. "She deserves an Oscar for that performance. Showing me the ropes, what bullshit." The toile-covered room swirled as I felt faint.

"Hannah, there's something I have to show you," said Maggie, who got up and opened a beautiful regency desk, taking a key from one drawer to unlock another stealthily. It was very *Dangerous Liaisons*, though I had no idea how much so until what followed. She handed me a stack of papers, which I immediately recognized as a computer chat between Maggie and Bee.

"I think it comes from my having been a lawyer," she said, watching me leaf through the pages. "I save everything."

There it was, the slow-cooking blossoming of the rumor that I was banging Tate Hayes. That bitch Bee planted the seeds of my so-called infidelity, watered it over time on her instant messages, and harvested it just when her own cheating had reached a fever pitch. I was a patsy. I didn't know whether to bawl or be pissed, but it was a little of both. I looked at Maggie and hugged her as I started to tear up.

"Thank you for showing me this," I said soberly. "Maggie, I need you to know, I never ever would cheat on my husband. He is my life," I said. Maggie hugged me and said she knew that, and the more she got to know me, the less she believed Bee's lies.

"I know," she said, handing me a tissue and patting my shoulder. "It's just she is bored, so bored, and so she dreams up this gossip—I can't tell you how many rumors she's started, to deflect from her own marriage or maybe even just because she felt like it, for no reason. I don't know, to fill the silences at the playground. She's the worst friend. And wife! This is the proverbial captain of the cheerleaders who always got so much attention, but she still craves more. Just having poor Parker's love got boring so she courted others. Pathetic. And poor Weston, she pretends to be this SuperMom constantly pontificating about what's the right sleep method or eating regimen or playgroup, but she never even sees him! He's raised by his team of nannies, and yet she goes around criticizing other mothers and making statements about child rearing. God only knows what she's said about me all these years," Maggie wondered. But it didn't matter now; Bee's reign over her frenemies was at an end. Maggie hadn't even called her to tell her about the birth.

"What about Hallie and Lara, do they know?"

"Not yet. I've realized, though, that they are Bee-worshippers. I hate being around them, too. They always compete and talk about the same damn shit."

I paused, smiling. "You mean Julia Charlotte's Mensa exam?"

Maggie burst out laughing. "Yes! I mean, gag!"

"You always seemed so much nicer than those girls," I said to Maggie, loving that the floodgates were open and that I now had a mom-ally. "I never understood why you were so tight with them."

"Inertia," she replied, shrugging. "I was too busy to go and make new friends, and I'm usually nonconfrontational and just didn't want to pull the plug. Then they'd really talk about me and have a field day. But now I don't care." She shrugged again. "Because you did your own thing, I knew I could too. I have my husband and my family, and now I have a new friend . . ." She gave me a hug and I was so happy she'd seen the light about her posse. But also about herself—that she was stronger than she thought and could move on without the clique.

AND THE FINAL EXCHANGE . . .

Instant Message from: BeeElliott

BeeElliott: Maggie, you there? I left two messages! Helloooo? My Buddy List says you're online. HELLO???

Maggs10021: Stay away from me, Bee. You lied about Hannah and so many others. You terrorize every mother to make them feel bad about themselves but really you're the sad one who doesn't even know her kid. And now you're out of my life. GOOD-BYE.

BeeElliott: WHAT?! WTF??

Maggs10021 is no longer signed on

Fifty-two

Josh was coming home that night and we hadn't spoken in two days; I had left messages on his cell but I knew he was probably hunting and was unreachable. He had left me a message when he landed, which was our longtime pact, but his voice sounded wounded and distant. He couldn't possibly come home fast enough, and I was shaking so much I thought my ass would register on the Richter scale. After I read with Violet, I prepared a beautiful dinner of butternut squash soup with fresh chives and crème fraîche and a roasted root vegetable lasagna with a vodka sauce on top. Hardly a four-star plate served with a silver dome on top, but my Food Network watching was definitely paying off. I needed to set the table and decided to ransack our boxes until I found our wedding china. After cracking open about six boxes I almost gave up, until I saw one box that said, conveniently, "Wedding China." I knew I was more organized than I'd thought! I unbubble-wrapped two place settings and carefully set the table, lighting candles and surveying the scene. It was truly the first effort I'd made to really make it like our old home; using our wedding china just 'cause, for no reason, not for guests, just us. I went online and found his flight had just touched down so I calculated forty minutes 'til he was home, since he never checked luggage.

As I looked around the living room, awaiting his arrival, I decided that very moment to shake the Etch-a-Sketch of my life and erase the messy mistakes I'd made. I wanted a clean slate, to turn the white knobs in totally different directions this time.

I thought about the havoc Bee's concocted drama wreaked, but in a way I was grateful, because it halted my time with Tate in its tracks and forced me to see what he really was—a male Bee who couldn't be happy with one person. Granted, he wasn't evil, although he obviously had no problem cheating on his wife, which to me meant a nonstop ticket to Hades. But it really stemmed from a desire to always be coveted, perhaps like the art he so salivated for. Bee, queen of the perfect Christmas-card picture, was like Tate is his breathless passion for the image. Controlled projections of perfection, or whatever it is the artist chooses for you to see. I thought about how Tate's love of images surpassed even his love of the real thing; perhaps for him true passion is only reserved for what is preserved in oils—not the actual starry sky, but van Gogh's heightened, saturated, swirling comet-filled crazy version of it. It's like he wouldn't be moved by a bunch of real wildflowers in a vase, only some painted collection of bursting hothouse buds. Funnily enough, as I reflected on this breakthrough of mine, I remembered how he had pointed out in a class once a still life that contained an assortment of different flowers that never actually bloom in reality at the same time of year. It was a surreal, contrived arrangement, just like his relationship with women. Trapped in a fantasy, and frozen, he might be wonderful—a flicker across a classroom here, a trip to a museum there—but he didn't love reality, only the hyperbolic, exaggerated, painted fantasy.

Way back when we shared this romantic moment that was arrested and frozen in time, this kiss that never went anywhere. Like a still life. And I suppose he preferred it that way.

But I need the real thing. The fruit instead of the painted fruit. The painted fruit never gets rotten, maybe that's why he likes it. There are no crags and bumps. With Josh and me, there were fights about radio stations or the toilet seat being left up, but we were bound together closer than Tate or Bee could ever be with anyone.

Because life, as we know, is not *still*. It's ever evolving, and a perfect moon in the sky doesn't have to be a faithful simulacrum in art to be perfect. What makes it so amazing is the fact that it's fleeting and tomorrow that big bloated moon will wane, and it's almost painful because it's *too* good. And it'll be gonzo with no rewind button, or pause button as the Old Masters tried to offer us on panel. Too bad for them. Because both Bee and Tate, always striving for that perfect image, that drama, will never be entrenched in reality and therefore will never, ever be truly happy.

Fifty-three

When my Josh walked in, I ran to him, tears streaming down my face. He matched my emotion in a hug so tight I knew he realized I would never betray him. I took him by the hand and led him to the feast I'd prepared. I didn't even need to whip out Maggie's printouts—exhibit 1A of the *Hannah v. Bee* meltdown in addition to my Trevi Nail eavesdrop of the century; he already knew all about it.

Parker had spoken with Bee from their trip and she had thought she'd hung up the phone with him, when in fact it was still on, leaving her husband to hear her phone sex with Troy on her landline. Stunned, he broke down to Josh, admitting he always suspected her of cheating. As Bee was suddenly proved a liar, Parker revisited all of her statements through the prism of her constant deception. He told Josh that he never actually believed it was true about me. Bee had either spread that lie to eclipse her own skankiness or just because she was truly mean.

"I knew deep down it couldn't be true," Josh said, hugging

me. "But Bee, she told these lies to Parker that she saw you kissing, and just the thought of it made me so sick and angry—"

"I can't believe you went through that," I said, still dewy-eyed. "Sweetie, you are my life. And honestly I would freak if you ever were friends with some woman and strolled museums. You were right to be creeped, although I would never lay a hand on him. You're the only one for me."

We hugged and went to watch sleeping Violet before a delicious dinner. And the dessert? Fresh baked brownies served with two Nine Inch Nails tickets for New Year's Eve sitting on top.

"Second row? No way!"

"Way." I beamed.

"How? How did you get these? I had my assistant calling every scalper in town! They are impossible."

"I went on Craigslist," I explained, telling Josh about the odyssey, which was very amusing, to say the least.

Because the ticket broker company was a corrupt cartel and evil to fans everywhere, the concert sold out in thirty-seven seconds, which would be nearly impossible except for the fact that scalpers had staffs of engineers to write code that bought up chunks of tickets the second the online purchase service was activated. So they were all snapped up and essentially no one on the floor actually paid face value, it was all markup. One dude scored a pair, only to then discover he was being sent to Chicago over New Year's and had to unload them via Craigslist, which I had scoured, naturally, along with countless other people. I e-mailed the guy and he e-mailed me back, "I have to leave the office soon. Whoever gets here first with the cash gets the tickets."

I threw Violet in her red stroller and literally ran over a mile to his looming glass office building on Sixth Avenue in the fifties. There was security galore in the enormous lobby where we'd agreed to meet. I was sweating like a pig and when I called his cell, he said he was downstairs already.

"Where are you?" he asked, seemingly peeved.

"Right in the lobby. By some potted fern."

"I'm here and I don't see you. I just see, like, some mom with a stroller."

I laughed. "That's me!"

I turned to see the preppiest-looking banker dude with a dumbfounded look approaching me holding a cell. He was wearing a blue button-down shirt and khaki pants and looked me over like I was an alien.

"You're joking," he said, looking at Violet. "*You're* the one buying my Nine Inch Nails tickets? Knock me over with a feather right now."

"What, you're so edgy, Brooks Brothers?"

"Touché."

I paid him the dough and we shook hands, wishing a bon voyage and bon concert extravaganza.

Josh was in stitches from the tale of my quest. "He must have thought you were bringing Violet, as like a sacrifice to the goths."

"It was so funny, such a New York moment."

"A New York, moment, eh?" Josh smiled—he knew I was finally getting it.

"I've had a lot of those lately," I admitted. "You have to come to Vi's class—it's all these Broadway actors, you'll die!"

"I can't wait," he said, taking my hand in his.

"Oh, and I had this idea, call me crazy, but I think maybe one good thing came of my museum trips with Tate Hayes: I had a lightbulb for a series of classes for moms. Normal moms. Not

Momzillas who need to stare at their kids interacting as Dr. Poundschlosser takes notes; this would be something to get moms outside themselves. I figured if I could get some women, maybe eight or ten, and their kids to sign up, I could lead them through a different part of the art world each week. Galleries in Chelsea, artists' studios in Brooklyn, museums, everything—"

"That is such a good idea," Josh said, putting down his brownie. "You're really on to something. Plus, you expose the babies to art at a young age, you stimulate the moms . . ."

"You think it could work?"

"I know it will."

Fifty-four

That weekend, sealed back madly in love and rock-secure in my marriage, Josh and I went with Violet to brunch at Lila's for our "sit-down." I was still wobbly over the cruel comments Bee had made about my not being worthy of Josh and how his mom didn't think I was up to snuff, but Josh never took his arm from my side and made me know I was the main woman in his life.

Lila's staff had prepared a huge spread, which we all ate to-gether before Watts retired to his walk-in humidor and Violet went down for a nap in our stroller. Josh and I sat with Lila on a huge overstuffed burgundy couch. And we began to speak. And we didn't stop for a very, very long time.

Josh said we didn't appreciate the pop-bys. He said that it was invasion of our privacy and that while we were happy to see her, the buzz from the lobby didn't work for us. I told her that I sensed her disapproval of my involvement or lack thereof in New York society and that I no longer wanted to be told that I dressed inappropriately or that Violet looked like a ragamuffin.

And then I told her about Bee. Her precious, perfect Bee.

"She would have cheated on Josh, too," I told her. "She can't be happy with anyone. And I may not be as put-together or wired or posh in your eyes, but Lila, I know one thing about myself: I am a damn good wife and a great mom. And that other stuff just doesn't matter to me."

Lila remained very quiet, sipping tea from a porcelain gold-edged cup as she drank in my words slowly, looking to her son and back at me.

"Are you finished?" she asked, smiling slightly.

I paused, drawing in a breath to regain confidence after my spiel.

"Yes. And I hope you are, too," I said calmly. "Finished with the school pressures, and the constant monitoring, and, after what I've told you, with quoting of Bee Elliott as the gospel."

After bottling up so much with Lila for so long, it felt like an amazing release to get it all out. And all the while, Josh sat beside me, his arm around my shoulder.

"You remind me of someone," Lila said, softly, looking me over.

Gee, who could that be? A stray dog? A *fille des rues*? A West Coast slob roller-skating on Venice Beach?

I must confess, I was stunned by her answer.

"Myself," she admitted, looking down.

"Really?" said Josh, happily. " 'Cause you stood up to Grandma and Grandpa just like that when you wanted to marry Dad?"

"Yes," she said, wiping a tear from an eye I'd been so sure had never wept. "And because I realized then, as you've reminded me now, that the nest you two build together with your children is all the shield you need from the outside. I forgot that for a while." She reached her hand to mine and held it for the first time ever. "I'm sorry."

Bee, the dream daughter-in-law in her eyes, was not such a dream anymore. And while I probably wasn't suddenly now the golden child, I knew I had one thing more important than admiration for my clothes or compliments on my hair: respect. It wasn't about the power shifting; it was that I no longer cared and was freed of my obsession to gain her approval, or the world's for that matter. What I needed to be happy was in our newly solidified cocoon, and when I realized that, I felt free.

Fifty-five

As I brewed and stewed over my new idea that could in some infinitesimal way enhance the lives of some knowledge-starved Nickelodeon-glued mommies, I threw myself full force into all of Violet's classes as fall turned officially into winter. Besides the nannies in her Milford Prescott class, I started, little by little, to bond with some of the other moms and as the weeks passed felt more and more comfortable. It was weird how at first everyone looked each other over, Mexican-standoff-style, and by the end of the semester, most of the ice in the circle had melted away just as it started to form on the trees and canopies outdoors.

One mom, Helena, even walked a few blocks with us after school, as we talked about how nice the group was.

"I have to confess," Helena said smiling, "I was kind of intimidated by you at first."

"Me?" I asked, incredulous. "Are you kidding? I'm a total loner! It's not like I had a posse!"

"No, but that's it—you did your own thing and had your cool earrings and stuff."

I didn't know exactly what that meant, but I did know this: everyone has initial hang-ups. While our kids instantly united with toys and row-row-row-your-boats, and we had to slowly feel each other out, like high school. Part Deux.

I don't know at exactly what point that innocence of hugging another child just because they're the same size fades. When does one stop getting excited over, say, seeing a monkey in the zoo? Or a circus? Or a pinwheel? I suppose there's no way to trace that delicate crossover from naïve and innocent to "over it" and jaded, but one thing I discovered was that the more I threw myself into everything, immersing myself and making an effort and not being so worried about other people, the happier I was. I don't know why I had been so initially plagued by Bee and her cohorts, but now that they were fully in my past—sure, I bumped into Lara and Hallie occasionally on Madison—they didn't bother me anymore. It was small talk, then sayonara.

Obsessed with my Broadway Babies class, I talked more and more with one really sweet mom, Tina, who asked me if I

wanted to join her at a cabaret where some of the teachers per-
formed. I happily accepted.

Josh and I went with Tina and her husband and had a total
blast—the performance was racier than the singers' normal
shiny happy two-year-old fare, but I felt so thrilled to be out
and enjoying the gifts of these incredible singers and still to
this day pinch myself that my daughter gets to be exposed to
such amazing talent.

By the time Christmas arrived, many people were solidify-
ing their JetSet Baby plans to hit Antigua or St. Bart's or Ly-
ford, but we happily plopped in New York City. The skyline
glistened under the snow, and the cold was chilling but comforting since we were cozy indoors as well as cozy in our lives,
finally in a place where I could exhale and enjoy the fact that
the raging tempests were outside my window and no longer in
my life. I made arts 'n' craftsy holiday cards and didn't feel the
least bit el-cheapo about them despite the fact I knew I'd be
receiving piles upon piles of Oyster Bay Printery—engraved
quadruple-ply cards; I liked mine. They were made with love.
And as I sat writing the names of the recipients, I realized I
had more nice people around me than I'd thought. And as I
hatched my plan to start my art world tours, I felt comforted by
the feeling that there were way more women in New York who
were like me than like Bee. Normal, nice, non—size 2 women
who just wanted to love their kids and enjoy their lives and
didn't make constant motherhood pronouncements beginning with the words "It's all about . . ." Sure, there would always be jerky, insecure, competitive type-A moms—hey, this *is*
New York after all—but they weren't as prevalent as I once
thought. Tucked between the probing questions about one of

Violet's outfits or preschool applications were exclamations of her sweetness and offers for playdates. These were women who were lower-profile than their shiny, stylish Momzilla counterparts, and that's why they were harder for me to find. Except Maggie, who was initially in that scene, then found the calm happiness in being just plain normal, one of the more spread-out, lower-key type of moms who didn't need their pictures in magazines to make themselves feel better. Moms who just wanted to be quiet and real, who didn't need to have their kids vaunted in other people's eyes, just in her own, in the way a mother reads to a child and looks into that child's and knows how deeply connected they truly are. I hoped the women like that would join me in my quest to not only expose them to great art and reinvigorate any latent desire to learn, but also to bring the nice mellow moms together.

Fifty-six

It was the morning of New Year's Eve, and the city was filled with fanny-pack-wearing tourists. I remembered how out of place I felt when we'd arrived, but now seeing people from all over wide-eyed and absorbing the flux and crunch and pulse of the city, I truly felt like a real New Yorker. Josh was worried I couldn't handle the Nine Inch Nails concert that night because I looked slightly Kermit-green and felt flu-ish when I woke up. But I told

him there was no way I would miss it and would pull myself together. I felt a pang as he went to work in his perfect man suit
(never a day off still, unfortunately), fastening each cuff link, in-
serting the collar stays. I loved watching his dressing routine,
except that I was a slob sacked out in bed with Violet. He kissed us
good-bye and we each took a ticket, ready to reunite twelve hours
or so later on the Madison Square Garden floor. I was happy to
see that he'd left me a note on the kitchen table of new porn titles:
Bi-Curious George, *Snatch Point*, and *Girl with a Pearl Necklace*.

After two hours of lounging and zoning in front of the
Nickelodeon lineup, we finally got motivated to go to the park.
The weather was cold, the first truly biting day. And then,
mid-walk, downy snowflakes started to fall on us. As the nip-
ping air rouged Violet's cheeks and the snow fell on her
tongue, I felt so elated to have seasons.

"Mommy, it's knowing!" which was how she said "snowing."

"I know, isn't it beautiful?"

My little girl would soon sled in the park. We'd make snow-
men and snow angels. I felt good, at peace, and when I saw Bee
Elliott walking toward me (why she was even in town instead
of St. Tropez I had no idea), I didn't even wince. Despite everything she'd done, I didn't hate her. Okay, I fucking loathed her,
let's be honest, but it wasn't an active, boiling hatred. Why?
Because she was so incredibly sad and pathetic. Because she
didn't even know her own kid, because she was always trying to
be the Queen Bee and not just keep up with everyone but sur-
pass them. Because she didn't have Josh and never could, despite her efforts. Because she didn't have real friends.

As she got closer and closer on Madison Avenue, I felt a
small pit and walked by saying nothing. I never saw her again.

See, she wasn't the queen of New York anymore, not because she'd fallen from grace and was a gossip's dream scandal now that Parker had left her cheating ass, but because I realized New York didn't have queens. Any girl who loves her life and her city can take it by storm. Her throne and court of followers vanished the day I heard how she decimated me behind my back, and the reason I didn't actively hate her and let her drain my energy is that I just stopped caring about her at all. I had her number, and now everyone else did, too. She was like a cancerous tumor that had now been excised from New York, her power cut off, her ability to poison terminated.

After a while in the cold air, Violet passed out in her fluffy stroller sleeping sack and I hit the drugstore to get some loot to help what was potentially ailing me. We came home and no sooner did we enter than the flakey snow turned into a blizzard, complete with biblical hail and a snowstorm that shut down the city. It reminded me of Seattle and how I took comfort in the pounding rain on my window; it always made me feel safe inside, curled up and cozy. The phone rang and it was Sheila Stone, Troy Kincaid's associate broker, telling me that we were accepted by the board into the co-op. Hooray! I exhaled a huge breath of relief, literally feeling the weight come off my shoulders. I surveyed the Ethan Allen–filled corporate apartment. *It's been fun, but adios*, I thought.

When Amber arrived that evening, I decided to blare music pre-date psych-up-style like the old days. I put on my coolest black skirt and blouse with some jet earrings and boots, and yes, maybe I was a tad overdressed, but despite the flu feeling I felt kind of sexy. Ready to go, I showed Amber where Violet's fish for dinner was and kissed my nugget goodbye. But as I headed for the door, something dawned on me. There was one more thing I had to do before the concert.

I arrived at the Garden to find masses upon masses of goth kids, face-pierced peeps sleeved in tattoos, and perhaps not so shockingly, yuppies. Beaming, I made my way to my seat, turning around to anxiously scan all the ticket-rippers to see if Josh was coming. I was starting to grow stressed that maybe he was trapped at work, when I suddenly saw his boyish face emerge among the metal. He came over and hugged me just as the light went out and the crowd roared. I yelled that we got into our building as the masses cheered, and Josh's thrilled shout added to their euphoric chorus.

As heated guitars opened the show, you could feel the ecstasy of the twenty thousand fans. The energy was so intense that every single soul felt utterly high. Josh wrapped his arms around me and we listened to the music and I started to think how perfect the moment was. Instead of feeling thirty and haggish, I felt twenty-two again. I truly felt younger than I had ever felt since motherhood, and I realized two very important things. One, you can have a sexy side and a life and interests post-stork. Babies tend to eclipse that for a while, but the moment beamed me back to pre-Violet days where I was so *me*, strong and centered. The second thing was that all the hipsters around us may have been really edgy and supposedly cool, but I had the coolest thing of all, a daughter at home who loved us, who we cherished more than anything on the planet. I felt unique; probably no one in our parent world was also at the show, and no one at the show looked like they had little critters sacked out in cribs at home. But as with everyone you see in New York, you just never know.

Suddenly, I felt my phone vibrate in my pocket. I looked at Josh, worried that Amber was buzzing that something had happened to Violet. I nervously whipped out the phone to see a text message which read: "I love my wife." Grinning, I texted back and Josh put his hand on my hair. Seconds later his phone buzzed. "I love my husband, and . . ." He was turning to look at me when his phone buzzed again with a new message: "I'm pregnant." Yes, I'd found out two hours before. I peed on the stick, and saw the little plus sign. And unlike Bee, Hallie, and Lara, who would have been speed-dialing Lucky Me Under Three before they even pulled up their lace thongs, I simply exhaled happily, knowing the only person I wanted to tell was the love of my life, Josh. Ecstatic, he bear-hugged me and we kissed, knowing little Violet would be a big sis in about nine months, and I couldn't have been in a better place to welcome the stork.

Follow-ups

smART MOMS: My company, smART Moms, launched the following winter and was instantly sold out. That spring, I added three more sections, all filled to capacity, with field trips visiting artists' studios galleries and museums in all five boroughs.

BEE ELLIOTT: Bee is still hot and heavy with Troy Kincaid, though she'll no doubt cheat again. After finalizing their divorces, they moved to London, leaving Weston behind with Parker. Bee never was truly connected with her son anyway, but before you grieve for mommyless Weston, see *Mr. and Mrs. Parker Elliott*.

CARNEGIE NURSERY SCHOOL offered Violet a place in their fall class. We passed and enrolled at the more charming Browne-Madison School. And something tells me Harvard's not automatically counted out because of it.

COUNT ALEXEI VON HAPSENFÜRER became so enamored of Josh's talent, he poached him away from his firm to be his main money manager in the States, setting him up with an office two blocks away and his own hours.

DR. EMILE POUNDSCHLOSSER was arrested on seven counts of tax evasion. Through the press of the trial it was revealed that the renowned parenting expert never even had children. He was cured of his Affluenza in an upstate jail.

MR. and MRS. PARKER ELLIOTT: After nursing his wounds and getting used to life as a single dad, Parker began spending a lot of time at our house. As did Leigh. Through the months they grew closer, and when I went into labor, they both took Violet for us. Leigh was crazy about Weston and Violet, and Parker saw how loving she was with his kid and ours, and by the end of the year, they were together, madly in love and happier than ever.

LUCY SLOANE ALLEN was born September 14, weighing in at seven pounds exactly.

VIOLET GRACE ALLEN loves her baby sister, New York, her new school, and her very happy mommy.

Acknowledgments

Thank you to genius editrix and do-it-all-mom Stacy Creamer for getting the idea, giving me ideas, and commiserating on some of the daunting aspects of dealing with Big Apple parenting. A big thanks as well to Joanna Pinsker and Julia Coblentz, for getting the word out, and to Laura Swerdloff plus the ICM gang: Amanda Urban, Jennifer Joel, Katie Sigelman, and Left Coaster Josie Freedman, as well as superlawyers Steven Beer and Mary Miles of Greenberg Traurig.

To the mellow moms: thank you for helping me laugh at the Momzillas, for sharing insane anecdotes, and showing me how it's done: Teresa Heinz, Laura Huang, Tara Lipton, Jane Timberlake, Alexis Mintz, Marisa Fox Bevilacqua, Liz Carey, Laura Hammam, Britney Spears-Federline, Isobel Case, The Group 3P.M.-ers, Leslie Coch, Carrie Karasyov, Robyn Foreman, Abby Gordon, Jennifer Nordstrom, B. J. Blum, Olya Thompson, Julia Van Nice, Lynn Biase, and Jenn Linardos.

Gracias also to sounding boards and supporters whose humor I worship: Richard Sinnott, Frances Stein, Alice Ryan, Liz Herzberg, Andrew Saffir, Daniel Benedict, Clara Pang, Kathryn Wender, Karen Quinn, Chris and Sasha Heinz, Andre Heinz, Michael Kovner, Jean Doyen, Naomi Waletzky, and especially Jacky and Jada Davy.

And to my sisters, the *chère* clan, I love you guys: Vanessa Eastman, Jeannie Stern, Dana Wallach Jones, Lauren Duff, and honorary *chère* Trip Cullman. And to the greatest note-giver on planet Earth, the brilliant Dr. Lisa Turvey, without whom this book would not have been possible.

Last but not least, thank you to the fam: the Kargmans, Robert, Sophie, Bess, Dana James, and my MiL Marjie (who is nothing like Lila!), and to my nana, Ruth Kopelman. *Merci mille fois* to my beloved mom, Coco, aka "Gwammy," who devotes so much to her kids and is the best role model I could ever have as a mother; to Arie Kopelman (Dad slash Poppy), thanks for your sage guidance and for always showing us that humor is the best medicine; and broddow Will for all your amazing love, support, and constant inspiration. To li'l Ivy and Sadie, any mommy stresses are worth it in spades with you two delish nuggets as my reward, and extra-special thanks to Harry, my beloved LC.